A

TREACHEROUS
TALE

A
TREACHEROUS
TALE

ELIZABETH PENNEY

St. Martin's Paperbacks

This is a work of fiction. All of the characters, organizations, and events portrayed in this novel are either products of the author's imagination or are used fictitiously.

First published in the United States by St. Martin's Paperbacks, an imprint of St. Martin's Publishing Group

A TREACHEROUS TALE

Copyright © 2022 by Elizabeth Penney.

For information, address St. Martin's Publishing Group, 120 Broadway, New York, NY 10271.

www.stmartins.com

ISBN: 978-1-250-78772-9

Our books may be purchased in bulk for promotional, educational, or business use. Please contact your local bookseller or the Macmillan Corporate and Premium Sales Department at 1-800-221-7945, ext. 5442, or by email at MacmillanSpecialMarkets@macmillan.com.

Printed in the United States of America

St. Martin's Paperbacks edition / September 2022

10 9 8 7 6 5 4 3 2 1

For Charlotte and CiCi

ACKNOWLEDGMENTS

First, belated but huge and grateful thanks to the authors who gave me blurbs for *Chapter and Curse*: Ellen Byron, Vicki Delany, Hannah Dennison, Diane Kelly, Molly MacRae, Shari Randall, and Paige Shelton. Your support and interest are appreciated more than I can say.

Again, many thanks to Nettie Finn, my editor at St. Martin's, and Elizabeth Bewley, my agent, for their help bringing this series to print. Sarah Haeckel, much appreciation for sending *Chapter and Curse* to the Edgar's judges—such a thrill to be short-listed for the 2022 Mary Higgins Clark Award. Thanks as well to Allison Ziegler, Katie Minerva, and Barbara Wild at St. Martin's for your excellent assistance.

Everyone is raving about this cover, which captures the story so well, and no wonder. A special shout-out to designer Danielle Christopher and illustrator Mary Ann Lasher!

Author's note: Many locations in the series are real, but Magpie Lane and its businesses, and the village of Hazelhurst are fictional. This story was partially inspired by the discovery in Cambridge of a young woman's Saxon burial site that included gold and garnet jewelry. East Anglian folk and fairy tales also provided elements I included in *The Strawberry Girls*, an original tale.

CHAPTER 1

Books, books, glorious books. Mug in hand—I love tea, but my mornings require coffee—I stood in the middle of the bookshop, reveling in the sight. Dusty, musty, gilded and plain, stacked on tables and crammed in shelves. Everywhere I looked, books.

How had this happened? I still couldn't quite believe that I was now partial owner of Thomas Marlowe—Manuscripts & Folios, a charming tumbledown Tudor bookstore in the heart of Cambridge, England. Was there a more literate city in the world? I thought perhaps not, considering Cambridge's thirty-one colleges, more than one hundred libraries, and numerous renowned writers through the centuries.

Puck, the stray black cat who had adopted me, twined through my ankles, mewing, and I picked him up with my free arm for a snuggle. Not only did I own a bookshop, I also had a cat—two counting Clarence, the bookshop tabby—new friends, and a wonderful man I was dating, Kieran Scott, owner of the bicycle shop next door. He was also the son of an English lord, something I hadn't quite wrapped my very American mind around.

"Molly? Ah, there you are." My great-aunt, Violet Marlowe, popped her head out of the door to the living quarters. "Breakfast is ready." Tiny and trim, with high-piled white hair and big glasses, Aunt Violet was almost the last in a long line of book-loving Marlowes. Earlier this year, she had written to Mum explaining her need for help, and here we were, uprooted from Vermont and transplanted back to the old country. An offer we couldn't refuse, especially since my town library job had been cut and my mother and I had found ourselves at loose ends after losing my dear father, a history professor. It was time for a fresh start.

"Great," I said. "I'm starving." A whiff of frying bacon had escaped through the open door and I sniffed with appreciation. Forget what they say about English cooking. Homemade meals made with local ingredients were fabulous, even if what they called bacon wasn't quite what I'd known back in the States.

"Come on, Puck." A loud thump behind me told me Clarence had jumped from his favorite armchair, always ready to follow when food was in the offing. "Clarence, you too."

As the three of us entered the kitchen, I asked, "Are we still going to visit Iona York today?" Later this month, Iona York, author of a classic children's book, *The Strawberry Girls*, was doing a reading for us in celebration of a new edition. One of my initiatives to revive the bookstore had been hosting author events. So far, they'd been very popular, despite the first being ruined by a murder in the garden.

"I thought we'd head over after breakfast," Aunt Violet said. "I want to nail down the details and start working on publicity."

A plate of scrambled eggs, bacon, and thick whole-wheat toast was already in front of my usual chair. I put Puck down, then sat at the table and dug in. The cats went to check their dishes and began crunching on kibble.

"There's an interesting backstory behind *The Strawberry Girls*," Aunt Violet said, sitting beside me. A plate for Mum, who hadn't come down yet, was warming on the stove. "I don't know if you've heard it."

My ears perked up. "You mean involving her husband?" All I knew was that Iona's husband had died before the book was published almost twenty years ago. Their daughters, Poppy and Rose, had been the inspiration for the main characters, so they must be in their mid-twenties now. A few years younger than me.

Aunt Violet nodded. "Nathanial was a lecturer in early medieval history at the University and his interests extended to East Anglian folklore and fairy tales. He came up with the idea for the story, incorporating some of those fairy tales, and Iona was going to illustrate it. After he died, she went ahead and wrote the book using his notes. The book was an instant best seller, as they say, partly because of the tragedy, I think."

"Which was?" I swallowed my impatience along with a bite of savory, salty bacon.

She leaned across the table, lowering her voice. "He fell off a tower in the grounds of Thornton Hall, which is right next door to Strawberry Cottage. After one of Geoffrey Thornton's wild parties." A flash of mischief lit her eyes. "I may have attended one or two myself."

"I don't doubt it." Aunt Violet might look like a sweet little bookworm, but she had quite a backstory of her own, as I was learning.

Her face sobered. "Anyway, the theory is that Nathanial's fall was an accident, after he became intoxicated at a Midsummer Night's Eve bash. Iona never understood why he was up there in the middle of the night, and no one else came forward as a witness."

A possibility chilled me. "Maybe he jumped." Gosh, I hoped not, especially since he left two young daughters and a wife. I knew all about the loss of a parent. "Did the police investigate?"

"I'm sure they did," Aunt Violet said. "They must have had a good reason to consider it an accident and close the case."

I wasn't quite as confident about police investigations, especially after Aunt Violet had become a suspect in the garden murder and was cleared thanks to me rather than the authorities, but I didn't comment further. At this point, any evidence contrary to the cause of death ruling was probably long gone.

Light footsteps tapped on the stairs and my mother, Nina Marlowe, entered the kitchen, dressed in a white skirt and pink sweater set, carrying a spiral-bound notebook.

"Good morning, all," she said, her smile including the cats, now licking their paws after breakfast. "What's on the agenda today?" She set the notebook on the table before heading over to the stove, where she retrieved her plate.

Unlike me, Mum was tiny, with short dark hair that suited her elfin features. I took after my father, medium in height and build, but I had Mum's hair, which I wore long, and the Marlowe nose. Such fun to see it in historic portraits and photographs. Our ancestors may not have passed down much money, but we had their distinctive, slightly long, elegant nose.

"Oh, this looks yummy," she said, joining us at the table.

"It's delish," I said. While we ate, I told her about our plan to visit Iona York in Hazelhurst and discuss the upcoming reading.

"That's nice." Mum stiffened a little at the mention of her hometown. She'd had a very unhappy family life, and after escaping to the United States with my father, she'd never spoken about her parents or her older brother, Chris. It was only after we'd returned to England to help at the bookshop that she'd reconnected with her brother. Uncle Chris was fine, his wife, Janice, not so much, and they had a son, Charlie, about my age. He was okay too. "I'll mind the store while you're gone and, between customers, work on a little something." She patted the notebook.

I hardly dared to ask. "A poem?" After my father's death last year, Mum, a well-regarded poet, had experienced a stubborn case of writer's block. She'd worried that it was permanent, but I'd hoped that time and healing would refill her creative well. If books were my life, poetry was hers.

Mum picked up a piece of bacon and nibbled. "Yes. The start of one, anyway."

"*So* great." I shared a smile with Aunt Violet. Moving to Cambridge had been a good decision after all. Not that I had many doubts.

•◉•

After breakfast, we walked down Magpie Lane to the garage where Aunt Violet kept her gold Cortina. Despite being older than me, the vintage sedan was spotlessly clean, with an engine that purred. Aunt Violet's good friend and sometimes handyman, George Flowers, kept the car in perfect working order. Reminded of George, I realized how much I missed his good-natured bluster. He was out of town, taking his first vacation in "donkey's years," as he put it.

With Aunt Violet at the wheel and me in the front left passenger seat, a position I still wasn't used to, we bumped up the cobblestone lane past the tea shop, the bicycle shop, and the pub. After working our way through the maze of one-way and no-vehicle roads that was historic downtown Cambridge, we merged onto the A14 and traveled out into the countryside. Once we left the highway, civilization gave way to hedges and fields and stands of ancient, ivy-covered trees.

After a few miles, a cluster of cottages appeared and then we were crossing an arched bridge over the River Ouse. On the other side, a pretty painted sign displaying a coat of arms announced: Hazelhurst.

The Scott family emblem, maybe? Kieran's parents, Lord Graham and Lady Asha Scott, lived in a magnificent edifice called Hazelhurst House, built in 1482. I admit it, I've Google-stalked his family and their drool-worthy home. Plus, after we started dating, I set up online alerts for photographs of us, which are published annoyingly often.

Kieran is considered one of Britain's most eligible bachelors, you see, so anyone he dates is scrutinized—and given a nickname. Mine, after they caught me with windswept hair and sporting a faded flannel shirt, was "a natural Vermont beauty." It could be worse, I suppose. They still call regular people like me commoners in this country—at least in the press.

We had reached Hazelhurst proper and were now creeping along a narrow street lined with historic brick, stone, and whitewashed storefronts. Window boxes, urns, and hanging planters overflowing with flowers added color and cheer.

"This is the high street," Aunt Violet said. "They have some good shops here." Even smaller streets led off the high street, providing enticing glimpses of cottages set among flower gardens. When we passed a stately church with arched stained-glass windows, a graveyard nestled next to it, I wondered if I had ancestors buried there. I was pretty sure Kieran did.

Since my mother never mentioned Hazelhurst, let alone came out here, I'd been glad when Aunt Violet suggested visiting Iona York. This way I could satisfy my curiosity without upsetting Mum.

Once through the heart of the village, we turned down a small lane lined with hedgerows, so narrow that I prayed there wouldn't be any oncoming cars. After we passed a few cottages, the hedges fell away to reveal fields on both sides. To the right, a tan two-story stone manor with six windows across and a triangle pediment above the entrance stood on a gentle rise. Stone pillars marked the main drive, which was lined with beech trees touching overhead.

"That's Thornton Hall," Aunt Violet said. "Strawberry Cottage used to belong to the estate."

"It's gorgeous." I stared at the manor until we had gone by, drinking in every detail. I wondered where the tower, site of Nate York's accident, sat on the property, since it wasn't visible from the road.

On our left, several people were crouched in the fields, bent over what looked like trenches. Pop-up tents sheltered them from the relentless sun. A runner in bright pink leggings and a black top stood watching them from the road, her face hidden by a low visor and sunglasses.

"What are they doing?" I asked.

Aunt Violet slowed, craning her neck to study the workers. "Oh, I heard about this. The University is doing a dig this summer. A farmer plowing the field stumbled on arti-facts from an Anglo-Saxon settlement."

Excitement fizzed in my veins. "An archeological dig? I've always wanted to go on one." I was intrigued by the idea of past lives below our feet, waiting to be discovered. In England, that meant any time from prehistory to the previous century, often in layers.

"Me too," Aunt Violet said. "Have you heard about the dig at Sutton Hoo? Britain's version of King Tut's tomb, I call it. They think this settlement is from about the same period."

"Oh yes, I have. They made a movie about it." A recent film detailed the 1939 excavation of a royal ship burial, the grave of a seventh-century Anglo-Saxon king. *The Dig* was already saved on my streaming list. "You think they'll find any treasure?"

"Maybe," Aunt Violet said. "What a thrill that would be, for the team and the landowner too." She made a little face. "Any treasure has to be reported to the Crown, but Geoffrey Thornton will get a cut if a museum wants it."

"What if they don't?" I asked. It didn't seem fair that he wouldn't own something found on his own land.

Aunt Violet hit the gas again, pulling out around the run-ner, who was still watching. I waved at her, but she didn't respond. "In that case, the landowner can keep it."

Better than nothing, I supposed.

A short distance up the lane, at the first drive past the manor, Aunt Violet slowed again and signaled a turn. Over-grown butterfly bushes covered with showy pink flowers crowded the entrance, hiding any glimpse of the house be-yond.

The cottage came into view gradually, only a glimpse of thatched rooftop among the trees at first. Then the drive swept around into a clearing.

"Oh," I said, stunned. "It's exactly like *The Strawberry Girls*."

The front of the white stucco cottage was smothered with pink climbing roses. Multi-pane casement windows stood ajar, and in front was a small but riotous flower garden hemmed in by a picket fence. When Aunt Violet shut off the engine, I could hear bees buzzing and the twitter of birds in the fruit trees.

As we climbed out, quietly to match the hush around this dream dwelling, I wondered why I had expected anything else. Despite being a fairy tale, *The Strawberry Girls* felt genuine, as if inspired by actual events. Crazy idea, right? Or maybe not. The girls were real too, like this cottage.

"I wonder where Iona is," Aunt Violet said, glancing around. "I don't see her car."

I didn't either, but I did notice something about the roof. "They're in the middle of a thatching job." I pointed to scaffolding at the far side. "I wonder if Uncle Chris is doing it." My uncle had a well-established thatching company, and since he lived in Hazelhurst, this area was his stomping ground.

"He might be." Aunt Violet tipped her head to study the thatch, turning when the noise of an engine was heard. "I bet that's Iona now."

A battered green Mini rattled into view, the woman behind the wheel waving when she spotted us. She parked beside us and climbed out, a small woman with dandelion fluff blond curls and a bewitching smile. "Sorry I'm late," she called. "I had to run an errand and it took longer than I thought." Tanned and freckled, she was dressed in linen, pale blue Capris, and a white sleeveless top.

"No problem," Aunt Violet said. "We just got here."

"You must be Molly," Iona said, advancing on me with her hand extended. "I'm so happy to meet you."

"Same," I said, shaking her hand. "I love your house. And your book too," I added hastily. "It's one of my favorites."

"Molly is a librarian," Aunt Violet said. "So her endorsement really means something."

"How flattering. Thank you." Iona grabbed a tote bag from the car. "Let's go in. I'll put the kettle on."

After ushering us along the path, Iona opened the front door, standing back to let us in. We stepped into a small entry area with a flagstone floor and a flight of stairs leading up. To our left was a comfortably furnished living room with a beamed ceiling and inglenook fireplace, open to the kitchen beyond.

"You should have seen this place when we bought it," Iona said, setting her bag on the counter. "Poky little rooms." She directed us to a long table under a casement window with a view of the back garden, which featured a white lattice summerhouse. The lawn ended in forest, and with a thrill I recognized the Deep Woods from *The Strawberry Girls*.

While Iona filled a kettle at the farmhouse sink and set it on the AGA in its brick-lined nook, I took in the picture-perfect cottage kitchen—an antique dresser displaying Blue Willow plates, copper-bottomed pans dangling from hooks, and pots of herbs along the windowsill.

Our hostess bustled back and forth with teacups, milk and sugar, and a plate of custard creams. "I'm really excited about the reading," Iona said as she poured steaming water into a teapot. "Haven't done one for years." She laughed. "Typical introvert, all hidden away with my pencils and paints."

"Nothing wrong with that," Aunt Violet said. "Hard to create in a crowd."

"We already have customers asking about the new book,"

I said. To build buzz, I'd put together a display of earlier editions with a poster announcing the upcoming release. My late great-uncle Tom had a deep love for children's literature and I was carrying on his tradition.

"I have an advance copy, if you want one." Iona slipped a tea cozy over the pot and brought it over. She pulled out a chair and sat. "I'll fetch it after tea."

Aunt Violet and I exchanged excited looks. "What a treat," Aunt Violet said. "Thank you."

"You're very welcome." Iona picked up the teapot and poured, then handed cups around. The next couple of minutes were spent doctoring our tea. I like milk, no sugar, and strong tea. Weak tea tastes like dishwater.

"We saw the archeologists digging at Thornton Hall," I said to break the silence. "How fascinating."

Selecting a biscuit, Iona nodded. "It is. Very. Both of my girls are working on the dig, which means I see them almost every day." She took a sip of tea. "Poppy is getting a postgraduate archeology degree, as is her fiancé, Ben. Rose is the dig sketch artist."

"I didn't know they still used artists," I said. "What a cool profession."

"It's quite technical," Iona said. "She's learning a lot. I don't know if she'll keep on with it or do something else."

"Maybe she'll illustrate a book like her mother," Aunt Violet said.

Iona smiled. "We're talking about doing one together. Poppy is going to write the text."

I got goose bumps at this news. "Wonderful. It's sure to be a best seller." I was pretty sure the publishing world would jump at another Iona York book.

"We'll see," Iona said, the smile lingering. "It's a long way from inspiration to completion." She lowered her eyes, her mood seeming to change as she traced a knot in the tabletop with one finger. "I do wish Nathanial had lived to see his book in print."

"Dreadful," Aunt Violet said with sympathy. "What a terrible loss."

Tears glittered in Iona's eyes as she reached for a napkin. "Sorry," she said, dabbing her eyes. "I didn't mean to get emotional. I love the new edition, and the money has been very welcome. But it's brought it all up again. Why was he on the tower? Why did he fall?" Her voice broke on the last word.

I froze, her grief triggering painful memories of losing my father. Why had my father died so young of cancer? Some questions didn't have answers.

Thankfully, since I wasn't able to move, Aunt Violet leaped up and went to Iona, soothing her with an embrace and murmurs of comfort. After a few moments, Iona gently pulled away. "Pardon me." She gave a little laugh before blowing her nose. "A meltdown wasn't on my agenda today."

"They never are," Aunt Violet said, returning to her seat.

"The worst part, well, not the *worst*, is that I didn't want him to go to that party." Iona crumpled the napkin in her fist. "Poppy had been sick and we were all exhausted. But when it came to Geoffrey Thornton, Nate could never say no. To be fair, Geoffrey's parties were a lot of fun. Intelligent conversation, good food, lots to drink. A great gang of friends, really. But Nate . . ." She pressed her lips together. "He was a bit of a binge drinker. I've come to realize that he was probably self-medicating. He hated taking medication for his depression. Said it made him fuzzy-headed and lethargic."

A chilling thought struck. Had Nate killed himself after all? The shadow in Aunt Violet's eyes told me she was thinking the same thing. Poor Iona: what a terrible thing, to be left wondering all these years.

"I'm so sorry," Aunt Violet said. "He was an absolutely brilliant man. I know he loved you and the girls very much."

Iona's distressed expression eased. "Thank you for saying that, Violet. It helps." Rising to her feet, she tossed the napkin into the trash. "Well, enough of my problems. Would you like a tour of the garden? It's lovely this time of year."

"I'd love one," I said, drinking the rest of my tea. Exploring the property would almost be like walking into the fairy tale.

We followed Iona out the back door, trailing along as she showed us the vegetable and herb garden, cherry, plum, and apple trees, berry bushes, and, naturally, a strawberry patch.

"Here." Iona plucked two red, ripe berries and handed them to us. She grinned. "In honor of the Strawberry Girls. We grow them every year."

Some of the rear roof had already been stripped, and I asked, "Who is doing your thatch?"

Iona studied the roof. "Chris Marlowe." She turned to look at me. "Any relation?"

"My uncle," I said. "I wondered if this was his job."

She drifted across the lawn, staring up at the thatch. "He was here earlier. I hope he's coming back. We might get rain later." Again, we tagged along as Iona wandered toward the far side of the cottage.

The first thing I noticed was a squashed hydrangea bush with the shape of an object I couldn't yet make out—surely the culprit—lying nearby. What a shame. Had Uncle Chris dropped a chunk of thatch, missing the skip waiting to collect the old roofing?

As we drew closer, the bundle in the bushes resolved into a heap of clothing. And, finally, horribly, I realized what it was. A man's body.

CHAPTER 2

The three of us huddled together like frightened ducklings. Although his van was gone, my first horrible thought was that Uncle Chris had fallen off the roof. After stealing a few brief peeks at the body, I realized I didn't recognize him. On the short side and slim, he had graying hair and was wearing trousers, a vest, and a button-down shirt with rolled sleeves. The angle of his neck made it clear he was dead.

"Who is it?" Aunt Violet whispered. "Do you know, Iona?" Reasonable question, since he'd obviously fallen off her roof.

Iona put a small, clammy hand on my arm. "It's Robin Jones. An old friend of mine. What was he doing up there?"

Good question. There were scaffolding boards on the roof but no railing to prevent a fall. I fumbled for my phone. "I'm calling the police. Why don't we go back inside and wait?"

"I'll make a fresh pot of tea." Iona ran ahead of us, her sandals flashing. Such a typical British response, I'd found. And tea was comforting under almost every circumstance.

I dialed 999, walking slowly as I waited for an answer, Aunt Violet keeping pace beside me. At the familiar inquiry, I said, "Hello, this is Molly Kimball. I'm out at Strawberry Cottage in Hazelhurst and . . . and we've found a man . . ." I paused to suck in a breath. "He's dead."

Keys clicked. "Was he ill? Was it an accident?"

"I don't know," I said. "It looks like he fell off the roof. Robin Jones is his name. The homeowner identified him. Iona York."

"Twenty Thornton Lane," Aunt Violet whispered. "That's the address."

I passed that along. "Someone will be right out," the dispatcher said. "Is anyone in danger? Is there any threat to your well-being?"

Her questions made fear jolt through me. I hadn't considered that someone might be lurking and attack us. "I hope not." I glanced around the yard and then into the woods. "I don't see anyone on the property." My voice shook. "I'm with my aunt and Iona York. None of us were here when it happened."

Aunt Violet and I hadn't pushed Robin off the roof. Had Iona? She'd been gone when we arrived, but perhaps that had been deliberate misdirection. She could have been down the road somewhere, watching for us. Death made you doubt everyone, I had learned.

"Do you need me to stay on the line?" the dispatcher asked.

"Maybe?" My heart was racing and my underarms were damp. "Please." Even if Iona—or anyone else—hadn't pushed Robin to his death, there was the undeniable fact that this was the second mysterious fall in this vicinity. It may have been twenty years ago, but Iona's husband's death had, from all I'd been told, been eerily similar . . .

A sudden gust of wind rustled through the woods, and despite the utter idyllic beauty of the setting, a chill ran through me. Maybe I was being overly imaginative, but I sensed that something dark lingered here. Was Robin's killer watching us from the forest?

•••

Rapping on the front door startled us. We'd been sitting around the kitchen table, tea going cold in front of us, lost in thought.

"Who is it?" Iona's eyes were wide with fear. I wondered if she was having a flashback to when Nate had died so unexpectedly, also from a fall off a roof he had no reason to be on.

"Probably the police," I said, unfolding my body and standing. "I'll get it." I shuffled through the living room to the front door, where I glimpsed a police cruiser parked behind the Cortina. An ambulance was pulling in.

I opened the door to reveal Inspector Sean Ryan and his frequent officer companion, Sergeant Gita Adhikari. Not that I saw Inspector Ryan a lot, but whenever I did he was working with the sergeant. Ryan was about Mum's age, very good-looking but quite intimidating. Sergeant Adhikari was gorgeous, with glossy hair tucked under her cap and striking features.

"Miss Kimball." The inspector tipped his head in greeting. "You called in the incident?"

"I did." I glanced over my shoulder at Aunt Violet and Iona, sitting frozen and staring our way. "Want me to show you, um, his body?" I would rather not, but I wasn't going to ask either of them to do it.

"Sergeant, why don't you talk to the other witnesses?" Inspector Ryan suggested. "Get their initial statements."

"Right away." Adhikari strode toward the door, all business instead of her usual friendly self.

I moved aside to let her in, then came out to join Inspector Ryan. "We can go around this way," I said, stepping onto a flagstone path that skirted the house, all too aware of the officer close on my heels. When we reached the corner, I stopped and said, "He's around back, underneath the scaffolding. He landed on a bush."

While Inspector Ryan continued on, I turned away, hugging myself. The side lawn ended in forest too, the trees and undergrowth so thick they appeared impenetrable. A squirrel ran along a branch overhead and chattered at me, scolding me for invading his space.

His face set in grim lines, Inspector Ryan hurried back around the corner. "Miss Kimball. I need to speak to the team and then I'll come talk to you." He glanced around. "Is there a good place for you to wait?" Another panda car had pulled in and officers were climbing out and slamming doors. The EMTs stood by the ambulance, waiting for instructions.

"How about on that bench?" I pointed to a carved wooden seat placed under a rose arbor. "I'll be over there."

The white roses over the arbor filled the air with sweetness. Tucked away underneath, I felt almost hidden as the officials got to work. Officers strode back and forth. Another car arrived. The pathologist, I guessed, since he was dressed in civilian clothing. Carrying a bag, he disappeared around the corner.

Seeing that no one was paying attention to me, I pulled out my phone and tapped *Robin Jones, Hazelhurst*, guessing that he lived in town. If nothing came up, I'd widen the search.

Aha. A list of links scrolled into view. The top one was Jones & Company Antiques, Hazelhurst. Clicking on it opened a website for an antiques store, filled with photographs of furniture, paintings, and decorative items. Whew. Pricy ones too.

Why had an antiques dealer been up on the cottage roof? Surely he wasn't interested in the moldy old bundles of thatch. It was all really strange.

A van eased down the drive, halting sharply when the driver saw all the parked vehicles. As an officer went over, the driver rolled down his window and I recognized his salt-and-pepper hair and attractive features. My uncle had returned.

I jumped off the bench and practically ran over. "Uncle Chris."

He bent forward, looking past the officer. "Molly. What are you doing here?"

"We came to visit Iona. She's doing a reading for us soon." The officer glared at me and I stepped back, knowing I was pushing the envelope.

My uncle's face had paled. "Iona," he croaked. "Is she all right?"

"She's fine. A little shaken up, but fine."

"Now, miss," the officer said. "I must ask you to refrain. Go back where you came from and wait for the inspector."

I couldn't resist giving him a saucy smile, despite the circumstances. "Yes, sir." I pointed at the bench. "I'll be right over there, Uncle Chris."

Sauntering away as slowly as possible, I heard the officer say, "Tell me, Mr. Marlowe, what's your business here today?" Obvious, but I supposed they had to start from scratch.

"I'm redoing the thatch," Uncle Chris said. "Took a break. Came back to all this. What happened?"

"We'll get to that in time," the officer said. He threw me a glare and I reluctantly moved faster.

Back at the bench, I opened the antiques store website again. In the "About Robin" section, I read: *Born with a knack for finding treasure in trash heaps, Robin has been dealing in antiques since the late nineties. His specialty is eighteenth- and nineteenth-century furnishings, decorative items, and tableware, with concentration in porcelain, silver, and gold plate. Robin also sells select fine art and estate jewelry.*

Okay, then. Still no clue what he'd been doing on the roof. Curious, maybe? Thatching was an interesting trade. I'd been hoping to go on a job with my uncle and watch him work.

I closed the website and opened a popular social media site. Robin had a personal page, fairly secure, but I could see a few posts and photographs. I squinted at the newest picture. He and a blond woman wearing sunglasses were seated at an outdoor café table, raising glasses of wine. She looked somewhat familiar, so I tried to enlarge it.

"Miss Kimball."

I jumped and the phone shot out of my hand and landed under the rosebush. "Inspector. I didn't see you." I wanted badly to retrieve my phone but thought I'd better leave it there for now.

My attempt to pretend it didn't exist was futile. Making a harrumphing sound, the inspector bent and teased my phone out from among the thorns, somehow managing not to get scratched. "I trust you weren't broadcasting the news on social media?"

If he saw Robin's page— I let out my breath when the screen went dark. "No. No, I wouldn't do that. I haven't even called my mother." That last was a tactical lob and I was rewarded when his ears reddened, just a little. I'd sensed a vibe between them during the first murder case, and although Mum wasn't ready to date, he didn't know that.

"Your mother." He gestured for me to scoot along and sat beside me. "How is she?"

"She's fine. Working at the bookshop." Lucky her. I clasped my hands together and waited for the questions, feeling like I was in the principal's office. Or sitting through a bad annual review at work. There was something about being interviewed by the police that was uncomfortable even if I was totally innocent. Of anything.

Inspector Ryan pulled out his device and sat, poised to type. "Miss Kimball. Take me through what happened, starting with why you're here."

I gave him an overview of our movements that morning, explaining that Iona York was one of the authors scheduled to do a reading. "Our meeting was at ten, so we got here maybe a few minutes before? She wasn't here, but she showed up right after we did. Uncle Chris wasn't here either."

"You didn't see Mr. Jones around the property, either in the garden or inside the house?"

"No. We didn't hear anything either when he fell." My hands were clasped so tightly my fingers hurt. "Or any footsteps on the roof, come to think of it. He must have been there the . . . whole time." How horrible to think that while we were drinking tea and eating biscuits a man had been lying dead outside.

"Who recognized him?" he asked. Another obvious question since I'd mentioned that in my call to 999.

"Iona. She said he was an old friend. I've never seen him before. I'm not sure about Aunt Violet. She knows quite a few people around here." Then I bit my tongue. The last thing I wanted to do was put my great-aunt into the firing line. She'd already been there once. "I'm her alibi, by the way. We were together all morning. She made me breakfast."

He lifted a brow, sending me a sidewise glance, but didn't comment. "Was Mr. Marlowe here when you arrived?" When I said no, he asked, "Did you see his vehicle on the way? Pass it on the lane or in Hazelhurst?"

Oh no. My uncle was in his sights, not Aunt Violet. It seemed my family had a talent for being nearby when suspicious deaths occurred—not what I'd expected from my British relatives. "Um, no, I didn't. In fact, I didn't even know he was working out here until I saw the scaffolding and Iona told me it was his job." I glanced toward the van. Uncle Chris was now standing outside it, smoking a cigarette. *Huh.* I didn't know he smoked. Then again, I didn't really know much about him at all given our family's estrangement had only recently lifted. Seeing me looking his way, he lifted the cigarette in a salute. I wanted to wave but held back, thinking the inspector would interpret it as a signal of some sort.

Ryan made a note. "I think we're all set for now, Miss Kimball. Once we're done talking to your aunt, you can leave." He gave me a closed-lipped smile. "We know where to find you."

I grunted a response to his attempted joke. "So, tell me. Was it an accident? Or . . ." I let my voice trail off.

He pulled back with a frown. "I can't possibly tell you that."

"Didn't think so." But it didn't hurt to try. As I got to my feet, a young man driving a Vespa buzzed into the yard, a young woman seated behind him. "We've got company."

Who was this? As they disembarked, taking off their helmets, I thought I knew. The young woman with Iona's hair had to be one of her daughters. After glancing around wildly at the ambulance and cruisers, she spotted Inspector Ryan and began to trot toward us. The young man was right behind her.

"What's going on?" she cried as she got closer. "Is Mum all right? Is Poppy?"

"Hold on," Inspector Ryan said. "Your mother is fine. Who is Poppy?"

"My sister." She glanced around wildly. "She left the dig and didn't come back." This must be Rose, the younger sibling.

"I haven't seen her," I said. Was *Poppy* involved with Robin's death? Had she come by, pushed him off the roof, then taken off? It was possible, although I had no clue why she would do that. I shook myself slightly. No need to speculate. That was the inspector's job, to put together the puzzle.

Inspector Ryan's antennae went up. "When did she leave?" His tone was sharp. "To clarify, you are talking about the Thornton Hall dig?"

"Of course," Rose said, her tone saying, What other dig was there? "What time was it, Ben? Um, maybe around nine? She said she had a quick errand and then was going to stop by here. She drives Daddy's old Ford Anglia, the one he restored."

I itched to look up *Ford Anglia* but refrained. "If she came by here, she left before we arrived," I said.

Her brow creasing, Rose stared at me. "Who are you? Not to be rude, but—"

"I'm Molly Kimball, from Thomas Marlowe. The book-store in Cambridge."

"Oh yeah." Her expression cleared. "Mum mentioned that she's doing a reading at your shop. Did you see Poppy's car on the road, maybe?" She sounded hopeful.

"I didn't see any traffic once we left the village," I said. "We got here around ten," I added to give her a point of reference.

She nodded. "What's going on, then? Is someone hurt?"

Inspector Ryan sighed. "I need to talk to you both. Why don't we go inside?" As he ushered the pair ahead of him, he glanced over his shoulder and said, "I'll send your aunt right out, Miss Kimball." Implied was the order to stay where I was.

I leaned on the hood of the Cortina while I waited, not daring to talk to Uncle Chris, who was still cooling his heels in his van. Officers were now combing the grounds in what the British police called a fingertip search. I hoped our tromping around hadn't obliterated any evidence.

Aunt Violet still hadn't emerged, so, dying to find out what was going on, I thought of a reason to go inside. Police vehicles were blocking us from leaving.

When I opened the front door, Rose was coming down the stairs. "She's not up there." Inspector Ryan, Iona, Aunt Violet, Sergeant Adhikari, and Ben were standing in a circle in the living room.

Ben's shoulders sagged. "I didn't think so, not with her car gone—"

Rose shrugged. "It was worth checking. You never know; she might have lent it to someone."

"I haven't seen Poppy this morning," Iona said, push-ing both hands through her curls. Her lips quivered and she pressed her mouth closed to stop them. "Or heard from her either. I have no idea where she is."

The obvious conclusion was that Poppy had come by while Iona was out. If so, I hoped she didn't have anything to do with Robin's death. This poor family had faced enough.

Ben pulled out his phone and shook his head. "She hasn't called or texted me either. Which is weird. We're practically joined at the hip."

Iona gave him an understanding smile. "As it should be when you're engaged." To me and Aunt Violet, she said, "Ben and Poppy are getting married this summer."

"Congratulations," I said. "That's wonderful." In light of their impending wedding, her lack of communication with Ben was troubling. If they were anything like the engaged couples I'd known, they were constantly in touch.

Inspector Ryan's brows drew together. "Miss Kimball. How can I help you?"

I flushed under his stern tone, but what could I expect? I had gone against his orders by coming into the cottage. "We're blocked in, Inspector. Can you get someone to move some cars?"

"Of course. I'll get someone right on it." He turned to Aunt Violet. "Miss Marlowe, you are free to go as well."

Aunt Violet didn't move. Instead, she said, "Iona, please call me if you need anything. And I do hope Poppy turns up soon."

Iona gave Aunt Violet a hug. "I'll keep you posted, I promise. Oh, and before you go." She darted over to a cardboard box next to the fireplace and pulled out a book. "This is for you and Molly."

I could see by the cover that it was the new edition of *The Strawberry Girls*. As Aunt Violet tucked it in the crook of her elbow and hoisted her bag with the other hand, I was comforted by one thing. Even in the face of unexpected death, police inquiries, and missing (temporarily I hoped) fiancées, the book business would go on.

CHAPTER 3

After much maneuvering, Aunt Violet and I made it out of Strawberry Cottage's driveway onto Thornton Lane. Uncle Chris had gestured that he'd give us a call, and I hoped the police would finish with him soon. I also wondered when they would let him continue with the roof. Within a day or two, I hoped, since the stripped sections might leak.

"Well, that was exciting," Aunt Violet said, huffing out a breath. "And I don't mean in a good way."

"They must think he was pushed," I said. "They're doing a full forensic investigation, it looked like to me." How did they determine the difference between jumping, falling, and pushing? Position? Signs of a struggle? I hadn't gone close enough to notice any.

"Sergeant Adhikari asked Iona if she knew of any reason for Robin to be on the roof. For example, checking the thatching job or looking for a leak."

I hadn't thought of that possibility. Maybe Robin helped Iona with household maintenance, even as an advisor. "What did she say?"

"She said absolutely not. She sees Robin around the village now and then, but he hadn't been to the cottage in years."

"So he went up there without permission. Really, really strange." We were riding past the dig now and I noticed that it was deserted. Seeing it reminded me of the missing woman. "I sure hope Poppy turns up. I hate to think she had something to do with it."

"Me too," Aunt Violet said. "It's tough enough for Iona to deal with a death at the cottage. But to have her daughter a suspect? Nerve-wracking."

"Tell me about it," I muttered, remembering when Aunt Violet was under suspicion of murder. Thinking of Poppy, I pulled out my phone and searched for *Ford Anglia*, learning that they were jaunty little sedans last built in the 1960s. "Wow. Her car is really cool. Look." The flying car in the Harry Potter books had been a Ford Anglia, I recalled.

Aunt Violet glanced at the photo. "They are lovely."

"I wonder what color she has. I like the pale turquoise." The shade reminded me of my bicycle, Belinda, an old-fashioned style with a wide, comfortable seat. I'd bought it at Kieran's shop. Everyone cycled in Cambridge.

Now that I was well away from the inspector, I opened Robin's social media page again. I scrolled up and down, but the picture of him drinking wine with a woman was gone. I even checked his photo albums. Not there. How could that be?

Then I got it. The person who tagged him had untagged him. Why? Was it his date? Or another friend? Were they trying to distance themselves from Robin? I closed my eyes trying to remember any details in the picture. They'd been sitting at a table with what in the background? I thought I recalled the glint of water. Along a river somewhere? That only narrowed it down to a million places, since pubs along the rivers in this region were very common—and quite delightful.

"What is it, Molly? You sound frustrated." I gave her an overview and she said, "Whoever did that must be involved. Think about it. Who even knows that Robin is dead? It hasn't been on the news yet."

"Good point, Aunt Violet." Maybe I should tell Inspector Ryan about the untagging. But then I'd have to admit I was snooping. And since I was . . .

The rest of the way back to Cambridge, I thoroughly analyzed Robin's page for clues. Status, single. Too easy if he'd been in a relationship, right? I took screenshots of his friend list and recent check-ins, then scrolled through his pictures. Attractive, with thick graying hair, a beaked nose, and a square jaw, he had a tendency to pose. Standing in doorways. Head and shoulder shots taken in front of windows. Lounging on a sofa, arms wide across the back, one ankle resting on the other leg. The jut of his chin was arrogant, the twinkle in his eyes both friendly and curious.

Robin had been an interesting character with his antiques business, rather big ego, and loads of personality. And now he was dead.

Swamped by a wave of sadness, I put the phone down. I hoped the police would find answers to the mystery of his death soon.

◂▮▸

"How did it go?" Mum looked up from the bookshop computer as we walked in the door.

Noticing that a woman was browsing within earshot, I handed Mum the new copy of *The Strawberry Girls*. "Here's the good news."

She was not stupid. "So what's the bad news?"

"We'll tell you in a minute," I said, moving aside as the customer approached the desk holding several books.

"I'll put on the kettle," Aunt Violet said, disappearing into the living quarters.

While Mum rang up the sale, I patted both cats and straightened a couple of shelves. Then I held the door for the customer. "Please come again."

"I will," she said with an eager smile. "I love this place."

As I started to close the door behind her, I spotted Kieran on his way over from the bike shop. "Hi there," I called.

"Hey, Molly." He gave me his easy grin, the one that lit up my insides. Not only was Kieran gorgeous with his dark curly hair, intense brown eyes, and chiseled features, he was also down-to-earth and really nice.

"What are you up to?" I stood back to let him enter the bookshop.

"I was wondering if you were free for a lunchtime bike ride and picnic along the river." He raised his brows, waiting for my answer.

What a perfect idea on this lovely day. "That sounds fun. What do I need to bring?"

"Nothing," he said. "We'll stop and grab sandwiches to go."

I glanced at my mother, then Aunt Violet, who had returned with the tea tray. Not that I had to ask permission, but I liked to be considerate of my business partners. "Fine with us," Aunt Violet said. "We can handle the shop."

"The answer is yes," I said. "What time?"

"Half an hour? I need to wrap up a couple of things." He said hello to Mum and Aunt Violet, then ducked back out of the shop.

Once the door closed, Mum said, "All right, spill. Quick before someone else comes in."

Aunt Violet handed Mum a mug of tea. "There's been another unfortunate death."

"No one we know," I added hastily. Then I reconsidered. "Well, you might know him. Robin Jones, an antiques dealer from Hazelhurst."

Mum blinked her eyes, one hand to her throat. "No, I don't know Robin. What happened?" Suspicion creased her brow. "More importantly, why are you telling me about it?"

Aunt Violet leaned against the counter with her mug. "He fell off Iona York's roof sometime this morning. I'm pretty sure before we got there. Iona wasn't home, she says, so she doesn't know what happened. Or even why he climbed up there. Your brother is in the middle of thatching the cottage, but he had left for a break. And strangest of all, Poppy, Iona's daughter, was supposed to stop by, but she's now missing."

"Wow, great synopsis," I said, impressed Aunt Violet had managed to get a whirlwind of a morning down to a few short sentences. "That's it in a nutshell. We were taking a tour of the garden with Iona when we found him. It was awful."

My mother must have seen something more than what I was saying in my face, because she put down her tea and held out her arms. "How dreadful. You poor thing."

"It *was* quite upsetting," Aunt Violet said.

Mum extended an arm to her. "Get over here." The three of us hugged for a long moment. Long enough for me to reflect on how fortunate I was to have these two in my life.

●I●

Before Kieran came back for our ride, I ran upstairs and changed into shorts, sneakers, and a T-shirt, hoping the change of clothes and scenery would help get the events of the morning out of my head. My hair went up into a pony-tail and I popped sunglasses on my nose. After filling my water bottle and grabbing a windbreaker and my helmet, I was ready.

We kept the bicycles in the garden shed, and as I wheeled Belinda out I couldn't help but smile at my pretty ride. One of the first things we'd done after moving here was buy bicycles. Mum's was pink and named Beatrice.

By the time I returned to the front, Kieran was already waiting, seated on a sleek black bicycle. Since he was wearing shorts and a T-shirt too, I couldn't help but notice his tanned, muscular legs and arms. His green T-shirt advertised Spinning Your Wheels, his bike shop. "Love your shirt," I said.

"Come with me and I'll give you one." He hopped off his bike and put down the stand. I followed suit and we walked over to the shop.

Tim, his lead employee, was behind the counter, tidying up. "Back already?" he asked with a grin. Lean and hand-some, with cropped blond hair, Tim was dating my friend Daisy from the tea shop. They made a great pair and we of-ten double-dated.

"Molly wants one of our shirts," Kieran said, pointing to the rack.

As I went over to pick one out—there were lots of color choices—Tim said, "Did you catch the noon news?" When we shook our heads, he said, "A man named Robin Jones fell off a roof over in Hazelhurst this morning. Do you know him, Kieran?"

Kieran thought for a moment. "I don't think so. Did they mention his age?"

"Fifty-one," Tim said. "The police are treating it as suspicious. They've put out a be-on-the-lookout for a woman named Poppy York."

"Poppy York?" Kieran looked shocked. "I went to primary school with Poppy. She was quite a bit younger. Back to Robin. Do they think he was murdered?"

"Sounds like it to me," Tim said. "With the police looking for Poppy and all."

"Unless they think she saw it happen," Kieran pointed out in his scrupulously fair and evenhanded way. He gave a snort of disbelief. "I can't imagine Poppy killing someone."

Over by the shirts, I was cringing, spinning the rack without really looking. I debated saying nothing but knew that holding back was futile. Sooner or later connections would be made. Aunt Violet and I might even be mentioned in news stories as witnesses.

"Um," I finally said, waving my hand. "We were there when it happened. Well, right after." They turned to stare at me with expressions of shock so similar I almost laughed. "Aunt Violet and I were visiting Poppy's mother, Iona York. She's one of our authors."

Kieran crossed the room in two bounds. "Are you all right?" His dark eyes roved over my face and body as if checking for injuries.

"I'm fine, Kieran," I said, touched by his concern. "It was awful, yes, but we came along after Robin fell. Or was pushed, which is a possibility. I was the one who called nine-nine-nine, and once they questioned us, they let us leave. I don't know much more, except that Poppy *is* missing. Earlier today, she left the dig at Thornton Hall. While we were still there, her sister and fiancé came looking for her."

"I hope to God she's not been hurt too," Tim said. "Maybe she got in the way of a killer."

"Yikes. I hope not." That was a theory I hadn't considered.

I prayed Poppy was merely off somewhere, not realizing that people would be worried. "They think she's in her car, so if you see a Ford Anglia, let the police know. There can't be too many of those around."

"That's right," Tim said. "They gave her vehicle and license plate. Love Anglias. Great old car."

Kieran pointed a forefinger. "I know the one, I think. I've seen a pale green Anglia around Hazelhurst."

"That's probably hers." Curious, I asked, "Have you seen Strawberry Cottage? It's right next door to Thornton Hall. That's where Iona lives."

He nodded, his eyes wide. "Of course I have. It's a beautiful old place." His lips curved. "I've even read Iona's book. My mother bought a copy."

"Which book is that, mate?" Tim asked.

"*The Strawberry Girls*," I said. "It's a children's book, a fairy tale."

Tim shook his head. "Never heard of it." He tipped his chin toward the shirts. "Did you find one you like?"

"No, not yet." I turned back to the rack. I grabbed a pink one in my size and held it up to my body. "What do you think?"

"It's you," Kieran said. "Put it on my account, all right, Tim?" To me, he said, "I track what I take out of inventory."

"Are you sure? I can pay for it." He waved that off, so next I asked, "Mind if I put it on?" The least I could do was wear my gift.

After I switched shirts in the changing room, we said goodbye to Tim, who said he hoped we would have a good time. As we walked back outside, I said, "I was going to tell you about Robin, promise." I didn't want Kieran to think I would hide anything from him.

He brushed that off. "My concern is how you're doing,

after a horrific experience like that." His gaze was somber as he studied my face.

"I'm okay." I pushed away the images crowding into my mind. "Getting some fresh air and exercise will help."

He took the hint and dropped the subject, instead telling me about our plan. "I thought we'd bike over to Midsummer Common for our picnic. A great sandwich place is on the way. How does that sound?"

"Absolutely perfect. I haven't been there yet." Although I'd been in Cambridge for a couple of months, I hadn't even scratched the surface when it came to exploring. I did know that Midsummer Common had been used for grazing since the twelfth century, meaning that yes, cows hung out in the middle of Cambridge. The common also bordered the River Cam, which wound through the city.

After I dropped my old shirt off inside the bookshop and we did a final check-over of our gear, we hopped on our bicycles and headed up Magpie Lane. At Trinity Street, we turned left, riding past Trinity College with its magnificent gate. Then we turned onto Market Street, which led us past a square full of vendor stalls. There had been a market here since Anglo Saxon times, which I found incredible to think about.

Kieran didn't stop at any of the food stalls, though. Instead, we continued onto a side street, where he pulled up in front of a small café. A sandwich board announced the day's offerings. "Tell me what you want and I'll go in."

"Oh, they all sound good." I studied the list, my mouth watering. "I'll have cheddar and tomato on wheat." Cheese sandwiches seemed to be more of a thing here, and I adored creamy yet savory English cheddar, good as any I'd had in Vermont.

"A bag of crisps?" he asked.

"Yes. And lemonade, please."

I waited with the bikes while he went inside and ordered. A poster in the window advertised the Strawberry Fair, which was happening a few days from now on Midsummer Common. Vendors, games, music, and no doubt plenty of fresh strawberries. It sounded fun.

Kieran emerged from the restaurant, carrying a sack under his arm. "That didn't take too long." He put the bag into his basket. "Ready?"

We climbed on and were soon underway again. "Do you go to the Strawberry Fair?" I asked as we rode side by side. "I just saw a poster for it."

"Wouldn't miss it," Kieran said. "The shop has a booth every year." He threw me a look of confusion. "So does the bookshop, usually."

I groaned in exasperation. "I guess we blew that. We didn't sign up." Aunt Violet must have forgotten and Mum and I were too new to know about the event.

"You can share our booth, if you want," he said. The path narrowed and he pulled ahead, to lead the way.

What a nice offer. I thought about what we could sell. Nothing too expensive, since the fair probably wasn't the venue for expensive and rare books. *The new Strawberry Girls books*. If we could get a box in time, they would be perfect.

The ride didn't take long, the distance barely a mile, and soon we were wheeling along the river looking for a free bench. We grabbed the first one we found, parking our bikes and sitting to eat.

To my dismay, I noticed they were herding the cattle on the common toward trucks waiting nearby.

"Where are they taking the cows?" I asked. "Did they

change their mind about allowing them to stay here?" Had the centuries-old tradition come to an end?

"They move them whenever there's an event," Kieran said. "They'll be back after; you'll see."

"Oh, good." Having grown up in Vermont, which was famous for its bovines, I loved that I could see a herd without leaving Cambridge.

Kieran unpacked the bag, placing our wrapped sandwiches on the bench between us. I picked mine up and peeled back the paper. "Yum," I said after a big mouthful. I wiped my mouth with a napkin, then reached for some crisps.

"Umm-hmm," Kieran agreed. After a few bites, he said, "There's something I've been meaning to ask you."

I stopped stuffing my face for a moment. "What's that?" His tone was serious, which made my pulse go up a notch.

He smiled. "Sorry, I didn't mean to alarm you. I, well, my—" He cleared his throat, then said in a rush, "My parents are having a garden party and I'd like you to come with me it will be fun promise."

I parsed apart his blurted words. Garden party. Hosted by his parents, Lord and Lady Scott. Then the heart of the matter hit me.

Kieran wanted me to meet his parents.

CHAPTER 4

"Garden party?" I squeaked. "You mean big hats, summer frocks, and a polite game of croquet on the lawn?" I was afraid to address the real issue, meaning that this felt like a big step forward in our relationship. Meeting *his* parents, I mean. Oh, he'd met *my* family, because how could he not, when we were neighbors.

So far, I'd been content to keep things the way they were, casual and fun. No pressure. No running the parental gauntlet. Which was way more intimidating than usual in this case. They probably wanted him involved with a member of the upper class. Gah, *upper class*. I couldn't believe I was even thinking in those terms.

"There might be croquet," he said. "No hats, though. It goes into the evening, so there will be a buffet dinner and dancing on the terrace. Mum goes all out decorating, even stringing lights through the garden. It's really lovely."

The party sounded amazing. How could I say no? Even if his parents didn't like me, what a great experience. It sounded like something out of a movie. "I should dress up, though, right?"

"Nothing too fancy. A short dress is fine." He lifted his sunglasses to look into my eyes. "Does this mean you'll come?" He mentioned the date.

Was I ready? Would I ever be? "Do a lot of people go?" I temporized, lifting my sunglasses too. I could stare into his eyes all day.

He guessed what I was really asking. "Dozens. Hundreds, even. You'll be lost in the crowd. It's very low-key, Molly, honestly."

Uh-huh. Low-key back home meant drinking beer around a bonfire, dressed in ratty jeans and a flannel. But at least an outdoor gathering wouldn't be as nerve-wracking and intense as, say, a sit-down dinner with the 'rents.

"I'd love to come," I said primly. "Thank you for the invitation." Now I had to find something appropriate to wear. Dressy enough to fit in but not too fluffy. I despised frills and bows and ruffles. Maybe Daisy could advise me.

Again, in that uncanny way he had, he read my mind. "By the way, Daisy and Tim are coming. You can ask Daisy about what to wear. She knows the drill."

"I was just thinking about asking her to help me. How do you do that? Know what I'm thinking, I mean."

Smiling, he slid his sunglasses down onto his nose and picked up his sandwich. "I'm a good guesser?"

No, it was more than that. Kieran *got* me. That's why I was dating him. It wasn't because I had fantasies of becoming Lady Molly. Not often, anyway—I wasn't made of stone.

"So," I asked after we ate quietly for a few minutes, "so, Robin Jones? He owned an antiques shop in Hazelhurst. Jones and Company."

"I've seen it," Kieran said. "Antiques are more my mother's thing than mine."

Since I certainly wasn't planning to ask his mother about Robin, I moved on to what was really bothering me. "My Uncle Chris might end up being a suspect."

In the middle of drinking water, he sputtered, then coughed. "Sorry," he said after he recovered. "How is your uncle involved?"

"He was thatching Strawberry Cottage," I explained. "Unbeknownst to us. He was off somewhere when we got there this morning, but came back right after the police arrived."

"So," he said slowly. "Because he was working on the roof, they think he was involved somehow?"

I inhaled, trying to ease the knot in my chest. "No one has actually said that. But maybe Uncle Chris is the reason Robin climbed up there." Saying these words aloud made my throat constrict.

"To talk to him, you mean?"

Unable to speak, I nodded. No scenario I could conjure would make Uncle Chris look good if he'd seen—or caused—Robin's fall. The fact that he hadn't called the police would weigh heavily against him.

"Did your uncle have dealings with Robin?" When I shrugged helplessly, since I absolutely had no idea, he reached out and took my hand. "Maybe Robin came to the cottage with someone—someone else entirely. And that person saw what happened." He paused. "What does Iona think?"

His reassurance had helped beat back the panic and my throat loosened. "She seemed as shocked as us when we found the . . . him." I didn't like calling a person, especially one who had recently been breathing, *the body*. "She was off doing an errand when Aunt Violet and I arrived, so she didn't even know Robin was there."

He exhaled. "Or so she says, right? Maybe she asked him to take a look at her roof for some reason."

"According to Aunt Violet, the police already thought of that and asked. Iona said Robin hadn't been at the cottage for years."

"Hmm." Kieran let that sink in. "But if he wasn't there to see your uncle or Iona, why did he go up on the roof?"

"I don't know. Isn't it strange? I don't think we're going to know until they find Poppy. Or another witness." Fingers crossed they didn't arrest Uncle Chris first.

❧

When we rolled back down Magpie Lane after lunch, Kieran stopped at the bike shop and I continued to Tea and Crumpets, across from the bookstore. I had to talk to Daisy.

Inside, Daisy was clearing a table, placing cups and plates on a tray. My friend was gorgeous, with blond curls and a curvy figure. Her uniform was a white bib apron over slacks and a T-shirt.

She looked up when the entrance bells jingled and smiled. "Nice hat." I put my hand to my helmet. "Oh, I forgot I had it on. Kieran and I just went for a ride." I glanced around, seeing only a few customers in the shop, tapping on laptops or reading a newspaper. "Daisy. He asked me to the garden party."

The smile widened into a grin as she continued to clear the table. "What did you say?"

I rolled my eyes. "What do you think I said? After I got over the shock, I mean. He told me you and Tim are going. You two can be my reinforcements."

"Reinforcements for what?" Daisy began carrying the tray toward the counter, gesturing with her chin that I should follow.

I was right on her heels. "When I meet his mother." I lowered my voice. "I'm petrified." Even as I realized how ridiculously backward this thinking was, I was worried Kieran's mother wouldn't like me. She might even encourage Kieran to dump me. How many books had I read and movies had I seen where the *commoner* was treated with disdain and even sent away in disgrace? The bottom line was, Kieran was from a different, less egalitarian world. People still believed in royalty here.

Daisy carried the tray through to the tiny kitchen, indicating I should follow. "She'll love you, Molly." She must have noticed I wasn't convinced, because she added, "What's important is that he cares about you. Kieran isn't going to let anyone tell him who to date." She slotted the dishes into a dishwasher basket.

"You're right. He really is fantastic." I felt a tiny bit better. Maybe I was jumping to conclusions. For all I knew, Lady Asha Scott had an enlightened worldview. "Want to help me find a dress? I've never been to a garden party."

"You bet," Daisy said. "We'll find something that will knock all their eyes out." She glanced out the window into the tea shop. "Tim told me about Robin Jones. You were there?"

I nodded, coming back to reality with a thump. "Aunt Violet and I were visiting Iona York. She's doing a reading for us soon." Mindful that new customers would probably interrupt us any minute, I gave her a quick overview of the situation. "Iona has had so much tragedy in her life." Thinking of Poppy, I continued, "I hope her daughter shows up soon and that she isn't involved."

"I remember when Nate died," Daisy said. She was also from Hazelhurst and had taken over the Cambridge tea shop from an aunt and uncle. "I was only a kid, but everyone in town knew the Yorks. They were such a beautiful couple and their daughters were adorable. They were a few years behind me in school."

"Have you read *The Strawberry Girls*?"

"It's one of my favorites," Daisy said. "I have a signed copy from when it was first published. My mum took me to a bookstore and Iona signed it for me. What a thrill."

"Well, you can have her sign the new edition for you at our reading," I said. *As long as Iona isn't in jail for murder.* I pushed that unpleasant thought aside. "We have a copy of the new book at the shop."

"I'll pop over later." Bells sounded and Daisy looked out into the main room. A trio of women was coming through the door. "I'd better get back to work."

"Me too," I said. "Oh, before I go, I'll take three of those strawberry scones." I'd noticed them on the way in and they would be perfect for our afternoon snack.

●●●

Back at the shop, I put my bike and helmet away and changed before joining Mum and Aunt Violet in the bookshop. After giving them the exciting news about the garden party invitation, I sat at the desk behind the counter to update our inventory system for the next hour or so.

Another part of my job was managing social media. Immediately, I thought about posting a picture of the updated Strawberry Girls book. The cover was so gorgeous, showing the two little girls riding a pony into the Deep Woods.

Then I had second thoughts. We should see what happened with Robin's death before launching a publicity campaign.

And speaking of which . . . I glanced around the shop to see what was going on. Aunt Violet was talking to a customer over in the history department, and Mum was waiting on someone at the counter.

Grabbing my laptop, I slipped away from the desk and headed to my favorite red velvet armchair. Tucked between two tall bookcases, the spot was secluded but allowed me to see new customers coming in. When I was working alone and it was quiet, I often sat there with Puck and relaxed. Knowing the ritual, he jumped down from a file cabinet and padded after me. Clarence, sprawled in his usual window, opened an eye and glared at us. "You can come too, Clarence," I said. He closed his eye and rolled over, feet in the air, as if to say, *I can't be bothered.* Clarence was definitely a cat with attitude.

First I checked the internet for updates about Robin Jones. Nothing new had been posted, only the same story Tim had mentioned. All right, then. Next I opened up Robin's social media page again.

The picture of Robin with the mysterious woman was still gone. I checked his photos again for any other sightings of her but was unsuccessful. Then I turned to his friends list and scrolled through, looking for blond women. There were quite a few. And wow, he had tons of friends. More than me. A few had heard the sad news and had posted their shock and dismay even though he obviously couldn't read them.

I thought about digging deeper into his friend list but decided to wait. My own friend list included people from elementary school, summer jobs, and college, other librarians, and almost complete randoms who knew other people I knew. His list was probably the same, meaning it could include people from fifty years ago all the way to someone he met last week. At this point I didn't have an inkling as to which of his acquaintances might be involved. Or might know something about his reason for visiting Strawberry Cottage.

On an impulse, I decided to look into Nathanial York's death. Two mysterious falls on adjacent properties seemed odd, especially since Iona had known both men. I didn't know if Robin had known Nate yet and didn't want to assume anything. The puzzle had piqued my research librarian instincts, so I went for it.

While searching for *Cambridge newspaper archives*, I found a site that allowed keyword searches of back issues. The date of Nate's death—June of 2003—was included in the available range.

My librarian Spidey senses tingled as I typed in the search bar. I adored research, which to me was like a treasure hunt—for information, not actual gold or gems. The thought of treasure made me think of the Thornton Hall dig. When I had a chance, I wanted to learn more about the project and Anglo-Saxon history in general.

While the search results loaded, I glanced around at the jam-packed bookshelves. We probably had a bunch of books on Anglo-Saxons. I'd take a look later.

"Local Man Plunges to Death" was the first headline I found. The article was short, with only the basics, stating that Nathanial York, thirty-one, of Hazelhurst, had been found at the foot of a "folly" tower on Thornton Hall property. The small headshot illustrating the article showed a good-looking man with a friendly grin and dark, curly hair.

There was a tower in *The Strawberry Girls*. I wondered how many spots around the cottage Nate and Iona had used in the book. Kind of a cool idea, especially since the book had been written for their daughters. The fact that it became a best-selling classic was a bonus.

Geoffrey Thornton had come across his friend's body while taking a morning walk. What a horrifying discovery. I was glad Nate's wife and children hadn't found him, at least.

I went back to the results and scrolled to an article that seemed to offer more information. "Writer Mourned after Tragic Fall. Police Investigating." As I scanned the text, the words *Robin Jones* jumped out at me. I think I even leaped a little in my seat, earning a glare from Puck, who was sprawled across my legs, sucking up heat from my laptop.

"Sorry about that." I gave him several soothing strokes along his back while I continued to read.

"It's a terrible shock," local antiques dealer Robin Jones said. "Nate was in good spirits at a gathering earlier that night [at Thornton Hall]."

So Robin Jones *had* been Nate's friend. He'd also been around the night Nate died. Did that mean something—or nothing? Now Robin had fallen to his death.

The article relayed that Geoffrey Thornton had held a party the evening before, attended by over fifty people. His parties were legendary, a villager was quoted as saying.

Aunt Violet had made a similar remark about Geoffrey's bashes. I kept reading, hoping to find additional names.

Another guest, Miranda Blake, was quoted: *"Nate was a dear," Blake, who owns a shop in the village, said. "Like many creative souls, he often struggled with depression. Or so he told me."*

The article managed to skirt making a definitive statement about why Nate fell from the tower—or the reason he was up there. No one seemed to know, nor did anyone claim to have seen him leave the party. Geoffrey Thornton was quoted as saying he was having the tower door and windows boarded up to prevent another tragedy. The article ended with a note that a coroner's inquest would be held shortly. Anyone who had witnessed Nate at the tower or spoken to him that night was urged to come forward.

The final article said that Nate's death had been ruled an accident. There was no mention of witnesses or new information.

I sat back, absorbing all this while patting Puck, who began to purr. What a sweetie. The main thing I had gleaned was that when Iona said Robin was a friend, it had been a long-standing relationship. Robin and this Miranda Blake had attended Geoffrey's parties. It sounded like they had known Nate quite well.

I did find it hard to believe that nobody saw anything. Miranda's remark implied that he'd committed suicide. The coroner hadn't agreed, apparently. No doubt speculations were running rampant back then, the villagers in shock at this young father's death. Since he'd been at a party, substances might have been involved. Had Geoffrey been worried about liability if Nate had alcohol or drugs in his bloodstream? Had they even tested him? People often looked for reasons, like depression or intoxication, because that felt safer than random bad luck. Had Nate climbed the tower as a late-evening jaunt on the way home?

At this point, decades later, it was probably too late to learn more. It was possible that Robin's death would give the police a reason to reopen Nate's case. Or the two tragedies could be entirely unrelated. This time, though, the police were treating the death as suspicious. I hadn't seen that wording in any of the articles about Nate.

I glanced at the laptop clock. Almost five. The afternoon had flown by and it was nearly time to go start dinner. The three of us took turns preparing meals, and I planned to grill chicken, bake potatoes, and make a green salad.

As I shifted in my chair, preparing to get up, a man wearing jeans and a T-shirt strode through the open store door. "Uncle Chris," I called, awkwardly carrying the computer and Puck out to meet him. I was dying to find out how it had gone with the police, but there were still a couple customers in the store. Aunt Violet wasn't anywhere in sight and Mum was helping someone choose a book in the fiction section.

He glanced around and spotted me. "Hello, Molly." An amused expression lit his face. "Got your arms full, I see."

Puck leaped down, tired of the way I was holding him, and stalked off, tail high and indignant. We both laughed.

"I really want an update," I said in a near whisper. "The store is closing soon. Can you hang around for a few?"

He nodded. "I knew you closed at five. I'll go browse." He headed toward the closest bookshelves.

I thought of something and followed him. "Do you want to stay for dinner? I'll bake an extra potato."

"That'd be nice, lass. Thank you."

Mum was herding her customer toward the cash register. As I placed my laptop behind the counter, I said, "I'm going to go start dinner. Uncle Chris is eating with us." She nodded in acknowledgement and started ringing up the sale.

Catching on that I was going into the kitchen, Puck and Clarence raced behind me, eager to check their dishes. "Give me a minute," I told them as they swarmed around my feet, almost tripping me. I filled their dishes before turning on the oven.

Pushing all thoughts about Robin and Nate out of my mind, I tied on an apron and focused on cooking, one of my favorite activities. I plopped potatoes in salt water to brine, then whipped up a marinade for the chicken. Olive oil, white wine, garlic, herbs, and spices went into a zipper bag along with the chicken. I plopped the bag into the fridge and pulled out vegetables for salad. Ruffled lettuce. A slender cucumber. Scallions. Big red tomatoes were waiting on the windowsill.

I'd been happy to learn that Cambridge was surrounded by small farms. Cloth bag in hand, I went to the Cambridge Market once or twice a week to visit my favorite vendors.

Aunt Violet had a stack of lovely old ceramic bowls with striped rims, and as I chose one for the salad I reflected on how much I loved living here. Cooking a meal in the same kitchen used by many generations of Marlowes, although upgraded fairly recently, made me feel connected with those who had come before.

June was such a lovely month in Cambridge, especially in our secluded nook in the heart of the city. The French doors were open to the garden, where birds chirped and flowers nodded in a soft breeze. Thanks to the automobile ban in the city's heart, we didn't hear much traffic, and occasional church bells were about the only ambient sound.

The potatoes went into the oven when it reached 400 degrees—or 204 Celsius. English recipes used the metric system for flour, sugar, and butter too. Thankfully, many recipes included measurement in cups as well. I continued chopping vegetables for the salad.

"Would you like a lager?" Mum asked as she breezed into the kitchen, Uncle Chris on her heels.

"I wouldn't say no," he said. "It's been a tough day."

Mum pulled a bottle of beer out of the fridge and popped the top. "Molly?"

"Love one." Beer was another department where England excelled. I often preferred beer, since many wines gave me a headache.

Holding his beer, Uncle Chris pulled out a chair and sat at the table. "Ah, it feels good to get off my feet. After they let me leave Strawberry Cottage, I worked on another job this afternoon."

"It's good you didn't lose the whole day," I said, covering the salad and popping it into the fridge before joining them at the table. Mum was drinking a glass of wine. "Where's Aunt Violet?"

"She went out on an errand." Mum turned to look outside. "Here she comes now."

Aunt Violet was coming through the back gate, a carrier bag in hand. By the time she reached the French doors, my mother was up and pouring her a glass.

"Good afternoon, Chris," Aunt Violet said, setting the shopping bag down on her armchair. Skeins of yarn poked out of the top, which answered the question about where she'd been. My great-aunt loved to knit, claiming that nothing else was as relaxing. I had a feeling this purchase was related to today's events. "How's the family?"

Uncle Chris made a face. "Janice and I have split up."

Mum and Aunt Violet made exclamations of surprise. I silently cheered. Sad to say, my aunt was a piece of work. She'd been abusive to my mother and I suspected to her husband as well. Spiteful, snobbish, a social climber—if Aunt Janice had any redeeming features I didn't know what they were.

"So you're going ahead with it, then," Mum said. "Divorce."

Uncle Chris pressed his lips together, his eyes bleak. "Looks that way. I did try, you know. Suggested counseling. Then a brief break, to see if we could reset our relationship, so to speak." His voice choked up and he took a swig of beer.

He set the beer onto the table and inhaled a big breath. "Janice had already started dating another man." As I was pondering the odd tense of his sentence, he went on. "Robin Jones."

CHAPTER 5

A stunned silence fell over the table. I was the first to speak, my voice rasping. "Aunt Janice dated Robin?" The implications made my head whirl. First, that she'd moved on so quickly, effectively pulling the plug on her marriage. Robin was a handsome man, probably well-off, and he had expensive tastes, judging by his antiques website. I could see Aunt Janice liking all that.

And, as his significant other, she should also be on the suspect list. I wonder if the police knew they'd been acquainted.

But the absolute worst thing about Janice dating Robin was, in addition to kicking Uncle Chris when he was down (where it counts), he now had a prime motive for murder. Even more damning, Robin had died at the site of a thatching job and Uncle Chris had been there that morning.

"They didn't arrest you?" I asked. Everyone turned to stare at me and I realized that of course they hadn't read my racing mind. "I don't think you're guilty," I said hastily. "I meant that the police might."

He dropped his gaze, pretending great interest in his beer

label. "They don't know." He must have felt our eyes boring into him, because he shrugged. "Seriously, I should tell them that my ex-wife was dating the bloke who just fell off my scaffolding?"

"Chris, you need to come clean," Mum said, sounding shocked but firm. "Get out ahead of this."

"She's right." Aunt Violet tapped a fist on the table for emphasis. "But before you do, call Sir Jon and ask him to represent you." Sir Jon was one of Aunt Violet's most fascinating college friends. The owner of another Cambridge bookshop, a barrister, and a former MI6 agent, Sir Jon had been knighted by the Queen for his very mysterious services. He was *good to know*, as they say.

Uncle Chris took a sip of beer. "I suppose I should. Call Sir Jon, I mean."

No promise to spill about Aunt Janice, not yet anyway. I wanted to nag, to tell him how bad withholding information would make him look, but somehow I managed to restrain myself. I could tell by the white lines beside Mum's nose that she felt the same. She was probably biting her tongue.

Aunt Violet had pulled out her cell phone. "I have his number right here." She peered over her eyeglasses at her nephew until he pulled out his own phone with a grumble. Then she read the phone number to him. "Got that?"

"Got it." Uncle Chris placed his phone on the table. "I'll give him a shout after dinner."

The mention of dinner reminded me to check the potatoes. They were about half-done, so a few more minutes and I'd pop out and start the grill.

I returned to my seat and picked up my beer. "How's Charlie taking the separation?" Charlie was around my age, but even so, I was sure seeing his parents go through a divorce was hard.

Uncle Chris pursed his lips. "All right for the most part. He says he understands. I try to leave him out of the middle, but I can't speak to the games his mother plays."

Mum made a gentle snort but didn't comment. "Charlie will be all right. Tell him to come by here anytime. We'd love to see him."

"I'll do that," my uncle said. "He's out of town right now, on a holiday with friends. They're climbing in Scotland."

"Cool," I said, picturing Scotland's breathtaking landscape and craggy cliffs. "I'd love to see his pictures when he gets back."

"I'll tell him," Uncle Chris promised. "Next time we chat." After a pause, he said, "Now that we've dissected my suspect status, I'd like to know what happened this morning. I didn't know you were coming out to Strawberry Cottage."

I glanced at Aunt Violet, who nodded, indicating I should lead off. "Iona is doing a reading later this month here at the bookshop. Aunt Violet and I went out to talk to her about that, which we really never got to. She was giving us a tour of the garden when we . . . um, found him."

"That must have been a horrid shock," my uncle said, shaking his head. "Awful. I started working early that morning, around seven or so. In this hot weather, I like to work when it's cool. Plus it's supposed to rain later. Thunderstorms. I took a break around nine and went out to grab a bacon sandwich and coffee."

"Did you see Robin at all?" I asked, the intensity in my voice surprising even me. "And what about Iona? Was she at the cottage when you left? She wasn't home when we got there."

Uncle Chris thought back, then nodded. "Her car was in the drive. I didn't say anything to her, since I come and go as

I like. I didn't see Robin on the property or along the road." His grin was crooked. "Or I might have been tempted to run him over."

His joke startled a laugh out of us. "Don't say that," Mum said. "Even in jest." She glanced around. "What if someone heard?"

"Don't worry, I know better than that," Uncle Chris said. "Besides, I didn't have a problem with Robin. I wasn't married to *him*. I barely knew the man." He twisted his lips. "Oh, I'd see him around town, at the pub, even church. We'd nod to each other. Janice was the same, until she went on that redecorating craze."

"She bought furniture from Robin?" I asked.

Uncle Chris nodded. "Several pieces. I'd come home and there would be something new, well, old, you know what I mean. I didn't have a problem with that. After I moved out last month, I heard through the grapevine that she was seeing him. Spending the night at his house." The back of his neck reddened. "What a way to learn something like that."

"I'm so sorry," Mum said, wincing. "How humiliating."

Aunt Violet made a snorting sound. "I hate to say it, Chris, but she's let you off the hook. You can make a clean break. Let her go and move on with your life."

Her blunt advice seemed to invigorate him. "Never thought of it like that. You're right, Aunt Violet. Not my choice, is it?"

To be honest, I wondered what would happen now that Robin was dead. Would Janice try to slink back into my uncle's life? I wouldn't put it past her. But she'd have to get through the three of us.

I rose to my feet. "Time to turn on the grill. Dinner in twenty." With Puck leading the way, I went through the French doors into the garden.

◀▶

Later that evening, in bed, I opened the new edition of *The Strawberry Girls*. The pages were glossy and stiff, the colors bright, the illustrations magical. My pulse rate went up in anticipation, a reaction any true book lover will understand.

At its most immersive, reading can feel like walking through a door into a different world. The new version of *The Strawberry Girls*, with expanded color illustrations and complementary but easy-to-read typesetting, didn't disappoint.

The Strawberry Girls

On a warm summer night, under the light of the Strawberry Moon, a little girl was born in a thatched cottage on the edge of the Deep Woods. Almost exactly one year later, while that same full moon shone, her sister came along. So of course the villagers called them the Strawberry Girls. "A sweet name for sweet babies," their mum said.

They were almost twins, but not quite, with identical dark hair and freckled noses. Poppy, the eldest, was a bit bossy. Rose was quiet—until she wasn't. They loved dressing up and dancing. Climbing apple trees in the fall. Wiggling their toes in the brook at the bottom of the garden. Until a fish nibbled Poppy's big toe. That put an end to that.

Their very favorite thing was having a picnic in the summerhouse smothered by a rambling rose. They liked to sit in the sweet-scented shade drinking milky tea and eating butterfly cakes and jam tarts while bees buzzed and birds sang. Then, one long, lazy afternoon, when it seemed like nothing new would ever happen, a girl on a fat white pony trotted out of the Deep Woods. They never had guests to tea, unless you counted a baby hedgehog named Ollie, who liked cake crumbs.

"Is that a crown on her head?" Rose asked with her mouth full.

"It looks like one to me," Poppy said. "And why is she wearing such a long dress? How can she climb trees?"

"Good question," Rose said. "Maybe I should give her a pair of my shorts."

Holding on to her crown, the girl slid off the pony—she'd been riding sidesaddle—and asked, pointing at the teapot, "May I have a cup?" She put a hand to her chest. "I'm parched."

At Poppy's nudge, Rose ran to get another teacup. When she returned, panting, she said, "Ooh, what a lovely pony. Can I ride him?"

The girl was already sitting cross-legged next to Poppy, stuffing a jam tart into her mouth. After she chewed and swallowed, she nodded. "Of course you can. Bramble is lovely."

Poppy, who had wanted to ask the same question but hadn't dared, said, "I'd better go first, Rose. To make sure that it's safe."

"He's safe as houses," the girl said. "By the way, I'm Audrey." She pointed her tart. "You're Rose. And you are?" Her brows went up as she stared at Poppy.

"Poppy." She poured a cup of tea for Audrey. "Very nice to meet you," she said in her best grown-up voice as she handed it over.

"Where do you live?" Rose asked, sitting with her

knees up to her chin. One had a scab and both were tanned dark from the sun.

Audrey gestured toward the woods but said nothing. She drained the cup of tea and held it out. "May I have another?"

After Audrey finished her tea, she helped Poppy climb aboard Bramble's broad back. "I can see so much from up here," Poppy cried with excitement as the pony ambled across the grass. "I can even reach the apples," she said, stretching her arm up into the tree.

"They're not ready yet," Rose said, impatiently waiting on the ground for her turn.

"I know that, silly," Poppy said, tossing her hair. Then she saw a nest among the leaves. The obliging Bramble edged closer so she could glimpse the fledglings, mouths gaping wide. "I found a bird's nest."

"I want to see." Rose strained on her tiptoes.

Poppy, kindly, slid down the tree. "Your turn."

Rose got on the pony for a peek, followed by Audrey. After, they played games in the garden, running and leaping and climbing trees. The sun was sinking low when Audrey said, "I have to go. May I come back and play another day?"

"Please do," Poppy and Rose said in unison. "We'd love to see you," Poppy added, the way her mother always did.

"Soon, then." Audrey flicked the reins and Bramble began to trot. "Goodbye." Girl and pony disappeared into the Deep Woods.

Audrey did return, and the three girls spent many days together in the garden. Then, one stormy after-

*noon, when the clouds gathered black and thunder
rumbled, Bramble trotted out of the woods alone.*

I closed the book there, knowing what was coming next
but wanting to delay the satisfaction and fun of reading it.
Now that I'd been to the real Strawberry Cottage, I could see
how faithfully Iona had depicted her home in the illustrations. It really was an enchanting place. No wonder she and
her husband had been inspired by their surroundings.

How especially sad it was, then, that Nate had died at
the stone tower, an important location in the book. It was interesting that she had included it at all, since the book had
been published after his death. Maybe she'd wanted to stay
faithful to his version, the early story she had fleshed out and
embellished.

I switched off the bedside lamp and lay down, Puck curled
beside me, but not too close. Summer air floated in through
the open window and it was too warm for his usual snuggle-
bear routine. "Good night, Puck." His response was a purr.

Breakfast was two local eggs over easy, served with thick
slices of homemade white bread toast with butter and strawberry jam, also homemade.

I sat in the back garden, leafing through the newest tabloids while I ate. Full of scandals and gossip, these lurid
publications were fun. Another reason I looked at them was
to find pictures of Kieran and me. Or just Kieran.

Oh, good grief. They'd snapped us sitting on the bench eating lunch. I had my helmet on and my mouth open. Why
hadn't I taken that thing off? Even worse was the caption.

"Kieran Scott dream date, complete with protection." I could hear the snickers all over Britain now.

Slapping the tabloid closed, I picked up my phone to focus on something far more important—Robin Jones. There were no updates. No news is good news, right? When you're expecting a relative to be arrested, that is.

Poppy York. A stab of concern made me pick up my phone again. I really hoped she'd shown up by now. Nothing new about her either. I checked her social media page, which had some public posts. *Poppy, come home.* So she was still missing.

Finished with my eggs, I slumped back in my seat and picked up my coffee mug. Where could she be? The most obvious conclusion was that she had killed Robin Jones and taken off.

What connection did they have, anyway? All I knew so far was that he was an old friend of the family. Had she worked for him in his store? Or, big ugh, had he been inappropriate with her? I sure hoped not. And again, why would they have a confrontation on the roof?

Her disappearance might have absolutely nothing to do with Robin. As far as I knew, no one had actually seen her at the cottage. It was only an assumption that she'd come by before leaving for who knew where, probably because she'd been working right next door. She might have taken off for a million other reasons. A fight with her fiancé. Or a disagreement with her boss at the dig.

The French doors creaked open and Aunt Violet emerged. "There you are, Molly." I must have had a strange look on my face, because she added, "I hope I'm not disturbing you."

I straightened in my chair. "No, just thinking. Wondering where Poppy York is and why she took off."

"Good question," Aunt Violet said. "I hope she's all right.

Her poor mother must be going bonkers." Leaving the door open, she took a couple more steps. "Sir Jon called. He wants me to meet him for lunch in Hazelhurst. Do you want to come along?"

That was an easy question to answer. "Yes, I'd love to." Then I reconsidered. "What about Mum? I hate to leave her alone for a second day in a row."

Aunt Violet waved that off. "Nina said that she'll be fine." Then she grinned. "If we let her take a spa day soon."

"Aww, spa day? Jealous." Maybe I could squeeze in a spa visit before the garden party, as long as I didn't try anything too harsh. A friend of mine once had a skin treatment right before an important date. Her face broke out and peeled in sheets. She ended up canceling. On second thought—no, I wasn't going to chicken out of meeting Kieran's parents.

I pushed back my chair and stood. "Lunch sounds fun." I squinted my eyes. "Unless you'd rather be alone with Sir Jon." My theory was that an old flame still burned between my great-aunt and her distinguished friend.

Aunt Violet laughed and shook her head. "If I did, I wouldn't have asked you, would I?"

"All right, it's a date." I gathered up my dishes. "I'll take care of these and go get ready to open."

The morning flew by, and soon Aunt Violet and I were headed to Hazelhurst in the Cortina. Our outing yesterday had ended with the discovery of a body. Today I'd gladly settle for a nice lunch and a pleasant afternoon.

The Saxon Arms was a rambling thatched building perched on the bank of the Ouse. The car park was almost full and the place had a bustling air, which boded well for the food.

"He's meeting us on the patio," Aunt Violet said as she pulled into a space and cut the engine. We gathered our handbags and climbed out, leaving the windows open a crack.

Not bothering to go inside, we made our way around the building to a flagstone terrace decorated with urns of flowers and partially covered by a pergola roof. Sir Jon was seated in the corner under the structure, a thick twining vine casting the table in deep, cool shade. His spot also had an excellent view of the terrace and grounds, I noticed. An old habit from his espionage days?

"Violet. Molly." With a smile of greeting, Sir Jon rose to his feet. At age seventy, he was dapper and trim with a full head of white hair. "So good of you to come." As always, his demeanor was formal, but today his outfit was casual, slacks and a polo shirt open at the neck.

"Nice to see you." Aunt Violet kissed Sir Jon on the cheek.

He shook my hand, then indicated we should sit. A server came bustling over, a curvy young woman wrapped in a big apron over a V-neck T-shirt and jeans.

"What can I get you?" she asked, handing us a small chalk menu. "Today's specials."

"The brown ale is good, Molly," Sir Jon said. He knew I loved beer.

"I'll have that. Are we ordering lunch now? And the fish pie." Fish pie was smoked fish in a delicious creamy sauce topped with mashed potatoes.

Sir Jon ordered steak pie and Aunt Violet chose fish pie as well. The server brought the ales and Aunt Violet's wine right over, plus three glasses of water.

For a few moments, we enjoyed our drinks while taking in other customers, the pub itself, and the garden bordering the river. Some tables had been set under tall trees on the lawn. That looked like a wonderful place to enjoy a meal.

"The ale is good," I said, wiping foam off my lip. The beer was nutty and dark, with a hoppy finish.

Sir Jon nodded in recognition of my comment. "I heard you had quite the time yesterday." He didn't need to elaborate.

"You could say that." I shook my head. "I've never been so surprised in my life." Well, almost never. "We were taking a nice walk in the garden when wham, there he was, lying in a bush."

Aunt Violet and I took turns describing our morning at Strawberry Cottage, pausing when our food was delivered. The server wore an odd expression when she set our piping-hot plates on the table, and I wondered if she had overheard our conversation.

She stood back and wiped her hands across her apron front. "Can I bring you anything else?"

Sir Jon looked into his almost empty pint. "Another, please." Aunt Violet and I shook our heads.

Still, the waitress hesitated. "I knew him, you know. Robin. He was a regular here." Troubled blue eyes took us in. "You must be the ladies who found him."

Despite the lack of detail in the police report, I wasn't surprised that she'd heard about us. No doubt all kinds of stories, true and false, were circulating.

"We are," Aunt Violet said. "We were visiting Iona York."

She winced. "That must have been awful. I can't imagine."

"I'm trying not to think about it," I said. "Did you know

him well?" I was curious to hear local people's thoughts about Robin.

"Not really," she said, tapping a finger on her chin. "He was here a lot, liked to sit at the bar and chat with the regulars."

My pulse gave a leap. The picture of Robin with the mysterious woman might have been taken at this pub. I also wondered about my aunt, if anyone beside my uncle knew she had been involved with Robin. "Was he ever here with a date?" Her brows knit in puzzlement, so I quickly added, "I'm thinking such a good-looking man must have had a significant other. How heartbreaking for her."

She nodded. "He did bring dates here sometimes. But no one steady." She gave a little laugh. "Not that I kept tabs or anything."

"Of course not," I said. Did that mean he didn't date anyone more than a few times or that his relationship with Aunt Janice was too new to be recognized as serious? I thought about showing her my aunt's picture, but that would be a bit over the top. I wasn't a private investigator on the trail of marital infidelity.

The server began backing away. "If there isn't anything else . . . I'll bring that beer right away."

"What was that about, Molly?" Sir Jon asked.

I glanced at Aunt Violet, who gave me a nod. I took that to mean she was okay with sharing family business. "My aunt and uncle recently split up, Janice and Chris Marlowe. According to my uncle, my aunt was having an affair with Robin." I curved my lips in a wry smile. "She brought him in to do some redecorating."

Sir Jon gave a snort. "I see." His gaze darkened. "Now I understand why Chris is under suspicion." The fact that he knew that didn't surprise me. Sir Jon was very well connected. "I had doubts that Robin climbed up on the roof to give him thatching pointers."

"I know." I shook my head. "It's so strange that Robin was up there. And yes, it does look bad for Uncle Chris." Would I feel the same if Aunt Janice was a top suspect? Um, probably not, to be honest.

Thinking that Sir Jon might know something, I asked, "Is there any sign of Poppy York yet? I'm really getting worried."

"I'm afraid not," he said. "I do know they're scouring the area for her vehicle, plus the airports, train stations, et cetera, on both sides of the Channel. They think her disappearance might tie into the international case."

"International case?" Aunt Violet asked. "What do you mean?"

Sir Jon glanced around to be sure no one was listening. "Interpol is investigating the sale of antiquities. Mr. Jones was helping them, as they say."

I immediately thought of the dig. Realizing I hadn't even tasted my lunch, I scooped up a bite of fish pie. Delicious. Creamy potatoes with flaky, tender white fish.

"What kind of antiquities?" Aunt Violet asked. "Is this related to our local Sutton Hoo?"

Sir Jon shrugged as he dug his fork into the shepherd's pie. "Not quite sure yet. Robin was tied into a network of dealers here and in Europe. Despite the tight rein governments try to keep on such things, some objects still end up on the black market."

"I've never understood the allure," Aunt Violet said. "Anything bought that way has to stay under wraps forever."

"For some, it's just possession that gives them a thrill," Sir Jon said. "Even more so if they're flaunting the law."

"Was Robin involved in a sting?" I asked, thinking how exciting that would be. Then I came down to earth with a thump. *Unless this mission had led to his death.*

"It's possible they were setting one up," Sir Jon said. "As you can see, this adds a whole new layer to the murder case. Someone might have gotten wind that he was working undercover for the Crown."

"Are you back at work, Jon?" Aunt Violet asked, a speculative twinkle in her eye. "Or is your interest purely academic?"

After a long pause, he said, "Academic, of course. I hung up my spurs long ago." I didn't quite believe him, especially when he added, "Want to visit the dig with me this afternoon? I'm delivering books to Geoffrey Thornton and he'll probably let us take a peek."

Get close to an ongoing archeology site? He didn't have to ask me twice. "I'd love to. Aunt Violet, can we go?"

"Wouldn't miss it," Aunt Violet said. "Ever since I read about King Tut, I've wanted to find an untouched tomb."

That sounded kind of gruesome, but I knew what she meant. The idea of discovering objects from a thousand years ago was fascinating. Everything—the dishes, grains of wheat, religious statues—spoke volumes about life in the past. Forensic examinations of mummies and bones provided new information about ancient diets and disease.

I focused on my meal, excited to finish eating and go see the dig site. Another thought popped into my mind. *And check on Poppy.* With any luck, she was back at work with the crew.

◆◗◀

We left the Cortina at the pub and rode to Thornton Hall in Sir Jon's Aston Martin, which had the top down. I loved this car, which made me feel like a character in a James Bond film. Except for that fact that I was squashed in the rear, in far from a glamorous position.

Traffic was crawling along the high street, which gave me plenty of time to gawk around at the businesses. I spotted a cute café and a boutique with some pretty dresses in the window. If Daisy and I didn't find garden party outfits in Cambridge, we could come out here—if Daisy drove. Skittish about driving on the left side of the road, I hadn't ventured behind the wheel of a car since we'd moved to England.

As the Aston Martin inched past Jones & Company, Robin's store, I saw a flash of movement inside. But the store was closed—a big sign in the window said so. "Stop," I shouted.

Aunt Violet turned with a frown. "We can hear you, Molly. What's the matter?"

I pointed at the dark plate-glass window. The movement flickered again. "Someone is inside Robin's store."

"Are you sure about that?" Sir Jon asked. He craned his neck to look past Aunt Violet.

"Positive." They must be in there without permission, I guessed, poking around in the dark like that. If it were the police, the lights would be on.

Flipping on his turn signal, Sir Jon turned down the alley next to the store so fast I had to brace myself. Braking sharply, he cut the engine, and we all jumped out. At the front door, Sir Jon rapped on the glass while I cupped my hands on the plate-glass window and peered inside.

"Can you see anyone?" Aunt Violet asked. No one had come to answer the door, of course.

"I think so," I said. "Yes." A tall shape sidled between looming shadows of furniture, barely visible in the faint light from a side window. Something fell over with a thud, followed by the sound of breaking glass.

CHAPTER 6

"That's definitely not the police. Call nine-nine-nine." Sir Jon took off running, skirting the building to go around to the rear.

Aunt Violet whipped out her phone and made the call. I gestured toward her, indicating I was following Sir Jon. The alley was narrow, barely wide enough for a car. I edged past the Aston Martin and ran as fast as I could in my sandals on the slippery cobblestones.

At the far end, the alley gave way to a lane behind the row of buildings. The area behind the antiques shop was fenced in, and that was where I found Sir Jon, staring at the open gate.

"He got away," he said glumly.

"Are you sure?" I edged closer so I could see through the gate. Inside was a small courtyard holding several garbage bins, a stack of flattened cardboard boxes, and a couple of clay pots holding dead plants.

The back door of the store hung open. I started to move

toward it, but Sir Jon put a hand on my arm. "Better not, Molly. Let the police handle it."

He was right. It did look like the intruder had escaped, unless they were hiding inside hoping we would go away.

Blue lights flashed down the alley, followed by the chirp of a panda car.

"There they are," I said needlessly.

"I'll wait here," Sir Jon said. "Go around and tell them what we found."

By the time I made it down the alley, a pair of constables was talking to Aunt Violet. One was a trim young man with dark skin, the other a woman with curly red hair. The cruiser sat at the curb, lights flashing.

"Molly, tell them what you saw," Aunt Violet said. "This is Molly Kimball, my great-niece. Molly, meet Constable Malago and Constable Johnson."

"I know you," the man said. "You were at Strawberry Cottage yesterday." He nodded toward his partner. "Johnson and I were pulled in to help."

His comment gave me the perfect intro. "We *were* there," I said. "Which is why I was staring at Robin's shop when we drove past." I pointed at the window. "I saw something moving around, which I thought was strange. If someone was inside with permission, the lights would have been on, right?"

The constables exchanged glances, acknowledging the truth of what I said. "What happened next?" Constable Johnson asked. She was taking notes.

"Sir Jon pulled into the alley and we all got out. He knocked on the door while I looked through the window. I saw someone moving around and then something fell over inside. Something big. Glass broke too." I paused to let her get that down. "Sir Jon ran around back and so did I. The back door and the gate are both open. They must have gone out that way."

"Did you go in?" the male constable asked.

I shook my head. "No. Sir Jon is still back there, guarding the place."

"Let's go round and talk to him, take a look inside," he said to his companion.

"Hold on, Gabe," she said, fingers busy on her tablet. "Almost ready." She regarded us with cool blue eyes. "You two stay here, all right?"

While the officers went to join Sir Jon, Aunt Violet and I stood close together on the sidewalk, trying to look nonchalant as passersby on foot and in vehicles gawked. Who could blame them, with blue lights flashing in front of a store owned by a dead man?

An older man walking a tiny white dog attempted to engage us in conversation. "What's going on?" he asked in a scratchy voice. "Did someone break into Robin's store?" We ignored his questions, but he stood there staring while his dog became very well acquainted with our shoes.

"We don't really know," I finally said. The officers would not be happy if we started gossiping.

"The police will sort it out," Aunt Violet said, a brisk tone in her voice. "I'm sure it will be in their report."

When the little dog lifted his leg over my foot, I jumped back. "Um, your dog . . ."

He glanced down and, giving a gentle jerk on the leash, started off again, muttering under his breath. His tiny pet scurried ahead, no doubt eager to find another target.

The minutes dragged past and I began to think about climbing into the Aston Martin to wait. Or nipping down the street to a café for a coffee to go. Then we heard voices and Sir Jon and the two officers came back around the building.

"We'll take it from here," Constable Johnson told us. "Thank you for calling in so promptly."

"Did someone break in?" I asked, eager to glean details.

The two officers glanced at each other; then Constable Johnson said, "No sign of forced entry. We did find a turned-over table and some broken dishes. The way they ran off gives me cause to believe they weren't supposed to be inside."

Lack of a forced entry must mean the intruder had used a key, assuming Robin kept the place locked. Someone close to him? Or maybe not. They might have stolen it. I wondered if the police had found keys on Robin's body, but I didn't dare ask.

"Is anything missing?" Aunt Violet asked. "I'm sure he had some valuable merchandise in his shop."

A rueful smile crossed Constable Malago's face. "It will take someone more expert than me to figure that out. The place is absolutely crammed with stuff."

Constable Johnson gave an eye roll. "He's right about that. Anyway, you're free to go." The shift in her tone told us we should leave now. "If we have any other questions, we'll give you a call."

As we drove away, the two officers were conferring on the sidewalk, staring up at Robin's building as though it held answers. I wondered if we would ever know who had been rummaging around inside—and why.

When Sir Jon turned into the drive at Thornton Hall, I clenched my fists in excitement, eager to get a closer look at this magnificent house. It wasn't huge, like Downton Abbey, but it was gracious and elegant with its tall windows and groomed landscaping.

The Aston Martin crunched on gravel as Sir Jon swept around a fountain and parked near the main entrance. We barely had time to climb out before a man in his fifties emerged from the front door. Tall and lean with stooped shoulders, he had hazel eyes, salt-and-pepper hair and beard, and a faintly sardonic, world-weary air.

"So good of you to stop by." As he shook Sir Jon's hand, his gaze roamed over us with frank curiosity.

"Geoffrey, let me introduce two very good friends of mine, Violet Marlowe and Molly Kimball. They own Thomas Marlowe in Cambridge."

Geoffrey shook Aunt Violet's hand. "Of course I know Violet. Thomas Marlowe is one of my favorite haunts." He turned to me, his eyes assessing but friendly. "You must be the American niece."

"That's me," I said. "Nice to meet you."

"I've got your books right here." Sir Jon retrieved a large bag from the rear seat.

Geoffrey took the delivery with thanks. "I was about to go across the street and check out the dig. Want to come along? Then, if you have time, we'll have tea on the terrace."

I suppressed a squeal. View an archeological dig and have tea at a manor house in the same day? I was living the dream.

"We were hoping to get a look at the project," Sir Jon said. "Lead on."

"Let me put this inside and I'll be right with you." Geoffrey disappeared into the house with the bag, and when he returned he was wearing a battered tweed hat and carrying a walking stick. Very much the English gentleman out for a ramble on his estate.

We set off down the drive on foot, strolling under the shade of the enormous beech trees. Plush lawns stretched to either side of us, ending in intriguing walls that must enclose gardens. I hoped I could tour them at some point.

As Geoffrey ambled along, swinging his stick, I wondered what he thought about Robin's death. Nate York had also died on his property, something else I'd love to ask him about. But now wasn't the time or place, so instead I said, "It must be so fascinating to have a dig on your own property."

He turned to smile at me. "It has been. To think that an Anglo-Saxon settlement has been lurking under my field all this time. When Rob Taylor, one of my tenant farmers, plowed up an Anglo-Saxon bone flute, well, we had to see what else is under there."

"A bone flute?" Aunt Violet said. "What a great find."

Geoffrey stopped walking and pulled out his phone. After scrolling through, he showed us a picture of the artifact, which yes, looked like a simple flute with finger holes. Goose bumps rose on my arms as I pictured the person who had played it a thousand years ago.

"I'll let Dr. Holloway fill you in on the rest of it." Geoffrey said. "He's the expert. Though I am reading up on the subject, hence the book delivery, Sir Jon."

We had reached the road, where we paused to allow a couple of cars to pass by. They of course slowed to almost a crawl to gawk at the dig.

"I'm guessing there's a lot more traffic along here right now," Sir Jon said, laughter in his voice.

Geoffrey looked both ways before leading us across the street. "You've got that right. Usually we hardly see anyone."

On the other side, we crossed a ditch and walked across the field toward the activity. As we'd seen yesterday, several people were hunched over trenches in the ground, including Ben and Rose. To my dismay, I didn't see Poppy, whose picture had been included on the latest Strawberry Girls book jacket, posed with her mother and sister. Was she still missing?

An older man wearing a helmet straightened up as we drew closer to the work site. He waved, then waited with hands on his hips.

"Good afternoon, Geoffrey," he said, his gaze curious as he studied our faces.

"These are friends of mine, Malcolm," Geoffrey said. "They came by the house and wanted to take a peek." He introduced us, and Ben and Rose both looked over in recognition.

"Nice to meet you," Malcolm said. He gestured at the field, at other test pits and other trenches. "It's a very exciting project. We think there were up to ten buildings here at one time. Similar to the site at Houghton, though smaller. So far we've found pottery shards, metal tools, and pieces of timber framing."

He invited us to step closer to the trench, where Ben was carefully brushing dirt away. "We excavate in layers, making a record of each step. While we do take photographs, Rose sketches as we go, artifacts and soil composition both."

Rose held up her pad, displaying a drawing of the trench. She had also noted exactly where items had been found.

"What a cool job," I said to her. "It must be fun."

She shrugged with one shoulder, a pleased smile on her lips. "It's fascinating, like a treasure hunt. You never know what you'll dig up."

Ben glanced up from his work. "Like the privy we found?" He grinned. "If anything is old enough, it becomes worthy of study."

Dr. Holloway cleared his throat. "Actually, many privies were used as garbage pits and, due to the nature of the use, quite frequently weren't disturbed."

An interesting factoid, to be sure. Obviously, the impulse to dispose of things in latrines was an old one.

"Are you going to excavate the barrows?" Aunt Violet asked, referring to several large, long burial mounds across the field. It was inside one of those ancient structures that the Sutton Hoo treasure had been found.

Malcolm glanced at Geoffrey. "We're discussing that. It will depend on funding, like everything we do."

Ben looked up with a laugh. "If we find enough interesting artifacts in this phase, additional funding will be a shoo-in."

"From your mouth to God's ears," Malcolm said dryly. "The department is always weighing competing projects. We've made a good start here, though. I'm very pleased." He turned to Geoffrey. "I had a call today about a television interview. Can I fill you in?"

"Please do," Geoffrey said. To us, he said, "Excuse me for a moment, if you would."

Sir Jon said to Aunt Violet, "Want to look at the other trench?" Another team was working a short distance away.

"Love to," she said. "Coming, Molly?"

Seizing the opportunity to talk to Ben and Rose, I declined. As Sir Jon and Aunt Violet walked away, I asked, "Is Poppy back?" My concern about her had been like a low-grade fever, nagging and constant.

Rose's mouth turned down. "Not yet. We haven't heard a peep either." She stopped sketching. "We were up almost all night driving around Cambridge and the countryside looking for her. Neither of us wanted to come to work today, but Dr. Holloway would replace us in a heartbeat. He's on a very tight deadline."

"I'm exhausted," Ben said with a groan. "But I can't afford to get booted. This dig is part of my independent research project." After a beat, he added, "Neither can Poppy. It's not like her to skive off." The bleak note in his voice told me that he was really worried. Glancing up at me, he brushed dark hair out of his eyes. "Something was bothering her. If only I'd pressed her for an answer."

Like what? I wondered. College? Family problems? Or Robin Jones and whatever he was up to?

"Don't beat yourself up, Ben," Rose said. "You know how stubborn she can be." But behind the bravado, she looked frightened.

"They haven't found her car?" I asked.

"No, not yet," Ben said. "No sign of it in the transport station parking lots, they said. Which means she must have driven somewhere."

That was bad news. Not only could she be anywhere on the island, she might have crossed the Channel through the tunnel. Poppy could be halfway across Europe by now.

Impulsively, I said, "If there's anything I can do . . ."

Ben threw me a nod as he returned to his work, but Rose tilted her head and studied me with narrowed eyes. "I heard about your involvement with that murder case. My mother was talking about it this morning." She paused, then seemed to steel herself to ask, "Do you think you can help us find her?"

I began to regret my offer, realizing that the task was way over my head. I didn't have a fraction of the police department's resources, for one thing. If they couldn't find her, how would I? And what if . . . I didn't want to go there. The truth was, Poppy might have met with foul play or been abducted. Or maybe she had killed Robin before running away, as the police seemed to suspect.

At the same time, how could I refuse to try? Maybe my efforts, however small, would uncover a clue to her whereabouts. To what had happened at Strawberry Cottage.

Both of them were staring at me now. My throat was bone dry I discovered, making it hard to swallow. "I'll try," I finally croaked out. "Although I'm no missing persons expert, I'm warning you. Where should we begin?"

"The bookshop is right across the street from the Magpie Pub, right?" Rose said. "Why don't we meet for a drink tonight and talk about it?"

I thought about my schedule, not that it was exactly jam-packed. Tonight was darts night and dinner with Kieran, Daisy, and Tim. "I can do that," I said. "I was planning to be there with friends anyway."

Geoffrey and Malcolm returned, followed by Sir Jon and my aunt. "I'm ready for a cup of tea," Geoffrey said. "Shall we go up to the house?"

When the four of us returned to Thornton Hall, a sleek black Peugeot was parked in the drive. Geoffrey smiled when he saw it, and a moment later I realized why.

The front door burst open and a beautiful woman in her late forties flew down the short flight of stairs. Slim, with long and curly dark hair, she wore a gauzy sequined dress, rings on every finger and bangle bracelets up her arm.

"There you are, darling." She flung her arms around Geoffrey's neck, making him stagger backward slightly.

He laughed before returning the embrace. "Now that's what I call a greeting." After releasing her, he left his arm around her waist. "Violet, Molly, Sir Jon, this is Miranda."

Still in the shelter of his arm, Miranda gave us a dimpled smile and a tiny wave. "Lovely to meet you. Won't you please come in?" She broke away from Geoffrey and led the way into the house, burbling on about tea on the terrace.

The entrance hall was paneled, with a staircase under an arch straight ahead and lush antique carpets underfoot.

Through another arch to the left was a double drawing room, and Miranda led us through there to the rear, where we exited through French doors.

On the partially covered terrace, a table was set for tea. Still acting as hostess, she ushered us to seats. From here, we overlooked a gravel walk hemmed with conical topiaries and flower beds. Beyond, on the lower level, were a tennis court, sunken garden, and croquet lawn.

Miranda caught me staring at the garden. "Aren't the grounds gorgeous?" She put a hand on Geoffrey's knee. "He's been restoring them to their former glory." She lifted the teapot and began to fill cups.

"You could say it's my hobby," Geoffrey said. "I found old plans and decided to restore a few features. The reflecting pool was a mess and the topiaries needed severe haircuts."

"You've done a lovely job," Sir Jon said. Wearing sunglasses, he sat back in his seat with folded arms, inscrutable and alert. I didn't know the former secret agent well, but I did recognize a shift to work mode. What was he thinking behind those Foster Grants?

"I'll give you a tour if you like. Meanwhile, dig in." Geoffrey gestured toward the tiered dishes holding tiny baked treats and tea sandwiches.

I was stuffed from lunch, but I tried the smoked salmon and cucumber sandwiches anyway. They were barely bigger than bite-size, so I was confident I could fit them in.

Miranda handed around the cups. "Wasn't that a shocker about Robin Jones?"

A dense silence fell over the table, broken only by the faint twitter of birds in the nearby trees. Because Geoffrey and Miranda were Robin's friends, I'd been wondering in the back of my mind what they thought about his death. I hadn't expected her or Geoffrey to address it so openly, though, and by the expression on Aunt Violet's face, neither had she. Sir Jon remained inscrutable.

Geoffrey shifted in his seat. "It was very upsetting," he mumbled. "Not sure it's a teatime topic, my dear."

Spots of color stood out in Miranda's cheeks, and her dark eyes darted from face to face. She settled on me. "You were there, weren't you, Molly? Iona told me all about it, poor thing. She's still in shock."

Feeling compelled to say something, I said, "Aunt Violet and I were taking a tour of the garden when we found him. What a tragedy. He must have slipped and fallen." This was entirely opposite of what I—and the police—believed, but I didn't want to discuss a murder case with Miranda. Not here, anyway.

Her response was to glance away with a sniff. "Yes. Well. Robin was always sticking his nose in. . . . Why was he even up on the roof? Any idea?" She wasn't letting it go.

I shrugged as I reached for another cucumber sandwich. They were so simple yet tasty, I decided to make them at home. "Interested in the thatching job, maybe? It is fascinating work. I'm going to go on a job with my uncle soon, hopefully. Chris Marlowe is my uncle."

Miranda touched Geoffrey's arm and said softly, "I didn't see Robin after breakfast. Did you?"

I stole a glance at Aunt Violet and Sir Jon. Robin had seen this couple the morning he died. Maybe they knew something, even if they didn't realize it yet.

Geoffrey's brow furrowed. "Come to think of it, no. I excused myself to make a few calls and I assumed he'd left. For the village, I mean."

Miranda tossed her hair. "I did wonder why his shop

wasn't open when I drove past." To us, she said, "I have a shop in the village. Titania's Bower."

"I've seen it," Aunt Violet said. "It's lovely."

Geoffrey cleared his throat to announce a change of subject. "Are you ready for the Strawberry Fair, dear? I'm available to help set up, if you need me."

Aunt Violet seized on the subject. "Are you renting a booth, Miranda?"

"I am." Miranda played with the bracelets on her arm. "I do it every year. My products are very popular." She smiled. "Especially my love sachets and potions. So perfect for June, don't you think?" She sighed. "Lovers under the Strawberry Moon."

I enjoyed herbal remedies and teas—spells and magic, not so much. But I could see why her novelty items would be popular. "We have an offer to share a booth." To Aunt Violet, I said, "Kieran and Tim said we could share theirs. I've been meaning to talk to you about it."

"Oh, good," Aunt Violet said. "The fair completely slipped my mind this year. Thomas Marlowe usually has a booth."

"Are you talking about Kieran Scott?" Miranda asked. Once again, she studied me with those intense dark eyes. "I thought you looked familiar. I've seen you in the tabloids, Vermont beauty."

Now it was my turn to blush. "Who hasn't? It's so embarrassing."

"Enjoy the moment, my dear." Miranda tossed back her hair. "The spotlight tends to move on."

That stung, as if she'd slapped my cheek. Several possible retorts crowded into my mind, but I managed to hold them back. Instead, I said, "One thing I'm sure I'll enjoy is the upcoming garden party at Hazelhurst House."

Her eyes flared with surprise. "You've been invited?"

"Of course," I said, injecting smugness into my tone. I wasn't generally such a social-positioning jerk, but this woman deserved it. "Kieran insisted I go with him."

"That party is the talk of the county every year," Aunt Violet said, giving me a look that said she saw right through me. "What a bash."

Miranda placed a hand on Geoffrey's forearm. "Like your parties. We should plan something casual and fun soon. Midsummer Eve maybe?"

His arm jerked away, which made me wonder if he was remembering another Midsummer Eve party almost twenty years ago. The one when Nate York had died. What was Miranda thinking? Her suggestion was, at the very least, thoughtless.

Realizing I needed a restroom visit, I asked for directions, then excused myself. The half bath was located in the hallway, in what had to be a former closet. After washing up, I decided to linger on the way back to the terrace, taking the opportunity to poke around this gorgeous house.

Adjacent to the drawing room was a formal dining room, and on the other side of the hall were a study and, most thrilling of all, a library. A dream library with floor-to-ceiling bookshelves reached by a sliding wrought-iron ladder, and soft leather furniture and window seats, perfect places to curl up in and read. If only I had time to browse the shelves.

Giving the library one last glance of longing, I noticed a collection of black-and-white photographs on one wall. Curious, I crept into the room to take a closer look.

The pictures were a series of candid yet artful shots taken around the manor. A group shot on the terrace caught my eye. Dressed in Shakespeare-era costumes, the gang was hamming it up, including Iona and Nate York, whom I recognized from the newspaper article about his death. The occasion must have been one of Geoffrey's famed parties.

Nate was cute in a jester's hat, while next to him Iona was stunning, flowers in her hair and wearing in a flowing gown. I recognized Robin, striking a pose in a doublet, and Geoffrey, a king's crown worn askew. Miranda, dressed like Titania the Fairy Queen, was front and center, the dramatic focal point. Typical, from what I'd seen so far of the woman.

Some of the other faces I didn't recognize, and acting purely on instinct, I pulled out my phone and took a picture. Maybe someone else in the group had some clue as to what had happened to Nate, why he'd fallen off the tower. Now, twenty years later, another of the happy band had died in a similar way.

"There you are," a voice said behind me. "I thought you'd gotten lost."

I jumped, turned, and almost dropped my phone, all in one move that almost sent me over. "Oh," I said, my heart pounding. "Geoffrey." I tried to laugh. "I admit it, I was being nosy. Your library is fantastic. A booklover's dream."

He gazed around the room, satisfaction plain on his face. "Isn't it? My great-grandfather started the collection and we've added to it through the years. You're welcome to visit anytime."

"Really?" My voice rose almost to a squeak. "That's so kind of you." Now I felt guilty for sneaking around without permission.

What he said next really surprised me. "Don't mind Miranda," he said, his voice almost a whisper. "She can be a little abrasive, but she means well."

"I'm sure," I said, because really, what could I say? Not only was Miranda rude, she was nosy.

Her probing for details had only made me more suspicious. Someone in this circle of friends must know something. I hadn't planned to investigate either death, leaving that to the police, but I kept coming across connections. Everything I'd learned only raised more questions. Even Poppy's disappearance might be—must be?—related. I'd already agreed to investigate that. Maybe by keeping an open mind, I could solve the mystery of two untimely deaths—both deadly falls.

CHAPTER 7

"I want toad-in-the-hole." Daisy slapped down her menu. The four of us—Daisy, Tim, Kieran, and I—were sitting in the Magpie, deciding what to have for dinner.

"All right then," Tim said, smiling at his girlfriend. He pointed at me. "How about you, Molly?"

The salad with prawns—similar to shrimp—sounded good, but toad-in-the-hole, basically juicy sausages baked in Yorkshire pudding, had an irresistible allure. "Same as Daisy. And a pint of brown." Ale, I meant. After several months in the UK, I was starting to use the lingo almost like a native.

"Coming right up." Tim and Kieran went to the bar to order and soon returned, bearing gifts of beer.

Once the glasses were dispersed, Daisy lifted hers in a toast. "To summer. Sweet and all too short."

"To summer," we chorused.

Daisy folded her arms on the table and leaned forward. "You had quite the day, Molly." On the way back from

Hazelhurst, I'd texted her and Kieran brief updates about our adventures, since I liked to keep my friends in the loop.

"I'll say." I thought back over the afternoon's events.

"What happened?" Tim asked, his eyes curious.

I gave him the highlights, including lunch at the pub with Sir Jon, followed by intercepting a break-in at Robin's shop, a visit to an archeology site, and tea with Miranda and Geoffrey. "My head is still spinning."

"Not surprised," Tim said, putting a hand to his head with a comical expression. "My head aches from just hearing about all that."

"Do you suppose you interrupted a burglary in progress?" Daisy asked. "Robin carried some very valuable silver and jewelry."

"That's the obvious conclusion," I said. "But whoever it was had a key." I took a sip of beer. "Maybe they were looking for something related to his death." I thought of the mysterious disappearing woman. Well, her vanishing picture anyway. *Aunt Janice might have killed Robin.* I'd been so focused on my uncle's possible guilt I hadn't even considered her seriously until now.

I must have made an odd noise, because Kieran looked at me with concern. "What is it, Molly?"

"My aunt, Janice. She was dating Robin. She and my uncle Chris are separated." I took another sip of beer to wet my throat. "When I first checked out Robin's social media page, there was a picture of him and a blond woman in sunglasses toasting each other with wineglasses. Before I could take a close look at her, Inspector Ryan interrupted me. Later, when I went back, it was gone. After Uncle Chris told me what was going on, I thought it might be Janice."

Daisy had picked up her phone and was searching. She

showed me the screen. "Is this his page?" When I nodded, she said, "I don't see it either. Maybe she deleted the picture to hide her tracks."

"Exactly what I thought." Why would someone do that unless they wanted to stay under the radar?

"Your aunt is blond?" Tim asked, and I nodded before he went on, "Hmm. Okay, she was dating Robin. Got it. Did she have a reason to kill him?"

"Honestly, I have no idea," I said. "She's not a very nice person, but would she go that far? Your guess is as good as mine."

"So they do think it was murder." Daisy unrolled her napkin and placed the silverware on the table.

Spotting a server heading our way with plates, I put up a finger to indicate a pause. "Toad-in-the-hole. Hot pot. Fish and chips," the server said, unloading the plates deftly. She then checked our beer glasses, which were fine. "Anything else?" At our headshakes, she whirled away.

Picking up my knife and fork, I cut into the golden puff enclosing a fat sausage, releasing gravy and savory aromas that made my mouth water. After we slaked our initial hunger, I picked up the conversation again. "From the way they were gathering evidence and questioning us, I'd say yes. I don't know if I told you this, Daisy, but my uncle is one of the main suspects. He's been thatching Strawberry Cottage."

Daisy stopped eating, her fork up in the air. "Your uncle is a suspect? Why? Because his wife was dating Robin?"

"Uh-huh. It's a very plausible scenario on the surface. Uncle Chris and Robin argued about Janice and my uncle gave him a shove. But he says he didn't do it, and I believe him." Uncle Chris's sincerity and distress had rung true to me. Not that I couldn't be fooled, but I couldn't imagine him as the killer. Being my grandmother's favorite, he may not have stuck up for my mom when they were growing up, but he was still family. He'd apologized to Mum soon after we moved here, expressing his regret and remorse. Both my grandparents were gone now, one reason my mother had felt okay about returning to England.

"Has Poppy York turned up yet?" Tim asked.

"No, not yet." My heart sank, the way it always did when I thought about Poppy. "Oh, here's another twist. Her sister asked me to help. She's going to be here later, along with Poppy's fiancé, Ben, and we're going to talk then."

Daisy's brow furrowed. "Help with what?"

"Look for Poppy. Iona mentioned to Rose how I helped solve Myrtle's murder, which somehow made Rose think I might be of use."

Daisy snorted. "You didn't help, Molly; you cracked the case. You're a real natural."

"Huh," I said. "Believe me, I never thought of myself as a detective. When Aunt Violet was framed, I had to jump in. This time I don't really know anyone. Not well, anyway."

"Which means you have a fresh perspective," Kieran said. "The main question is, do you want to get involved? You're not obligated to."

"No, I'm not." I couldn't hold back a rueful smile. "But I am curious." I hoped my curiosity wouldn't lure me in over my head. Or, in my inexperience, make a mess of things.

⚫

Rose and Ben showed up while Tim and Kieran were in the middle of a game of darts. Daisy and I were standing at a tall table, drinking beer and watching. Well, actually we were talking about dresses for the garden party while checking out royal events on my phone for outfit inspiration. Was this really my life?

"Something pretty but not too frilly," I was saying when Daisy nudged me. I looked over to see Poppy's sister and her fiancé carrying plates and glasses to another tall table. They backed up onto stools and began to eat hungrily.

I gave them a few minutes before excusing myself and strolling over to their table. "Hi, guys," I said.

"Hey." Rose grabbed a napkin and wiped her mouth. "Molly." She grabbed her beer and took a long swallow. "Sorry we're late. Holloway kept us."

Ben groaned, putting a hand to the back of his neck and arching back. "I'm permanently hunched from working in that trench." Despite the sunscreen I was sure he used, his face was slightly sunburned and he had the exhausted air of someone who had been outside all day in the hot sun.

"Holloway is a real pain," Rose said. She held her sandwich with both hands and I could tell she was dying to keep going. "Getting worse by the day."

"I'll let you finish and then we'll talk." I pointed to the table where Daisy stood, giving us covert glances while pretending to be on her phone. "Come over when you're ready."

"See you in a few," Ben said before stuffing chips into his mouth.

Back at my table, Daisy showed me her phone. "What do you think?"

The dress in question was slim and sleeveless with a slit up the front, the fabric a watercolor floral pattern with small splashes of poppy red and periwinkle blue.

"I love it." I took the phone for a closer look. "It's perfect."

"Isn't it?" Daisy smiled. "Even better, a local boutique has it. That's from their page."

"Which one? Oh, Bella Mia in Hazelhurst. I've driven by it, I think." I remembered the nice dress shop on the high street. I checked Bella Mia's address to confirm.

Daisy took her phone back. "They have some really cute stuff. Let's go over soon."

"Really soon," I said. "Before someone else buys my dress." I already felt possessive. I was relieved that my dress problem had been solved so easily, without a marathon shopping trip around Cambridge.

Kieran and Tim had finished their game and were sauntering over to join us. "What are you two whispering about?" Tim asked, a teasing tone in his voice.

Daisy held the phone against her chest. "It's a secret. Go away." In response, Tim slung an arm around her neck and began nuzzling her. Daisy shrieked in mock dismay.

Kieran rolled his eyes as though to say, *Those two.* "Do you want to play a game, Molly?"

I glanced over at Rose and Ben, who were finishing up their meal. "Not right now, thanks. Poppy's sister and fiancé are here and they want to talk."

Kieran craned his neck to look. "Rose I know. Ben I haven't met."

"He's a graduate student at the University."

Tim and Daisy stopped giggling and fooling around long enough for Tim to say, "We're going to head out."

I gave Daisy a hug. "See you tomorrow. We'll talk about shopping."

She returned the hug, looking past me at Rose and Ben. "And everything else."

"I'll keep you posted, don't worry." I patted her shoulder.

Kieran and I chatted about this and that after our friends

left, but I could barely concentrate. After Rose and Ben finished eating, they grabbed their drinks and came over.

"Hello, I'm Ben Sykes." He put out his hand for Kieran to shake.

"Kieran Scott." He smiled at Rose. "Rose and I have met."

"Understatement." Rose rolled her eyes and flapped the neck of her T-shirt as if to cool off. "My sister and I had the biggest crushes on you at primary school. You were one of the big boys we adored."

I didn't doubt it. Kieran had always been a heartbreaker, I was quite sure. Not only was he so devastatingly good-looking, he also was nice. Kind. Considerate. Practically perfect in every way. At least for me.

Kieran responded to Ben's questioning look, "I'm from Hazelhurst originally. Now I own the bicycle shop across the lane."

Ben's eyes lit with recognition. "Yes. Spinning Your Wheels. I get my bike tuned there."

"Good choice," Kieran said, grinning. He eyed everyone's glasses. "Who wants another round?" Everyone did, so he went to the bar, thoughtfully leaving me alone with the pair.

At first neither of them spoke, probably wracking their brains the way I was on how to begin. "Why didn't I ask her what was going on?" Ben burst out in a moan. "I knew something was wrong. She was so *different* all of a sudden. Moody, lost in her own world. Even snapped at me a few times, which she never does."

"She doesn't," Rose verified. "They're so happy together it's sickening."

Okay, so it seemed we were diving right into it.

"When was this?" I asked. "Did anything happen right before she changed?"

"It started a couple of weeks ago." He stared into space, his expression abstracted. "School was fine; the dig was going well." Answering my unspoken question, he added, "*We* were fine. Talking about the wedding this summer."

"It's going to be at Strawberry Cottage." Rose's forehead furrowed as she amended, "Well, it *was*."

Wincing, Ben shut his eyes briefly. "Don't go there. I can't even bear to think . . ."

"You're right. Sorry." Rose straightened her posture, as if forcing herself to buck up.

"Anyway, Molly, we hoped you could take a look at my flat," Ben said. "Since the dig ramped up, we've been boarding at Thornton Hall. But over the last week or so, Poppy spent several nights here in town."

"I'm not a real detective," I felt compelled to say. "Didn't the police search the flat?"

Ben nodded. "Yeah, they did. But there's more to the story. The last couple of weeks Poppy was reading her father's notes related to *The Strawberry Girls*."

My heart gave a little leap and it wasn't because Kieran was walking our way clutching four beers. "Your father left notes?" I asked, trying to restrain my excitement. They might offer an intriguing glimpse of his thought process while developing the story. As for clues to his daughter's disappearance, I didn't quite see the connection.

"Mum used them to finish writing the book," Rose explained. "She started with what he'd drafted and kept going."

Arriving at the table, Kieran handed round the glasses of beer, then came to stand beside me.

"We're talking about Nate's notes while writing *The Strawberry Girls*," I explained to Kieran. Then I asked Rose,

"You really think there are clues in there that will help us find Poppy?"

"I know it sounds far-fetched," Rose said. "But when you read them, you'll see. He was thinking about real people when he developed the characters. A lot of writers do that, don't they? But in his case, he died soon after." Devastation haunted her eyes. Her father might have died almost two decades ago, but for Rose the grief was still fresh. My heart broke for her; my own father had passed more recently, but on the other hand I had years of memories with him Rose would never have with her own. I guess that's why it's impossible to compare tragedies.

Rose continued, "Now one of Dad's old friends is dead and my sister is missing. Coincidence? I think not."

"Not that we think she killed the man," Ben said hastily. "As I'm sure the police are theorizing. She might know something that has put her in danger."

The police were also theorizing that Uncle Chris had done it, which I didn't believe. Perhaps I could find clues that would send the investigation in a different direction.

"I agree, the notebook is worth checking out," Kieran said. "Maybe she saw something that's been overlooked."

Rose gave him a look of approval. "Exactly. Poppy is one of those intuitive thinkers. I can't tell you how often she's been right when everyone else is busy pooh-poohing her." Her mouth turned down. "Like Dr. Holloway for example."

"What was that about?" I asked.

"Poppy wants to investigate the tumuli more closely," Ben said, referring to the barrows. "She's pretty sure they're significant burials. Holloway wouldn't even look at her reasoning, all the information she pieced together about them." His voice rose to a squawk of indignation. "He told her to stick to her assignments and master those first."

"Ugh." I sympathized with how humiliated and frustrated Poppy must have felt. "You don't think she quit in protest?"

Ben jabbed a thumb toward his own chest. "And leave this perfect specimen of manhood behind? I don't think so."

"Sorry," I said, snickering at his hyperbole along with the others. "I had to ask. One more question. You don't want to analyze your dad's notes yourself, Rose? Or have your mother do it?"

"I tried already, but I'm too close to it all," Rose said. "So is Mum. Plus she's super upset right now. About Robin dying that way. And Poppy being missing." She propped an elbow on the table and cupped her chin. "So, Molly, are you in?"

I slid a glance at Kieran, our gazes locking. *It's up to you*, his expression seemed to say. *Whatever you decide, I'm right behind you.*

"All right." I inhaled deeply. "I'm in." I put up a hand. "One step at a time. I'll look at the notebook—"

"And the flat," Rose interrupted.

"And the flat," I continued. "And then we'll see. I can't guarantee anything, but I'll do my best, of course. I want to help." There was the crux of it. I didn't need to prove myself as an investigator—how ridiculous—but if my efforts might help find Poppy, then I had to try.

A scene from *The Strawberry Girls* floated into my mind. The princess was missing and the sisters felt compelled to look for her. Interesting parallel. Only this time one of the sisters had vanished and we didn't have a magic crown to help.

We finished our beer and left the Magpie Pub to walk

over to the flat—we'd decided that if I was going to look into Molly's disappearance it was best to start right away. Ben and Poppy rented a place in Elderberry Close, a miniscule comma of a lane off Earl Street. Their building was identical to the others, sandy brick with two windows down and three above. The door was red.

Ben unlocked the door and we climbed the stairs, the wood creaking. Inside the flat, the air was close and warm, as if the place had been shut up.

Rose wrinkled her nose. "The bin needs to be emptied."

"Right. Sorry." Ben darted into the tiny alcove kitchen and began closing up the garbage bag.

"Hold on," I said, hurrying to catch up with him. "Check the bag first."

"Why?" His hands stilled.

"See if there's anything new in there," I said. When he looked confused, I clarified, "Something Poppy might have tossed if she came here after leaving the dig."

"Got it." Ben pulled the bag open wide again and began poking around the discards with one finger, his nose wrinkling. "These coffee grounds? I threw those away last time I was here."

The grounds coated the rest of the garbage like wet confetti. "Okay. Good. Just wanted to check." I went back into the main room, which held a comfy sofa and matching armchair. Two desks stood under the windows, both stacked with books, papers, and the typical student debris. A slice of bedroom was visible through a half-open door, the bed neatly made.

Rose pushed the bedroom door open. "Poppy?" She stepped inside.

I hovered beside Kieran in the middle of the living room,

uncertain what to do next. I didn't want to start poking around without permission.

"She's not in there," Rose said when she returned, her voice flat. "I thought maybe she'd be taking a bath . . ."

I thought of an obvious question. "Did she take anything with her when she left?"

Ben emerged from the kitchen, hefting the closed garbage bag. "No. Her clothes and toiletries are still in the room at Thornton Hall. Not her laptop or phone, though. She had those with her."

No luggage spoke to a hasty, if not involuntary, disappearance. "What about her passport?"

"I don't know," Ben said. "I'm not sure where she kept it."

"Wouldn't the police know if it had been used?" Rose said.

"Yes," Kieran said slowly. "I would think so. Any border checkpoint would have a record."

Rose sank onto the sofa. "We haven't heard anything one way or the other. Mum's been calling them for news. I'm going to start calling myself tomorrow."

I would hope that the police would be compassionate enough to provide updates. On the face of it, if Poppy's passport hadn't been used overseas, then she was probably in the UK somewhere, which was still a large enough landmass to be daunting.

"I'm going to run this out," Ben said, still holding the bag aloft. "Be right back."

I wandered around the room while we waited for him to return. Framed photographs on the wall showed the couple enjoying travel—the Eiffel Tower, Stonehenge, and a castle somewhere. A pencil sketch showed two girls riding on a fat white pony. I squinted at the signature. *Iona York*.

Rose moved to my side. "That's a preliminary sketch for

the book." She stretched her fingers out as though to touch the glass but stopped short. "It's one of my favorites."

"It would be mine too," I said. "I adore the book; I'm reading the new edition now."

Still staring at the sketch, she gave a nod of acknowledgment. "After the book was published, Poppy and I got a lot of attention. People recognized us when we went out in public, even." Her features screwed up in a frown. "But it was weird. Those girls in the book weren't us, really, but people acted as if we were one and the same."

"The same thing happens to actors in a popular role," I said. "People mix them up with the character. They have trouble moving on to new projects."

"Yeah, that must be a pain." She straightened the frame gently. "Not that I'd ever want to stop being Poppy's sister."

Footsteps sounded on the stairs. "That's taken care of," Ben said, coming through the door. "Where do we begin?"

I sidestepped the question by asking, "Everything here is as you left it?"

Ben scratched his head as he took in the room. "Far as I can tell, yes. I haven't been here since last weekend. Poppy and I stopped by and did some wash, went out to dinner, then headed back to Hazelhurst."

"How about her desk?" I asked, drifting in that direction. I wasn't sure which was hers, not at a glance.

He went to the one on the right and stood looking down at everything. "Looks the same to me." He leafed through papers and checked a stack of books. "Not that I memorized it, you understand. But nothing jumps out at me." Then he frowned, pulling his head back before bending to pick up a small object. He held it up for us to see, a stone oval in a pretty shade of pale green. "I've never seen this before."

Rose took it from him. "It's a worry stone. You rub your thumb in the hollow." She demonstrated. "See?"

I muffled a groan. If there had been a fingerprint on the stone, it was gone now, literally rubbed away by Rose's thumb.

"Do you know if it was Poppy's?" Kieran asked Rose.

"No idea," Rose said. Her brow furrowed. "Who else's would it be?"

Kieran looked at me and I guessed what he was thinking, because I had the same unpleasant suspicion. "Maybe someone else was in here," I said. They'd made a big mistake leaving the worry stone, although such small objects were easily misplaced.

"But how?" Ben asked. "There are only two sets of keys. Well, three, counting the landlord."

"Four," Rose said. "I have a set." She checked her handbag and showed us a key ring. "Still do."

Ben plopped down on the desk chair as if suddenly boneless. "What if someone came in here using Poppy's keys?" Resting his elbows on his knees, he cradled his head in his hands. The implications of that didn't need to be voiced. We all understood immediately.

"If that's true," I said, "and it's a very big if, what would they be looking for? Figure that out and you might be able to tell who it was."

Ben lifted his head. "I have no idea why someone would break in here. We don't own anything that's especially valuable." He flipped through the papers again with a dry laugh. "Maybe they were trying to crib off Poppy's essays."

That would have to be one desperate student to kidnap a rival and then break into her apartment to steal her work. The stone probably belonged to Poppy. She might well have bought the worry stone somewhere, an impulse buy. I'd seen bowls of them beside cash registers in gift shops, alluring heaps of colorful, polished stones. Without the potential fingerprints, or Poppy herself, we couldn't know.

"Want to take a look?" Ben slid out of the chair and stood. "I'm too confused to make sense of anything right now." He wandered toward the sofa and sat. Kieran joined him, a nice move showing solidarity.

I put my hand on the back of the desk chair, preparing myself. What was I looking for? How could I tell what was important?

Maybe I didn't need to figure that out right now. I could take an inventory of what was here and maybe later something would point us in the right direction. There was also a faint chance I would find a real clue, like an itinerary detailing Poppy's plan to skip town, for example. But I doubted it. Nothing was ever that easy.

"What can I do?" Rose asked, standing over my shoulder.

"I'm going to see what's here, make a note of it, see if anything jumps out," I said. "Why don't you grab that other chair and sit beside me? You can be a second pair of eyes. Plus you know your sister much better than I do, obvs."

As Rose dragged the chair over, I heard the pop of beer bottles and the low murmur of chatter. Kieran was distracting Ben, which was great. The poor guy must be close to a nervous breakdown.

Most of the papers and books had to do with coursework. I fanned the essays out and snapped a picture. "In case one of these topics comes up," I said. Besides textbooks, Poppy had a few books on Anglo-Saxon history and hoards like Sutton Hoo. That made total sense, given the dig she was working on.

After a few minutes, I realized what was missing. "You had mentioned your father's notes," I said. "Do you see them anywhere?"

Rose searched on top of the desk and then I moved aside to let her look in the drawers. "Hmm. Where are they?" She paused for a moment, thinking, then gestured for me to follow.

Feeling slightly intrusive, I trailed behind Rose into Poppy's bedroom. Furnishings included a large bed with a nightstand on each side, two dressers, and an antique bookcase, the type with glass doors above a cupboard.

While Rose squatted down and opened the cupboard, I looked at the shelves. They held a number of photographs, family shots. Iona and Nate's wedding. A large headshot, a graduation photograph, maybe. The sisters, at a very young age, on the beach, wearing swimsuits and with arms wrapped around each other's necks. Trinkets too, seashells, rocks, and other small mementos.

Rose was pulling photo albums out of the bottom. "As you can see, this bookcase is Poppy's family shrine. She's designated herself keeper of our history." More albums landed on top of the stack. "Not that it's a bad thing."

I thought it was nice, actually. Maybe we should do something similar in a corner of Thomas Marlowe—a lineup of ancestor booksellers and maybe a selection of old ledgers, stationery, and other memorabilia.

"Found it." Rose dusted off a brown leather notebook and handed it up to me. "I thought it might be in here. Poppy's fussy about keeping things together."

"I'm glad she is," I said, opening the cover and beginning to flip through. The pages were covered in dense, faded ink scrawls with occasional sketches here and there. Then I noticed additional jottings in a different hand, penciled in the margins. "Do you recognize this handwriting?" I thought maybe Iona had gone through and made her own notes.

"That's Poppy's handwriting," she said after a moment. "She wasn't only reading Dad's notebook; she was annotating it." She gave it back to me. "Maybe you can figure out why."

CHAPTER 8

Soon after the discovery of Nathanial's notebook, we left Ben and Rose and walked back to Magpie Lane. This late in the evening, I was glad to have Kieran beside me as we strolled hand in hand along quiet streets past dark alleys and gardens. The spotlights illuminating features on historic college buildings created a beautiful nightscape under an inky sky freckled with stars. We didn't say much, and as we ambled along, the tension I was carrying started to drain away.

"I enjoyed our walk," I said when we reached the bookshop. A huge yawn burst out of my chest. "I'm totally relaxed now."

Kieran laughed. "I can tell." He gave me a quick kiss. "It's been a long day."

"You can say that again." Most nights we liked to hang out and talk for hours, but tonight wasn't going to be one of them. "See you tomorrow?"

"Definitely." He gave me another kiss, then waited while I unlocked the door. As soon as I was safely inside, he waved and set off up the lane to the bike shop, where he had a flat.

After greeting Puck and Clarence with appropriate levels

of adoration, I poured a glass of water and headed upstairs. Nate's notebook went on the bedside table, but I decided not to start reading it tonight. I was too tired to fully absorb any new information.

Instead, once I was ready for bed, I reached for *The Strawberry Girls*. The princess was missing and I couldn't wait to find out what happened next.

The Strawberry Girls, cont.

"Where's Audrey?" Rose asked the pony. Of course he didn't answer, merely tossed his head and made his harness jingle.

Poppy pointed at the saddle's pommel, where the princess's crown hung. "Look, Rose. Her crown."

Rose's eyes went wide. "Has something happened to her?" As if in answer, Bramble stomped his front hoof and snorted. "Do we need to go find her, darling Bramble?" He snorted again.

Poppy was staring at the crown. The woods. The patient pony. "We should look, don't you think? She's probably hoping we will."

"I think so too," Rose said with a shiver of excitement. The girls had never ventured very far into the Deep Woods. Their mother had warned them that they might get lost. Wild animals lived there too.

But if the princess was in trouble, it was up to them to rescue her.

Using the summerhouse railing, the girls climbed aboard Bramble, Poppy in front, Rose behind, clutching her sister. Then, copying Audrey, Poppy kicked her heels gently and clicked her tongue. The pony obediently began to amble toward the trees.

"Do you think we'll see a bear?" Rose whispered.

Thick leafy branches leaned overhead, while on both sides, the forest pressed close. Bramble's hooves thudded on the dirt path.

"No, silly," Poppy said. "Bears don't live here anymore." *She hoped.*

Flowers covered a twisted hawthorn tree, a cloud of white in the dark woods. As they got closer, Rose saw the flowers move and realized that white butterflies were nestled in the blossoms.

"How beautiful," she said. "So many butterflies."

Poppy made a strange sound and Bramble jerked to a halt. Poppy took one of Rose's hands. "Touch this." Rose felt the cold of metal against her fingers. "Now look at the flowers again."

The butterflies were actually tiny fairies all dressed in white, with white fluttering wings. "Fairies like hawthorn trees," Poppy said.

"Is this a magic crown?" Rose asked. She let go and the fairies were butterflies again. Touched it and there they were, twinkling and laughing and darting about.

"It must be," Poppy said. "Which makes me think the princess was magic too."

Duh, Rose thought. *She'd known that from the moment Audrey had emerged from the forest wearing that long dress and sitting on a pony, looking like someone out of a fairy tale. Besides, real princesses lived in London.*

One fairy flew close, darting about as though studying Poppy and Rose from every angle. "Where are you going, girls?" Her voice was like silver bells.

"We're looking for the princess," Poppy said. "This is her pony."

The fairy landed on Bramble's head and sat. "I

thought I recognized him." She touched his mane with a tiny hand. "Where do you think she is?"

"We have no idea," Poppy said. "Do you?"

A strong gust of wind blew through the trees, making their leaves flutter. The sky darkened. The fairy sitting on Bramble flew straight up, her toes pointed in alarm. "Must go."

"Help us, please," Poppy called. "How can we find the princess?"

"Keep looking," the fairy said, joining the other fairies in a swarm that went this way and that and then up. They were gone.

The wind died and the two girls were alone in the forest. Well, Bramble was still there of course. "Her advice wasn't at all helpful," Rose said.

Poppy flicked the reins and Bramble started off again. "No kidding." She sounded grumpy.

Rose reached into her shorts pocket, where she kept emergency supplies for bad moods and disappointments. She fished out a Cadbury mini egg, left over from Easter, and slipped it into Poppy's hand.

"Yum. Thank you." Poppy popped it into her mouth.

Rose leaned against her sister's warm back, dispensing more mini eggs as Bramble ambled down the trail. Even if they didn't find the princess, this was awfully nice.

◆◆◆

I was still thinking about the book the next morning while I photocopied pages from Nate's journal. *The Strawberry Girls* perfectly captured the close relationship between the sisters. Even though I hadn't seen them together, I could tell the bond was still strong just from talking to Rose. She was like one half of a whole.

As I turned a page in the notebook, spread it flat, and lowered the printer cover, I wondered if losing their father had drawn them even closer together. Sometimes siblings grew apart over the years, as they matured and went their separate ways. Not these two, it seemed. They were even working in the same field, archeology.

"What are you doing?" Mum asked, returning to the desk. She'd been waiting on a customer and had walked the woman out, chatting all the way.

I showed her the notebook. "Copying Nate's journal. I'd rather work with a copy than keep leafing through the original."

She came over to stand beside me. "Anything interesting so far?"

"I found a cool map." I put the notebook down and flipped through the copied pages to find it. The hand-drawn map depicted Strawberry Cottage, Thornton Hall, and other locations on the estate property in tiny thumbnail sketches, including the tower where Nate had fallen to his death. Dotted lines showed where trails wound through.

"I love hand-drawn maps," Mum said. "This is enchanting."

Looking at the page, I said, "I'm going to enlarge this. To make room for notes." To be honest, I was still groping in the dark as to how the children's book related to real life, if in fact it did. I placed the page on top of the glass and hit the right buttons.

She leafed through the journal. "You actually think this is related to Poppy's disappearance somehow?"

The printer made its usual grinding noises as the enlargement snailed its way out.

"I know; I had doubts too," I said, reaching for the page.

"But Rose is convinced Poppy found something important in there. Ben said she was preoccupied recently, plus spending a lot of time with the notebook." I exhaled before voicing my deepest suspicion. "If she did, I'm wondering if it's related to Nate's death."

Mum tilted her head. "Tied to Robin's death as well?"

I shrugged. "Maybe? You have to admit it's strange she disappeared the day he fell off the roof. Robin was a friend of Nate's. So was Miranda." I found my phone and showed her the article quoting them both.

She skimmed the article. "Miranda as in Geoffrey Thornton's significant other?"

"Exactly. She's a strange one." Mum had already heard the blow-by-blow of our visit to Thornton Hall, but I went through it again.

She looked up from my phone. "What do you say to running out to see Iona this morning? Take her a treat from Tea and Crumpets and see how she's doing. We used to be school chums back in the day."

"Really? I didn't know that."

My mother looked a little sheepish. "I should have been there for the first meeting. It's time for me to stop avoiding Hazelhurst."

"Don't worry about it. We understand." In light of her difficult relationship with her parents, the whole village was probably one big trigger for her.

Mum set my phone down. "If you're finished copying, do you want to pop over to Daisy's for treats? Pick whatever looks good."

"Not an easy choice," I said with a smile. "Everything she bakes is delicious." I stacked the photocopies neatly and placed them in a manila folder. The notebook went into an envelope, for safekeeping.

"I know." Mum rolled her eyes and patted her trim middle. "I have to ration myself."

"Right." I rolled my eyes in return. Like Aunt Violet, Mum was naturally slender. She had to *try* to gain weight, unlike some of us. Setting the folder and journal on the desk, I said, "See you in a few."

"Hey, Molly," Daisy called out when I walked into the tea shop. She was clearing one of the tables, placing the used dishes into a bus pan. Other than one man sitting in a corner typing and muttering to himself, the place was empty. "How did it go last night?"

I joined her at the table, helping to clear. It was amazing how many crumbs some people made. "Really interesting," I said in a low voice. "Rose let me borrow her father's journal. I can't wait to dig in."

Daisy set the pan on a tray stand and pulled a damp rag out of her pocket. "You think it's related to her disappearance?" Exactly the question Mum had.

I picked up the container of sugar and artificial sweetener packets so she could wipe the table. "I have no idea, honestly. Rose said Poppy was obsessed with it before she disappeared, so I'm going to check it out. See where it leads." I set the container down and picked up the flower vase. "She didn't take any clothes or other belongings, Daisy. It doesn't look good."

Daisy finished wiping with a swirl. "Which means she either ran away in a panic or—" Grimacing in dismay, she tossed the rag into the bus pan. "It doesn't bear thinking about."

"Totally doesn't," I said, placing the vase in a good spot and tweaking the mini rose into position. "It's horrifying. Doing something, no matter how small, makes me feel like I'm helping." I followed as she carted the pan toward the counter, where she went around and into the kitchen.

While she disposed of the dishes, I studied the contents of the bakery case. Today she had a variety of scones, lemon curd bars, raspberry tarts . . . and strawberry butterfly cakes. Butterfly cakes are basically cupcakes filled with cream, with the cut-out part divided into two and placed like wings on top. These had pieces of strawberries for wings instead and looked delicious.

Daisy bustled back into the room. "Do you know what you want?"

"Sure do. Three butterfly cakes. No, make it four." I would get one for Aunt Violet.

"Coming right up." Daisy slipped on gloves and opened the bakery case.

"Mum and I are going to visit Iona at Strawberry Cottage this morning," I said. "I think these cakes are perfect."

"They sure are," Daisy said. "I can't keep anything strawberry in stock this time of year. Especially with the fair coming up." She gently set the last one in the box and closed the lid. "Here you go."

"Thanks," I said, pulling out my wallet. "With any luck, Poppy will turn up today." Or Robin's killer would be arrested. Waiting for something to happen was excruciating.

Daisy crossed fingers on both hands. "Here's hoping. Keep me in the loop."

"Always," I said, swiping my bank card. "Oh, let's plan a shopping date." While the transaction went through, we talked about when to go, finally settling on the next afternoon. Then I picked up my cakes and charged off, excited, against all odds, about another trip to Hazelhurst.

◂▮▸

"How does it feel?" I asked Mum. "Driving on the left, I mean."

Mum was behind the wheel of the Cortina for the first time since we'd arrived in England. The beauty of living in Cambridge was, you could walk or bike just about anywhere.

"I'm doing all right," she said, glancing in the rearview and then the side mirror. "Takes some getting used to."

"I bet." When I finally got behind the wheel, it would be in the most isolated spot I could find, free of traffic, intersections, and the dreaded roundabouts, what we called rotaries in New England. I didn't like them there either.

Mum heaved a sigh of relief once we were out of the city and on country roads. She rested an elbow on the open window ledge, the air ruffling her hair. "It's so pretty out here. I'd forgotten."

"Reminds me of home," I said. "Vermont, I mean."

She threw me a glance. "Do you still think of Vermont as home?"

"Not really," I said. "It was more a figure of speech. I like it here, Mum, even more than I thought I would." Having Aunt Violet to welcome us had made all the difference, I believed, since we had instant family and support in a foreign country.

"I'm so glad, Molly," Mum said. "After moving to Vermont with your father, I learned that home is wherever your heart is." Judging by the tender, almost pained expression on her face, I guessed she was thinking of Dad.

We wallowed for a moment, and then I said, trying to lighten the mood, "Well, getting to help run the coolest bookshop ever didn't hurt the transition."

Laughing, she reached out and patted my hand. "No, it didn't. By the way, how are you enjoying the new edition of *The Strawberry Girls*?"

"It's as wonderful as I remembered. I'm reading it slowly, only a few pages a night, so I can savor it." I'd brought the envelope with Nate's journal, figuring I could leave it with Iona, since I didn't know when I'd see Rose or Ben again. It should be safe there.

"It's a special book, that's for sure. So many good books in the world but only a few that grab you and don't let go." She clenched one fist as though to demonstrate.

"I love the butterflies that turn into fairies." That comment sparked a discussion of Cicely Mary Barker's *Flower Fairies* and other children's titles we liked. The original—and magical—*Mary Poppins. The Secret Garden.*

Before we knew it, we were through Hazelhurst and on the lane leading to Strawberry Cottage. "We're almost there already," Mum said in amazement.

I was glad our conversation had distracted her from thinking about her parents.

We slowed as we went past Thornton Hall. "I always loved that place," Mum said. "It's almost as magnificent as Hazelhurst House."

"It's pretty cool," I said. "Maybe we should pop in on Geoffrey sometime." I also needed to look up Hazelhurst House online. I hadn't so far because it felt like creeping on Kieran. What difference did it make where he grew up?

"Maybe we should stop and see him." Mum turned to look at the other side of the road. "So that's the famous dig. When we were kids, we used to make up ghost stories about those mounds. A few times we sneaked through the fields at night, thinking we might see something scary."

"Did you?" I asked, imagining my mother as a young girl creeping around the burial mounds. Not much different from my own childhood visits to the local cemetery with my friends.

"No, I'm afraid not," she said with a laugh. "Although after visiting the British Museum, I hoped we'd see a mummy wandering around. Wrong continent."

"The cottage driveway is just up here," I told Mum, although she probably remembered. It was hard to see, though, with the bushes so overgrown.

Mum signaled and turned and we crept at a snail's pace down the bumpy drive. I watched her carefully when we came around the turn and she didn't disappoint. "Oh, I love it," she cried. "It's exactly like the book." As an afterthought she added, "Which I should have known, right?"

"Did Iona grow up here?" I asked as we rolled to a stop.

"No, no. She lived near me, on the other side of town. She and Nate bought this place. I was already in the US when they got married."

Uncle Chris's van was in the drive, which meant the thatching job was underway again. I was glad for his sake—and happy he hadn't been arrested.

The slamming of our car doors brought Iona to the front door. "Nina," she cried.

Mum stared at her long-lost friend and then broke into a trot. They met halfway down the path. "Oh, I've missed you," Mum said.

"And I missed you." Iona pulled back, hands still on Mum's arms. "You look lovely. Not a day older."

Mum giggled. "Neither do you. You always were a beauty."

Iona made a dismissive gesture. "Come in, come in. I've got the kettle on."

"And we've got cakes. Molly?"

"Yes, Mum." In the joy of watching their reunion, I'd forgotten, and by the time I retrieved the box from the back seat Mum and Iona had gone inside.

In the kitchen, Mum was seated at the table while Iona filled a teapot with boiling water. "Tell me all about Vermont. I've heard it's beautiful."

"It is," Mum said. While tea was served and cakes passed, the two of them discussed Vermont, Dad, and our move to Cambridge. The windows were open to the warm breeze and now and then I heard thumps as bundles of old thatch came off the roof.

I sensed Iona was glad to talk about something else beside what must be weighing heavily on her mind, namely her missing daughter and Robin's death. The atmosphere was so congenial right now I wasn't going to be the one to bring them up.

"I adore butterfly cakes," Iona said. She took a big bite and whipped cream ended up on the tip of her nose. Mum gestured and Iona dabbed it off with a laugh. "I always was a slob."

"I'm glad to see some things never change," Mum quipped. They laughed again.

A shout came from outside. The two friends looked at each other with identical expressions of alarm. My mouth was probably hanging open too.

"Want me to go see?" I offered, pushing back my chair. Not that I was eager to witness another disaster or problem.

I ran out the back door to where I had a good view of the roof, seeing that almost half had now been stripped. Uncle Chris was up on the scaffolding, hunkered down and looking at something.

"What's going on?" I called up. "Are you all right?"

"Molly," he said. "Hello. I'm fine. I found something, that's all, and it startled me." He rose to his feet holding a rectangular metal box in both hands. "This was under the thatch."

"Wow. I wonder what's inside." I waved my arm. "Bring it into the kitchen. Iona is going to want to see it."

He nimbly climbed down the ladder, the box under his arm, and together we went into the house. "All is well," I announced. "Uncle Chris found treasure under the thatch."

Iona rose to her feet. "Treasure? I wish." Her gaze fastened on the box. "I wonder how long that was under there."

"Probably since the last time they thatched," Uncle Chris said. He started to set the box on the counter, then reconsidered after checking the bottom. "Got something I can put this on?"

Iona put a piece of cardboard on the counter and my uncle set the box down. He tried to lift the lid. "It's either rusted shut or locked." He turned to Iona. "Maybe you can get someone to open it."

Dying to look inside, I held back a groan of frustration. Mum looked equally disappointed.

"Can you do it?" she asked. "It doesn't look like a valuable antique, does it?"

Uncle Chris examined it. "No, it's your ordinary metal lockbox. I'll need to grab a tool from my van."

"Go ahead," Iona said. "If you can do it without damaging whatever is inside."

We followed him outside, where he set the box on the stone step before going to his van and rummaging around. He returned with a hammer, and after a couple of blows he broke the latch and lock and the lid flew open.

"These locks are meant to discourage people, not safeguard the Crown Jewels." He stepped back. "Want to do the honors?"

A velvet bag lay inside the box, and despite the earlier jokes about treasure, my heart began to pound. That type of bag was often used to hold jewelry.

With shaking fingers, Iona reached into the box and pulled out the bag. She felt around, pressing the velvet before pulling on the drawstring. She peeked inside, then put her hand in and pulled out a circular gold object set with colored stones.

A crown.

CHAPTER 9

"Blimey!" my uncle exclaimed. "Is it real?"

Iona held the crown in both hands, turning it back and forth. Sunshine refracted from the gems, creating beams of colored light. "I think it might be. It's heavy enough."

"Is that the crown from the book?" I blurted. Had Nate been inspired by a real crown? One he'd seen—or hidden? Where had he gotten it, if so?

Iona's eyes flared wide at my remark. She pressed her lips together and shook her head as if in denial. But I knew I was right. It looked exactly like the illustrations in the book.

My uncle shifted his stance. "I don't know the book you're talking about, but that thatch hasn't been touched for twenty years or more. You can tell by the condition of the straw."

"We had the roof worked on around the time Nate died." Iona's voice was low, almost meditative. "I can't believe . . . Oh, what did you do, Nate?"

Mum glanced at me with concern in her eyes, and I knew she was thinking the same thing, that Nate might have stolen the crown. Had he hidden it in a safe place, planning to retrieve it later and sell it? Had Iona been in on it, subconsciously revealing her knowledge by using this design in her illustrations?

What should we do now? I knew one person who could help. "I'm calling Sir Jon," I said. "He knows all about antiquities."

"Brilliant," Mum said. "I certainly don't remember the laws for finding treasure."

Iona didn't protest the idea of contacting Sir Jon. Instead, she remained seated on the step, almost cradling the beautiful object. I wanted to hold it, but the way she was crouched over, almost guarding it, discouraged me from asking.

I grabbed my phone from my bag and moved a short distance away to make the call. Thankfully, he picked up. "Sir Jon," I said. "We need you."

"Now that's music to an old man's ears," he said with a laugh. "What's up?"

"I'm at Strawberry Cottage. Uncle Chris was working on the roof again and he found something really amazing." I paused. "A crown. Literally. Round, gold, and set with gems. It was in a metal box under the thatch."

"Under the *thatch*?"

I guessed where he was going, that Robin might have left the box up there just before falling to his death. Why he would do such a thing was beyond my comprehension. "Uncle Chris said it had been there a while." I inhaled. "We think Iona's husband put it there."

"Nate York? Hmm." Sir Jon was silent for a long moment. "You'll need to report this. . . . Hang on, I'll buzz out. Don't do anything until I get there, okay? No social media, Molly."

Oh, he knew me too well. Although I did plan to take a few snaps of the crown. How could I not? "I won't post anything, promise."

"Sir Jon is coming out right away," I told the others after I walked back over. "He said not to do anything until he gets here. Should we wait inside?"

"I could use another cup of tea." Iona gave a little laugh. "Or something a trifle stronger."

She started to put the crown back into the bag, and I said, "Hold on a sec. I think we should document everything ourselves. And no, none of this is going online." Not until I was cleared to post it, anyway.

"Good idea." Iona posed with the crown and I took a shot of her with the box and velvet bag. Then she slipped the crown inside the bag and placed the whole thing in the box.

"Why don't we take pictures of where you found it, Uncle Chris?" I suggested.

He adjusted his brimmed cap. "We can do that." He gestured and I followed him around the house while Mum held the door for Iona, who was carrying our treasure.

"Up the ladder you go," Uncle Chris said. He watched me closely as I clambered up, trying not to think about the distance to the ground.

Holding my breath, I stepped onto the scaffolding and edged along to where the roof was stripped of thatch. *Don't look down.*

He was right beside me. "I was removing that area." He pointed. "The box was tucked right underneath. It's a wonder it didn't go flying when I pulled off the old straw."

Up close, the blackened straw gave off a dusty, grassy aroma that took me back to Vermont barns. I still found it unbelievable that plant matter, no matter how deep, could make an adequate roof.

"Straw really works?" I asked rhetorically as I took several photographs. The box had been resting on wide, ancient boards that formed the structure. "I know, that's a dumb question. It's only been around for centuries, right?"

Uncle Chris chuckled. "Few millennia, more like. They used thatch in the Mesolithic era."

An ancient art, like that wielded by the goldsmith who produced the crown. How old was it? I wondered. A thought struck and I almost dropped my phone. Was the crown of Anglo-Saxon origin, like the artifacts they were discovering next door?

"When did they start the dig at Thornton Hall?" I asked Uncle Chris. "Do you know?"

"First I heard of it was last summer, when a farmer came across some artifacts." He gave me a sharp look. "Are you thinking that crown came from there?"

"Maybe," I said, temporizing. "It would make sense, though, wouldn't it? Nate might have come across it and decided to keep it. Then he died and no one knew it was here."

"We might never know," Uncle Chris said. "The big question is whether they'll let Iona keep it. Or, if the Crown takes it, give her some money. If it was stolen, well, they can't put a dead man in jail, can they?"

No, but they could arrest her, if they thought she was involved. I took a couple more safety shots, then said, "I'm ready."

We were coming around the corner of the house when we heard the whine of a motorcycle in the lane. A moment later, Sir Jon bounced down the drive, astride a vintage motorcycle. We met him near the front door, where he cut the engine, then pulled off his helmet.

"BSA Lightning," Uncle Chris said. "Nice. What year?"

"Sixty-seven," Sir Jon said. "Bought it new."

"Even better." Uncle Chris eyed the machine. "You've kept it in good shape."

Sir Jon patted the handlebars. "One of my babies." He rubbed his hands together. "So, what did you find?"

"It's inside," I said, leading the way. Once we stepped through the door, I spotted the crown right away. Iona had set it on a table in the living room, resting on top of the bag, the metal box beside it.

Sir Jon stopped short. "Oh my. What a find."

"No kidding, right?" Uncle Chris said. "I thought someone had hidden some money, maybe. But a crown?" He gave a long, low whistle.

Mum and Iona had been in the kitchen and now they came to join us. Iona perched on the edge of a sofa, her hands clasped. "I had no idea that was on my roof." She lifted her chin as if expecting Sir Jon to challenge her statement, and I noticed that her lips were trembling.

Sir Jon didn't respond as he crept closer to the table, his keen eyes taking in every detail of the crown. After a general once-over, he pulled out a jeweler's loupe and studied the gems.

I bit back a laugh, my eyes meeting Mum's. She looked equally amused. Sir Jon never ceased to surprise me with his talents, connections, or knowledge.

"Ah, yes," he finally said, removing the loupe from his eye. "Those are precious gems. If this piece is the age it appears to be, it's priceless."

Although we'd already suspected that, we all gasped.

Sir Jon already had his phone in his hand. "The county coroner will want to see this, since found treasure falls under his purview." He glanced around the room, his gaze somber. "In light of what happened here earlier this week, I'm also calling the police. There's a possibility this is related to Robin Jones's death."

None of us could argue with that conclusion. Had Robin been up on the roof searching for the crown? If so, why now? The thatch hadn't been disturbed for over twenty years, according to Uncle Chris and Iona. Had the antiques dealer stumbled across something that indicated Nate had hidden the crown there? Or had an old memory suddenly made sense? Unfortunately, the answer had gone with Robin to the grave.

Unless Robin had mentioned the crown somewhere, say in an email or text, or confided in someone. In which case, that person will probably come back to search, if they hadn't already.

"Hey, everyone," I said. "I have something important to suggest." They all turned to look at me, including Sir Jon, who was in the middle of dialing. "We should keep this discovery quiet. If Robin was looking for the crown, then someone else might come over here and try to find it."

"You think that's why he was on the roof?" Mum asked. "What am I saying? That must be the reason." She turned to her brother. "He thought he could find it before you did."

"Why didn't they come over . . . after?" Iona asked. Her fingers plucked at the fringe on a pillow.

Although she had a point, I thought I could guess why not. "There's a possibility the killer didn't know about the crown. But if they did, then they were probably scared off by the police. They wouldn't know whether or not the police were still searching the crime scene."

"You could be right, Molly," Sir Jon conceded. "I'll ask the authorities to keep the crown quiet for now, for this very reason." He nodded at Iona. "May I suggest setting up some surveillance cameras and perhaps an alarm? That way we can catch any intruders."

Uncle Chris raised his hand. "I'd be happy to help set them up, since I'm already climbing about up there. We can attach cameras to the chimney, front and back."

Iona looked doubtful. "That sounds all right, but can you give me some advice as to what to get?"

"Sure can." Uncle Chris pulled out his phone and swung into action. "I've got them at my place and I can use my phone to monitor, see?"

While my uncle discussed security cameras with Iona and Mum and Sir Jon spoke to the authorities, I slipped into the kitchen to call Aunt Violet. Not only were we going to be super late, I also wanted to give her an update.

I know, I know; it was my own suggestion to keep the crown a secret. But after all, Aunt Violet was family. "Hey," I said when she answered the shop phone. "It's me. I have some news."

"Not another dead body, I hope," was the answer.

"No, this is good news." I glanced at the crown glimmering in the sunlight. "Mostly. I think."

Aunt Violet laughed. "Tell me, please. I'm on the edge of my seat."

Hurriedly I told her about Uncle Chris discovering the box under the thatch and what it held, a crown exactly like the one in *The Strawberry Girls*. That Sir Jon was calling in the police and coroner's office and Mum and I needed to wait here until we were dismissed.

After she absorbed all that, Aunt Violet said, "What a perfect hiding place. No one would ever think to look under a pile of thatch."

"Although Robin was on the roof, remember," I pointed out. "He must have gotten a heads-up the crown was there." If there was another reason, I couldn't imagine it.

"That makes sense," she mused. "I wish I'd been there this morning."

"It was thrilling," I said, allowing a wave of enthusiasm to sweep over me. "Now I know what it's like to be an archeologist. Sort of. And without all the tedious digging."

In the background, I heard the bookshop bells jangle. "I'd better go," Aunt Violet said. "Don't worry about the shop. Do what you have to do."

After hanging up, I moved the kettle onto a burner and turned on the flame. Might as well make tea for the troops. As I moved around the kitchen, I studied the little framed pictures hung in unexpected corners, tiny watercolors painted by Iona. Flowers, cottages, her daughters when they were young.

Anyone who only saw her paintings would believe that Iona led an enchanted life. The reality was a little darker. Her husband's mysterious death. The disappearance of her daughter. A murdered man. And the discovery of a priceless treasure.

Not for the first time, I reflected how one couldn't judge people's happiness by how their life looked on the surface. This realization kept my envy in check—and made me appreciate my own blessings that much more. We'd had our own losses, we Marlowes.

The kettle boiled and I made tea, then set the pot with cozy on a tray along with milk, sugar, and cups. When I carried it out to the living room, I saw Mum and Iona on the sofa. Iona was crying and Mum was comforting her. "I know, I know," she crooned. "You miss him." The way Mum missed Dad.

"I just don't understand," Iona said, crumpling a tissue in her fist. "He had so many secrets. So many questions he can't answer. And now Poppy . . ."

"Your daughter?" Mum's tone was deliberately hearty. "She'll turn up; you'll see."

Oh, how I hoped so. I placed the tray on the low table in front of the sofa. "Who wants tea?"

"Thank you, Molly," Mum said. "I'll pour."

Sir Jon and Uncle Chris were standing to one side, chatting, and now they came over to join us, taking seats in the wing chairs opposite.

Tires sounded on gravel outside. "I'll go," I said, figuring I was closest to the door. A panda car and a sedan were pulling into the drive. Doors slammed after Inspector Ryan and Sergeant Adhikari got out of the police vehicle and a young man dressed in shirtsleeves and trousers climbed out of the other vehicle. From the coroner's office, maybe?

Then, in a reprise of the other day, a scooter buzzed down the drive. Ben and Rose must have seen the police car go by the dig and wondered what was happening. Under the circumstances, I didn't blame them a bit.

They hastily climbed off the conveyance. "Inspector, Inspector," Rose called. "What's going on?"

Inspector Ryan paused, waiting for the couple to reach him. "There's no news," he said. "Yet. Or any developments regarding Mr. Jones. We're here about an entirely different issue."

To put the poor things out of their misery, I hurried over. "We found something," I said. "It's very valuable. An artifact."

Rose glanced at Ben, who said, "Here? Did Iona dig it up?"

"Not quite," I said. At the inspector's glare, I made a zipping motion across my mouth. "Come in and see." I ushered them all through the open front door.

The officers and the other man stood back to let Ben and Rose enter the cottage first, to be polite, I thought. Then I wondered if Inspector Ryan's decision was a little more calculated.

Rose gasped when she spotted the crown. "It's exactly like the one in the book." When her eyes shifted to take in the metal lockbox, her mouth dropped open and she sagged down onto a convenient ottoman. "Daddy . . . Daddy had that box. I remember."

Iona sat upright, her mug clattering as she set it on the tray. "You do, sweetheart? When?"

Rose squeezed her eyes shut as if to help bring the memory into focus. "Poppy and I were playing in the garden. He . . . he went up the ladder, carrying the box. We asked him what was in it, but he wouldn't tell us."

"Are you sure?" her mother asked again. "You were pretty small at the time."

Her daughter nodded. "Yes, Mum. Remember how we were obsessed with treasure hunts back then? Daddy even drew us a map once." She laughed; then, tears shining in her eyes, she put a hand to her mouth as if to stifle her emotions. After a moment she continued, "The map was all tea stained and crumpled to make it look old. He hid it for us to find and then helped us follow the instructions. Ten paces from the apple tree . . . that sort of thing. When we found the spot, he'd written a big *x* on dead leaves." Her laugh pealed out. "The buried treasure was a jar full of choc and biscuits. It was years before I figured out he'd put them there. Poppy and I thought they were ancient and it was magic that made them still taste good."

What a great story. Nate must have been a wonderful father.

"So, when we saw Daddy with the box, we asked him if it held treasure. He said, 'Something like that, ducks.' Then he put a finger to his lips. 'Don't tell Mummy, okay?'"

One mystery solved, if Rose's memory was accurate. Nate had hidden the box in the thatch. Figuring out where the crown had come from could now be the focus, as well as if he'd obtained it legitimately.

Big questions I fortunately didn't have to answer.

CHAPTER 10

Mum and I were questioned by Inspector Ryan first and released. Although duty called at the bookshop, I wasn't quite ready to return to town. "Want to take a walk in the woods before we go back?" I asked Mum once we stepped outside.

"What was that?" Mum sounded and looked abstracted. "You mean behind the cottage? I'd love to, haven't been out there for years."

I gestured toward the lofty trees surrounding three sides of the cottage. "I thought since we were here . . . reading the book again makes me want to see the setting in real life."

Mum glanced toward the door. "Let me pop back in and ask Iona if it's all right. I wouldn't want to prowl around without her permission." The pink tinge in her cheeks made me wonder if Iona was the only person she wanted to see again so soon.

During our last case, Mum and Sean Ryan had started to become friends. They hadn't seen each other for a while—that I knew of—and I thought I'd intercepted a significant look or two. It was hard to tell when he was on the job, though. He became quite frosty and aloof.

She went back inside, returning a moment later. "Iona is fine with it. She also asked me to call her later." An eager expression shone in her eyes. "I think we're on the way to becoming close again."

"I'm glad, Mum. We all need a friend to hang with." I hoped Iona wouldn't be arrested for Robin's murder. That would definitely put a damper on any rekindled friendship.

We strolled around the house to the woods path. What an idyllic spot this was. The garden slumbered in the sunshine, bees mobbing the fragrant roses smothering the summerhouse. If I squinted hard enough, I could see the two young sisters having their tea party all those years ago. I resolutely avoided looking at the area where we'd found Robin's body.

Leaves rustled as we entered the woods, as if acknowledging our presence.

"There it is," I cried, spotting the hawthorn tree mentioned in the book. Staying well back from its fearsome thorns, I studied the gnarled yet attractive tree. "It's so much fun finding Nate's inspiration."

Mum studied the tree, which still held a blossom here and there, although the main flowering time was May. "The butterflies turn into fairies, right? I always thought that was really magical."

"It is." We continued strolling, the woods becoming more and more silent and dense as we went. One of the oddest things to me, as a native Vermonter, was the scarcity of forests in England. In my hometown, one could travel for miles through unbroken forest. This spot, right here and now, felt like that isolation, yet we were only minutes from houses and roads.

Mum halted at a trail junction. "I remember this now. The left branch goes into a swamp, the right toward Thornton Hall, and straight ahead is the tower."

"The tower," I said. "I want to see the tower. It's amazing in the book." Then I remembered. *Nate fell to his death there.* Nausea churned in my belly.

My discomfort must have shown on my face, because Mum asked, "Are you feeling all right?"

I shrugged. "I'm okay. I'm upset about Nate dying there, though."

"So am I," Mum said. "It's horrible. You know what? After finding that crown, I'm starting to wonder how much of *The Strawberry Girls* is real. I mean in the sense that Nate, and then Iona, included elements from what was going on then. Was the book Nate's attempt to communicate truths he was afraid to share?"

She had a point. "Maybe so, since it looks like those truths might have killed him. Unless his fall truly was an accident, which I'm starting to doubt." Robin. Poppy. The crown. The three mysteries spun around in my head as if on repeat.

"Ready?" she asked. We continued ambling in single file along the narrow path, pausing now and then to take in interesting trees, rocks, or plants.

"We must come back next April," Mum said, halting at a clearing surrounded by thick old oak trees. "This is a bluebell wood, a sign of a very, very old forest."

I'd only seen pictures of blooming bluebells, which formed an enchanted carpet winding through stands of trees. "The Bluebell Wood is in the book," I said. "This must be it." I couldn't wait to get back to *The Strawberry Girls*.

"I bet you're right. I'm going to have to read it again myself."

"Let's take turns," I said, not wanting to hog our copy. "I'm reading it slowly, to savor it."

We rambled on, following the path as it wound uphill and down, around stands of trees or right through them. In my mind, I pictured the landscape, trying to figure out where we were in relation to Strawberry Cottage and Thornton Hall.

I caught a sweet scent drifting through the air, accompanied by the hum of bees. It almost smelled like apples, which was odd, because they wouldn't ripen for another three months or so.

Mum lifted her face and inhaled. "Sweetbriar roses. Amazing how a smell can take you back."

Around the next corner, we encountered the hedge, taller than we were and extending a good distance in both directions. The path seemed to end right here, at the brambles.

"Now what?" I asked, hoping the answer wasn't to push through that dense, thorny mass. It was gorgeous right now, though, covered in thousands of pink roses. This close, the aroma was almost enough to knock you off your feet.

Mum gestured as she sidled to the right, between the hedge and the woods. "Come this way."

We picked our way over the uneven ground, careful not to brush too closely to the tangled brambles, which seemed to extend clutching fingers toward us.

"Yes," Mum said. "I hoped it was still here." An arched and open gateway provided a way through the hedge, and beyond, in a small clearing, stood the tower.

About three stories high and built of rough stone blocks, the tower was topped with battlements and pierced with arched windows that had been boarded up.

"You can see for miles from up there," Mum said. "The tower used to be open, and we would climb up there and pretend we were princesses and princes."

Decades before Nate had fallen to his death. I remembered now the article I'd come across stating that Geoffrey Thornton had boarded the windows and door afterwards to prevent another tragedy.

"I wish we could go inside," I said. "What was it like in there?"

"Pretty plain," Mum said. "All stone. One big room on each floor and a winding stone staircase around the outer wall. We loved it, though."

"Was Geoffrey ever with you?" He was about Mum's age, I thought. Late forties or early fifties.

"Maybe once or twice. He was usually away at boarding school." She smiled at her memories. "He missed all the fun."

We'd drifted closer to the tower, which rose like a dark finger into the blue sky. There was something ominous about the place, forbidding even. Besides the buzzing of bees, the clearing was silent. A lone crow perched upon the battlements, cocking his head and glaring at us with his beady eyes.

My mind, which never seemed to stop working over the mysteries—Robin, Poppy, the crown—landed on a thought, an idea so awful it made me gasp.

Robin might have found out about the crown from Poppy. *Or that her father had hidden something on the roof,* I qualified. This was the terrible part. What if Robin was responsible for Poppy's disappearance, the only person who knew where she was?

And now he was dead.

The crow, perhaps tired of our intrusion, rose into the air, black wings flapping. His raucous cry was the perfect punctuation to my fears.

"Drink this." Mum thrust a bottle of water under my nose. It must have been hidden in her bag, which was slung across her chest.

Shifting my buns on the mossy stone tower step—not very comfy—I accepted the bottle and drank, gradually coming out of my funk. Wanting a moment to gather my thoughts, I'd claimed the need to sit down. The steps were the best option.

"I had a terrible thought," I finally said. "What if Robin had something to do with Poppy's disappearance?"

Going white around the lips, Mum sank down beside me. "Oh no. I sure hope not."

I gulped another swig of water, trying to dilute the dread that still clenched my midsection. "Maybe we should say something to Inspector Ryan. I wonder if they've searched Robin's store for clues. Or his home. I wonder where he lives. Lived, I mean."

"Over the store, maybe?" Mum suggested. "There's a flat up there."

We sat in silence for a long moment while the crow cawed and flapped around the clearing. "He really doesn't like us being here," I said.

Mum squinted at the crow, now sitting on the very tip of a dead branch in a tree. "Probably not. He's had the place to himself for ages." She stood, then rubbed the seat of her skirt. I decided not to mention the moss stain until we got back to town, where she could do something about it. "Ready to go?"

In answer, I stood, handing her the water. "Aunt Violet is going to be wondering where we are."

"True. Let me call her." After capping the bottle and tucking it into her bag, Mum placed the call to the store. "She said to take our time. Want to go back a different way?"

"Sure. Why not?" We should take this opportunity to explore the Deep Woods. We might not have another chance.

Mum put away her phone and led the way out of the clearing, away from the creepy tower and its guardian crow. He gave one last caw as we slipped through the arched gate.

"'And stay away,'" I said, pretending to translate his croak.

Outside the hedge, Mum chose a path leading away from Strawberry Cottage. "We're not going to get lost?" I asked. Although the woods weren't huge, we could still be wandering around for a while. Plus I was starting to get hungry for lunch.

"We won't get lost," Mum said. "Promise."

The trail led us downhill to a tumbling brook, where we crossed over a wooden bridge. That was a good indication civilization was near.

"'The Crystal Stream,'" Mum said, quoting the book as she paused to watch the water as it burbled by. "We used to toss branches on one side and run to the other to watch them float out from under the bridge."

"Like this?" I found a twig and dropped it over the rail.

We both rushed to the other railing and waited until we saw the tiny piece of wood skimming along.

"This is a nice place to hang out," I said, enjoying the cool air of the glade, which was hemmed by moss-covered rocks.

"One of my favorites," Mum said. Now I knew why she had wanted to keep exploring. She was on a memory tour of sorts, and I was glad this visit had proved there were still happy memories for her in Hazelhurst.

We tossed a few more twigs in before continuing on, passing through Ferny Glade and Stone Canyon, which forced us to squeeze between two huge boulders.

"Want to climb the boulder?" Mum asked, a teasing tone in her voice.

I glanced up, considering. "Maybe another day. Besides, you're not wearing the right shoes." She was wearing sandals, with good tread, but still.

"Come on, chicken," she said. With a few nimble moves, she clambered up the rock face and stood on top, hands on her hips, beaming. She wasn't even breathing hard.

I had no choice, obviously. A little less gracefully, I climbed up the rock, trying to remember where she'd put her hands and feet. On the fairly level top, I straightened and looked around. "This is great." I could imagine having a picnic up here.

Mum was strolling around, checking the view from every side, and I did the same.

Glimpsing a thatched roof through the trees, I asked, "Is that Strawberry Cottage?" On my mental map, the location didn't really make sense, but it was always possible the walk through the forest had me turned around.

"No." Mum's smile was gleeful. "It's the Witch's Cottage."

"Oh yeah. I remember that. It's real?"

Mum was already moving toward the edge, ready to climb down. "Mrs. Dobbins isn't an actual witch, no, but yes, the cottage is real. Let's go say hello."

A short while later, we reached the cottage, which was tiny, charming, and set among abundant flower beds. "I'm so jelly," I said. "I'd love to live here."

"Me too," Mum said, her hand on the gate latch. "I used to imagine this was my house when I was little."

Once we entered the garden, I noticed the hens pecking around and a couple of cats lounging in the sun. The back door creaked open and a very elderly, frail woman emerged, back bent but sprightly in her movements. She wore a bib apron over a print dress and sneakers on her feet.

"Can I 'elp you?" she asked, her gaze roving over us. Then her expression brightened. "Nina? Nina Marlowe?"

"Yes, it's me." Mum rushed forward to embrace Mrs. Dobbins, careful not to squeeze too tightly. "I've been away. In the States."

Mrs. Dobbins gazed up at Mum, glowing warmth in her eyes. "That's what I heard. You married a Yank and crossed the pond, they said."

"That's what I did. Mrs. Dobbins, I'd like you to introduce you to my daughter, Molly."

"Hello," I said. "It's so nice to meet you."

Mrs. Dobbins eyed me thoroughly for a moment. "And I'm glad to meet you, Molly. Your mum was a lovely girl and so are you."

I found myself blushing at this praise, as if I were still a little girl, not a woman of almost thirty. Not able to think of an appropriate response—*thank you* would sound too weird—I smiled and nodded.

"Will you stop and have a cuppa with me?" Mrs. Dobbins cleared a cat off a chair placed at an old wooden table. "Go on, you rascal." The calico eyed her with disdain before it moved only a few inches away and began to wash.

Reminded of Clarence and Puck, I couldn't help but laugh. "What do you think, Mum?" I was hoping she'd say yes.

"I'd love a cup," Mum said. "Do you need a hand?"

Mrs. Dobbins made the same shooing motion toward Mum that she used on the cat. "No, no. Please, have a seat. I'll be right out."

We pulled chairs out and sat, looking around at the over-grown but charming garden, pots and urns supplementing the beds. A clematis vine bloomed over the trellis shading us, and lavender, lemon thyme, and mint plants scented the air.

"I should plant an herb garden," Mum said. "Maybe in containers so I can bring them in during the winter."

"Good idea," I said, picturing pots of herbs clustered next to the kitchen French doors. "I love using fresh herbs when I cook."

Mrs. Dobbins had left the house door ajar and she now pushed through, teacups rattling on a tray. The hens and cats ran to their owner, clustering around her feet, but somehow, she managed not to trip.

"Ah, here we are," she said, releasing a breath. She took the chair between us and began to pour. "A rum do at Strawberry Cottage, eh?"

I exchanged glances with Mum. Which "rum do" was she referring to?

She slid a teacup toward Mum. "I used to see that young man walking quite a bit," she said. "He was always polite, stopped to chat most days."

"You mean Robin Jones?" I ventured.

"Yes." Mrs. Dobbins finished pouring my tea. "That's him. Owned the antiques store downtown. He was a good friend of Geoffrey Thornton, up at the big house."

After adding a splash of milk to my tea, I asked the obvious. "Did you see him the day he fell?"

"I did. He walked by around eight thirty. I was out here weeding." Mrs. Dobbins filled the third cup and set the pot down. "Have a biscuit." She pointed to a plate of custard creams, one of my favorites. "What was he doing up on that roof, I wonder?"

"Everyone wonders that," I said. "My aunt Violet and I were visiting Iona that morning. It was dreadful."

She nodded solemnly. "I heard you found him. Such a tragedy." A shrewd light shone in her dark eyes. "But you might say he shouldn't have been up there."

True. "Did you see anyone else around?" If she had, that might clear my uncle, Iona, and perhaps Poppy. I refused to believe that any of them had killed Robin, which was not exactly an unbiased approach.

Mrs. Dobbins put up a gnarled forefinger. "Only a woman running, right after he went by." She chuckled. "I get such a kick out of watching them trot by in their spandex. I want to tell 'em, come help me dig, that will give you some exercise."

With a jolt, I recalled the woman standing by the road and watching the dig. "What did she look like?"

The older woman nodded sagely. "I see where you're heading. You think she might have pushed Robin off the roof."

Maybe. I squirmed in my chair, not wanting to admit that. "She might have seen something. Or someone."

She took her time answering, adding milk to her tea and stirring, a hand propping her chin. "I couldn't see her face, really. She had on sunglasses and a hat. But her outfit? Enough to take your eyes out. Bright pink."

The runner I'd seen had worn pink leggings and a black top. "Pink leggings, you mean?"

She shook her head. "No, top and bottom were pink. Maybe even her shoes." She snorted. "I haven't worn pink that bright since nursery school."

Was her memory accurate or had she seen the same runner I had? Either way, it was unfortunate she hadn't recognized the woman.

"If I see her again, I'll try to get her to stop," Mrs. Dobbins offered, mischief lighting her face. "Do a wee bit of detective work for you."

"That's a kind offer," I said. "But what if she's the killer?" I couldn't live with myself if I put this sweet lady in harm's way.

Mrs. Dobbins made a scoffing sound. "Ah, don't worry. I'll talk to her about gardens and cats and chickens. She'll never know my real motive." She winked.

"All right, then," I said, digging in my back pocket for a Thomas Marlowe card. "Hopefully you'll see her again." I handed her the card. "Call that number," I suggested, thinking that was easier than giving her my cell number.

To my surprise, she whipped what looked like a brand-new cell phone—with a multi-colored Bubble Wrap case—out of her apron pocket and punched in the digits. "Thomas Marlowe. I'd heard you two were helping Violet run the place. I'll try to get into the city sometime soon. I don't have a car anymore, but I can take the bus."

"I hope you do," I said, kicking myself for making assumptions. "Stop by anytime and we'll put the kettle on."

CHAPTER 11

"Ah, this is so nice." I sat back in my chair, beer in hand, and surveyed the bookshop garden. The three of us were eating dinner outside, big salads featuring local vegetables and a tantalizing array of toppings.

"What a day," Mum said. "My feet actually hurt." She wiggled bare toes. After our lengthy trek through the Deep Woods, we had returned to Thomas Marlowe to find Aunt Violet surrounded by demanding customers from a bus tour. We'd jumped right in to answer questions, guide book choices, and ring up sales.

"I'm starting to regret adding our shop to the bus tour list," Aunt Violet said, stabbing her fork into her salad. "It seemed like a good idea at the time."

"They spent a lot of money, at least," Mum said. "Swarmed in like locusts, bought everything in sight, and left."

"True," Aunt Violet said. "Oh, wanted to tell you. I finally added upcoming tours to the desk calendar. Today's totally slipped my mind."

I poked around in my salad, trying to decide what I wanted in my next mouthful. Chickpeas, avocado, or a chunk of cheese. Maybe all three. "We wouldn't have left if we'd known," I said. "The bookshop is our priority."

Aunt Violet's smile was mischievous. "You mean over discovering an Anglo-Saxon crown? I still can't believe it."

"Me either," I said. "The coroner's office carried it away for safekeeping and I guess there's going to be an inquest. I hope Iona can keep it. Or at least get some money for it." I was pretty sure the crown would be declared to be treasure and thus have to go to a museum.

"I wonder where Nate found it in the first place," Mum said. "Did he dig it up in the back garden?"

"That's a possibility, I suppose," Aunt Violet said. "That would probably mean that there's a grave there. A piece that valuable wasn't disposed of by accident."

I shivered at the idea of a grave behind Strawberry Cottage. Although Thornton Hall's fields were dotted with barrows, so it wasn't that far-fetched.

"Why didn't he tell his wife about it?" Mum asked. "If they found it fair and square, they could have gotten some money."

I couldn't help but think that there was more to the story and Nate had hidden the crown for a reason. I was about to say so when a shrill voice hailed us from the back gate.

"Violet. Nina. Can I come in?" Aunt Janice stood at the gate, fiddling with the latch. After discovering a murdered woman in the garden a couple of months ago, we had installed a bolt. A little too late, but an instinctive reaction.

Shifting in her seat, Mum huffed in annoyance. "I'll go," I said. "Hold on, Aunt Janice. It's locked."

She continued to flick the latch. "Why? It's never been locked long as I've been coming here."

I didn't bother to answer. As I hurried across the grass, I wondered how she dared to show her face after the way she'd treated my uncle—Mum's brother. Surely she didn't expect to get sympathy from us. Aunt Janice had been awful to my mother for years.

Sliding the bolt, I said, "Try now. It's open." Not waiting for her to make it through the gate, I returned to the table and continued eating.

Aunt Janice's expression was sheepish as she reached for a chair. "May I?"

"Would you like a glass of wine?" Aunt Violet belatedly kicked into hostess gear. "Or something else to drink?" She rose from her seat, prepared to nip into the house.

"A glass of wine would be lovely." Aunt Janice appeared to relax at the invitation, perhaps realizing we weren't going to ice her out. While Aunt Violet was inside, she smiled at us tentatively and said, "Lovely evening, isn't it?"

"It w— is." Mum swallowed hard. Setting her features, she stared daggers at her sister-in-law, warning Janice that the ball was in her court and Mum wasn't going to play.

Aunt Violet burst out of the house, glass of wine in hand. "Here you are. Would you like something to eat? Cheese and crackers?"

"No, no. I'm fine. Really." Aunt Janice sipped the wine, then placed the glass carefully on the table. "You must be wondering why I'm here."

Ya think? We all stared at her and said nothing. Even Puck, who was curled up on a lounge chair nearby, glared.

To my incredulous disbelief, my snooty, arrogant aunt let out a huge sob, her chest heaving. "I have nowhere else to turn. Will you . . . will you help me?"

··

Aunt Janice wept and sniffled and choked and cried, practically destroying one of Aunt Violet's cloth napkins by the time she was done.

"All right, Janice," Aunt Violet said, handing her a glass of water. "What's going on?" Her tone wasn't unsympathetic, but it wasn't all warm and fuzzy either.

After gulping down half the glass, Aunt Janice blew her nose. "The police have been questioning me." Her lips quivered. "About Robin. He and I, well—"

"We know all about you and Robin," Mum said crisply. "Chris told us."

"Yes, well, ahem." Aunt Janice's face was already flushed, but now it became truly beet-like.

"They're questioning Chris too," Mum went on. "Which is all your fault, by the way. Because you had an affair with Robin, they think Chris killed him out of jealousy." She snorted. "Ridiculous."

"Chris wouldn't kill anyone," Aunt Janice said, her voice wavering.

"True, but that's not what I meant." Mum's eyes gleamed with barely suppressed rage. "If Sean—Inspector Ryan knew you better, he'd can that theory pretty quick. Chris is lucky to escape. I'm sure he was applauding your little fling."

As Mum delivered this truly epic tirade, Aunt Janice's head bent lower and lower. "Go ahead. Give it to me. I deserve it." Biting her bottom lip, she hunched over as if expecting a blow.

Aunt Violet put a hand on Mum's arm. "I don't blame you a bit for losing your temper, Nina, but we must think of poor Charlie." My cousin, one reason why we had to maintain some civility with his witch of a mother.

Mum nodded. "I'll stop now. But I'd like to hear why you

had the nerve to come over here." She picked up her wine and drank. "It better be good."

Aunt Janice dared to raise her head a fraction. "I had nowhere else to turn, to be honest. Chris won't talk to me."

"Do you blame him?" I asked. "You pulled the trigger, right?" I meant on the breakup.

She looked puzzled, then seemed to decipher my slang. "I suppose so, yes. Chris and I had already been talking about divorce. Robin . . . well, we were good friends." Tears flooded her eyes again. "He never approached me until . . . until after we agreed it was over."

Her version was slightly different from Chris's, but maybe that was to be expected. None of us challenged her story. I think we just wanted her to get on with it.

"Were you and Robin serious?" Aunt Violet asked, venturing where angels feared to tread.

She started to nod, then shook her head instead. "I thought we were." Ducking her head, she fiddled with the hem of her top, muttering something.

"What was that?" Mum's voice rang out like a bell. "I can't hear you."

Aunt Janice's ears flushed. "I said, he broke up with me. He thought my situation was too . . . messy." She wrinkled her nose.

Since she and Uncle Chris weren't divorced yet, then yes, it was messy. "When did that happen?" I asked, my senses alerting. Here was a motive all wrapped up with a bow.

She still wore the expression of distaste. "A few days before . . . I saw him the morning he . . ." Her voice trailed off and she wouldn't meet our eyes.

Now we were getting somewhere. "You saw him the morning he died? Where?" My words fired out like bullets and she flinched as though I had hit her.

Stalling, my aunt took a long drink of wine. "I was out running and saw him walking along the road. So I followed him to the cottage." Now her voice was almost robotic as if she was trying to get it all out. "We had an argument, right there in the garden. Then I ran away."

Okay. "You told the police all this?" I asked, to confirm. She said the police had questioned her.

But she shook her head. "I haven't told them. It puts me right on the scene." She rapidly blinked the tears back. "Do you think I should?"

We three exchanged glances, then said in unison, "Yes."

"Your husband—" At her protest I put up a hand. "You're still married, right? Your husband is the prime suspect. Because of *you*."

Her mouth worked. "I was worried about that. When I heard, I mean. Chris was pretty angry when he found out Robin and I were—"

"Do you blame him, lady?" I said, injecting my tone with sarcasm. "If you don't want your son's father to go to jail, I suggest you have another chat with Inspector Ryan."

"Chris wasn't even there, though," she said. "Iona's car was the only vehicle in the drive." She wrinkled her nose. "Loud classical music was playing, which is probably why she didn't hear us."

Another fact we hadn't known before now: Iona, or at least her car, had been at Strawberry Cottage when Robin, and apparently Janice, had been there. Had *Iona* killed Robin after all? Maybe she had known about the crown and was trying to prevent Robin from finding it. Then logic kicked in. If so, surely she would have retrieved it before Uncle Chris got to that section of roof.

"Another reason to talk to the inspector," Aunt Violet said. "The timing that morning is really critical."

It certainly was, with people coming and going the way they had been, and not only behind the wheel. Aunt Janice had been on foot. Had the killer also been a runner? Or someone who followed Robin from the manor? He had eaten breakfast with Geoffrey and Miranda, I recalled.

"What were you wearing?" I asked.

Aunt Janice pulled back. "What does that matter?"

Mum got it. Mrs. Dobbins and her runner dressed in pink. "There's a witness who saw a someone in the area," I said.

"A witness? Who?" Aunt Janice scowled at me.

"I'd rather not say," I said, not wanting to throw Mrs. Dobbins under the bus. I could just see my aunt storming over there and trying to bully her.

"Then I'd rather not tell you." Aunt Janice drank the rest of her wine and set the glass down a little too hard. "I guess I'd better get going." A strange look crossed her face. "I have something to do." She got up abruptly and set off for the back gate.

"Bye," Mum called. "Take care."

Aunt Janice's response was a flippant wave of her hand. After she stormed through the gate, leaving it open, we sat quietly for a few minutes. The air felt turbulent as though a squall had whipped through.

"I really hope she calls the inspector," Aunt Violet said.

"We can make sure he knows about it." I dug around in my bowl for the last avocado pieces. It wouldn't be the first time I'd shared theories with him, not that he encouraged it. "He'll need to follow up, of course. Or not."

"She was actually there that morning," Mum said in a musing voice. "She could have done it."

I imagined Aunt Janice chasing Robin up the ladder onto the roof. A heated argument, a sudden shove—and whoops. She slides down and runs away, pretending nothing happened.

"She's as viable a suspect as Uncle Chris," I said. "And don't forget, according to Aunt Janice, Iona was home when Robin arrived."

"Which means she could have done it." Aunt Violet took up the tale. "Janice left and Iona had an argument with Robin. It's very possible."

"I hate to think that," I said. "I like Iona. Which probably means I'd be a lousy detective. I'd want to pin crimes on people I don't like."

Mum swirled her wine thoughtfully. "One thing about Sean is, he's very fair." She hesitated. "I've been meaning to tell you . . . he asked me out."

Emotions cascaded through me at her announcement. Once the shock ebbed, that is. Although I had seen it coming. I missed Dad terribly and I knew Mum did too. At the same time, I didn't want her to be alone forever. Dad wouldn't want that either.

"We're just friends, Molly," Mum said when I didn't respond verbally. "We're going to an outdoor concert."

"Mum, it's fine," I said. "I was struggling with my big-girl panties." We both burst into laughter.

Aunt Violet stared at us, confused. "What's this about panties?"

"Knickers," I said. "It's a saying. It means you need to grow up and face life." I lifted my beer in a nod toward Mum. "Like when your widowed mother decides to start dating again. Which is awesome."

"You're really okay with it?" Mum asked. "I could beg off . . ."

"Don't you dare." I shook my head firmly. "He's a good man. Dad wouldn't want you to lock yourself away from life."

"Your father." Mum's expression was tender. "I loved him so much. Still do."

"He knows that. And so do I." My throat had clogged and I sipped my beer to clear it.

"Let me get this straight," Aunt Violet said. "Inspector Ryan asked you out, Nina. You said yes. Are you going to pump him for information about the case?"

Her saucy remark had the desired effect. We laughed again, and while the memory of Dad lingered like a sweet aroma, the mood lightened.

"I have an idea." I tapped the table. "Who wants a bedtime story? I'll read *The Strawberry Girls* to you."

The Strawberry Girls, cont.
The pony ambled deeper into the forest. "Are we ever going to get anywhere?" Rose asked.

"I don't know," Poppy said honestly. "I'm letting Bramble lead us."

As if understanding her words, the pony stopped and lifted his head. A tinkling, silvery sound was carried on the breeze, like the ringing of tiny bells.

"What's that?" Rose asked.

"Let's go see," Poppy said. She jostled the reins and Bramble started plodding along again.

The trees opened up, revealing a woodland glade carpeted with bluebells. The tiny flowers were swaying, and when the sisters looked closer they saw that blue pixies were pushing them. The pixies were tiny, with wings and pointed ears and bell-shaped hats.

"Pixies are real?" Rose asked, her mouth agape.

"As real as fairies and magic crowns, apparently," Poppy said. She slid off Bramble's back and held her hand out to help Rose down.

They crept closer to the edge of the flowers, fascinated by the tiny creatures cavorting about.

"Come play with us," one called, his voice as tuneful as the bluebells. Others joined in until a chorus of pixies gathered, their tiny faces and voices an echo of the flowers.

Rose started to walk toward them, but Poppy grabbed her arm. "It's not safe, Rose. Don't you remember the story about the pixies? They want to steal you."

"Steal me?" Rose crossed her arms and scowled. "Would you really do that, pixies?"

They shook their heads. "No. We wouldn't," they said in unison.

"Don't believe them," Poppy said. She whirled around. "What do you think you're doing?"

A group of pixies had climbed onto Bramble's back. One or two clung to his mane and another swung on his tail. They laughed at Poppy and began to urge the pony on. Thankfully, Poppy was holding the crown or they probably would have stolen that too.

Rose gasped. "I remember now. They like to steal ponies." She ran toward them, waving her hands. "Shoo, pixies. Shoo. Bramble belongs to us."

"He does not," said the pixie swinging from Bramble's mane. "He belongs to Princess Audrey. You stole him."

"We did not," Poppy insisted. "The princess is missing and we're trying to find her. We think she's in danger."

"Danger?" the pixies cried in unison. They began to chatter, a clashing sound like bells ringing out of

tune. The ones on the horse slid down his tail and those in the field ran around as if in a panic.

"Come on, Poppy," Rose said. She ran to Bramble and somehow scrambled up onto his back. Poppy climbed up too, and when she gently kicked the pony's side he began to move.

"That was a narrow escape," Poppy said. "If they'd taken Bramble, we would have been stranded."

Rose turned to look at the Bluebell Wood. The pixies had vanished. "Why were they so afraid? I wonder. And oh, I wish we could sit among the bluebells. I've never seen anything so pretty in my life."

CHAPTER 12

The Bluebell Wood section of *The Strawberry Girls* was so magical it filtered into my dreams. I was still thinking about the pixies the next morning while I dusted the bookshelves in the shop. Clarence and Puck were lounging a safe distance away from the dust, unlike me, who was right in the thick of it.

I'd just trumpeted a few vigorous sneezes when Kieran walked in. "God bless you," he said, looking slightly taken aback.

Exactly how I wanted to greet my boyfriend. *Not.* "Sorry," I said, eyes streaming and nose running as I dug around in my jeans pocket for a tissue. "Dusting." After mopping my face, I blew my nose and felt almost human again. "These shelves were extra dusty."

Moving closer, he scanned the titles. "I can see why. *Electric Bells and All about Them. Flow of Fluids through Valves.* Hmm, riveting."

"No, that's right here." I pointed to bound vintage copies

of *The English Mechanic*, which featured Victorian engineering techniques.

"Ha-ha," he said, getting the joke. "You're punny."

"Thanks," I said. "Anyway, how are you this morning?"

"Great, thanks." Puck and Clarence had come over to greet Kieran, who had crouched down to pat them. Using both hands—so as not to slight one or the other—required quite a feat of balance. "Just wanted to say hello. I wondered how you're getting on for the fair tomorrow."

"Oh, that's right. It really snuck up on me." I glanced toward the counter, where boxes of *The Strawberry Girls* sat. "The new books came in, barely on time. And I've got to get a table display poster printed sometime today. Do you know where I can go?"

"Yes, I do." Kieran rose to his feet, leaving two disappointed cats sitting and staring up at him. "I'll walk over with you, if you want. We can also stop for a coffee."

"Great on both counts. I'll be right with you." I put away the dustcloths and grabbed the flash drive holding the poster image. After I told Mum and Aunt Violet where I was going, we headed out into the sunshine.

"I told Mum I was bringing you to the party," Kieran said as we ambled up the cobblestone lane.

My steps hitched. I was almost afraid to ask. "What did she say?"

His expression was quizzical when he turned to look at me. "She's looking forward to meeting you." His face creased in a grin. "She wants to see a 'natural beauty' up close." Kieran was referencing the term tabloid reporters used when they printed pictures of me. As opposed to his unnatural beauties, I suppose.

I slapped at his arm, connecting with solid muscle. *Yum.*

"Seriously?" He ducked back with a headshake. "You are so bad."

We fell into step again and I thought about meeting his famous parents, which immediately led to the thought that I had to go shopping. Daisy and I were planning to go this afternoon, but if we didn't have any luck in that Hazelhurst boutique we would need to try here in the city.

"What else is new?" he asked as we dodged pedestrians on Trinity Street. This whole area of downtown was off-limits to vehicles, but people on foot and cyclists could be almost equally as dangerous.

"Where to begin?" I said, thinking over the events since I'd last seen him. "Oh, guess what? My uncle found an old metal box while stripping the thatch at Strawberry Cottage." Even though no one around was paying attention—obviously—I lowered my voice. "Inside was a gold crown set with gems. We think it's Anglo-Saxon." I brought a picture up on my phone to show him.

Kieran stopped to study the picture, his brows rising in amazement. "Wow. It looks like the real deal. And from the same period as the dig at Thornton Hall?" He was so good at connecting the dots. "Who put it there?"

I tucked the phone back into my handbag. "We think Nate York. Iona said the roof was last redone when he was alive. His daughter remembers seeing him climb up onto the roof carrying the box." I filled in some of the details while Kieran listened, fascinated. If I couldn't trust my family and Kieran, who could I trust? "The police and the coroner's office both came right over to take custody of it."

"Could that be why Robin Jones was up there?" Again, he reached the most logical conclusion with lightning speed.

"We were all wondering that too." A sour taste flooded my

mouth. Thinking of Robin led naturally to Poppy. I prayed he hadn't killed her or hidden her away somewhere, and that the secret of her disappearance hadn't died with him.

"Any news of Poppy?" Kieran asked, as if reading my mind. "I've been seeing a number of posts on social media reporting her missing."

"Not that I've heard," I said. "Unless something happened since yesterday." The longer she was gone, the more likely something horrible had happened to her. I really needed to spend some time studying the pages from her father's notebook, just in case they held a clue. When I got back to the shop from this errand, I resolved to pore over them.

"The print shop is down here," Kieran said, indicating we should turn down a side street. He waited outside while I went in and placed the order. They weren't busy and promised to have the posters ready in half an hour, so we carried out Kieran's original plan to grab a coffee.

After stopping at a kiosk, we found seats on a bench in the marketplace square. I thought back to when I'd eaten my first kebab with Kieran right here, on this bench. And now he was my significant other, which was a huge upgrade from friend/personal tour guide, as far as I was concerned. While we sipped coffee, we watched people browsing the various booths, which offered produce and prepared foods, clothing, household goods, and junk.

Kieran grew up in Hazelhurst, so I asked, "Have you been to the stone tower on the Thornton Hall property? Mum and I took a walk out there yesterday."

"Oh yeah, I have. My friends and I loved that place. Before it was boarded up, we'd climb up inside."

"My mum did too, when she was little. It sounds like all the kids in Hazelhurst used to play out there." Oh, for the days when children could safely, or at least mostly safely, roam the outdoors. I had done the same as a child, and those were some of my most cherished memories.

"Climbing the tower was a rite of passage," Kieran said. "Or used to be. Those woods are great, all those trails twisting around. We called it the enchanted forest. We never did find the tunnels, though, which is probably a good thing. We might have gotten trapped underground."

"Tunnels?" Not that I'd want to crawl through any, but they did sound intriguing.

"A lot of old properties have them, like my house for example. They were used for various purposes. Smuggling goods, hiding priests, or escaping an attack. We have secret passages and staircases too."

Kieran's "house" was even more magnificent than Thornton Hall, but I didn't comment on his modest description. "I adore secret staircases. Will you show me yours?"

He reached for my hand. "Anytime, babe, anytime." We laughed.

After a sweet moment of quietly enjoying each other's company, I asked, "Where are the tunnels at Thornton Hall?"

"I'm not exactly sure," Kieran said. "Someone told us there was an entrance in the old cemetery near the chapel, inside a vault. We were too afraid of what else we might find in there to break in."

"Ugh, I bet." I pictured opening a mausoleum and discovering ancient caskets. No thank you. "I suppose I can ask Geoffrey Thornton next time I see him. Not that I want to venture inside. I'm curious, though."

"Me too," Kieran said. "Let me know what you find out."

I took his hand again. "You'll be first to get updates." Well, after Mum and Aunt Violet, but they lived with me. Daisy, too, as my best friend. I was pleasantly surprised by how long the list of my friends and family here in Cambridge was becoming.

He let go of my hand and leaped up. "Hold on," he said. "I'll be right back."

Bemused, I watched as he beelined toward the stalls, going around a corner so I couldn't spot his destination. He soon popped back into sight holding a gorgeous bouquet. Smiling widely, he presented the flowers to me with a bow.

"Oh, Kieran, they're beautiful." I put my nose into the mass of peonies, white irises, sweet peas, and pink roses, inhaling the sweet scents.

"They're grown locally," he said, pride in his voice. He knew how committed I was to supporting small farms and businesses.

"Thank you." I wanted to give him a kiss but refrained since we were in public. One of the few downsides of dating Kieran. If someone snapped us kissing, it would be all over the internet within minutes. "I hate to say it, but I'd better pick up my order and head back to work. And put these into some water." I leaned close. "I'll give you a proper thank-you when we're alone."

His face lit up. "Let's go."

◄►

Back at the shop, I found myself in a very good mood. I placed the bouquet on the counter so everyone could enjoy it, and got to work. We had a quick lunch of sandwiches and then I dug into my real task for the day—studying Nate's notebook.

The bookshop was in an early-afternoon lull, so I carried the folder of photocopies to the back room where we held readings. I hoped we'd be hosting Iona here soon, an event sure to draw tons of fans. Not only was *The Strawberry Girls* on many people's list of favorite childhood books; there was the local connection also.

I opened the folder and pulled out the copies, arranging them in chronological order. When I tweaked the arrangement the third time, I realized I was stalling.

What if I don't find anything? Or worse, missed it? I scrubbed my hands down the thighs of my jeans, unable to bear the idea of failure, of letting Poppy down.

I let my gaze scan the pages, hoping something would jump out at me. Nate had created an outline of sorts, I realized, keyed to the map.

Yes, there was the hawthorn tree and the fairies. What was that? *Queen of the Fairies—M.?*

Miranda? She had that shop, Titania's Bower, named after the Queen of the Fairies in Shakespeare. Wanting to confirm every theory as I went—plus continue to stall—I reached for my phone. A few clicks confirmed that Miranda had founded her shop twenty years ago, so she'd owned it when Nate had worked on the story.

Miranda was Queen of the Fairies. So far in the book, not a nice character because she scared away the white butterfly fairies. Well, that wasn't stated in that scene, but I remembered that she brought storms with her when she appeared later on. The implication was there.

Nate had been so sly. I pictured him coming up with that characterization and grinning at his own wit.

Something struck me, hard. The setting was based on a real property, the grounds of Strawberry Cottage and Thornton Hall. Poppy and Rose were actual people, of course. Were all the other characters based on Nate's friends too?

I flipped over a piece of paper and picked up a pen, deciding to make a list. Besides the girls and the Fairy Queen, we had the fox, Lantern Men, the Good Witch, hermit, and mole. Bramble the pony and Princess Audrey.

After meeting Mrs. Dobbins, I had a good idea who the Good Witch was. What a sweetheart. Right now I could probably take a guess about the other characters, but maybe I should keep reading, take a fresh look at everything.

My discovery had led me to another conclusion. If all the same players were still around, then had Poppy made the same connections? Was that why she was missing? Was that why Robin was dead?

The Strawberry Girls, cont.

At Poppy's urging, Bramble trotted away from the Bluebell Wood, his hooves thudding on the path. Had he been afraid too, Rose wondered, afraid that the pixies would keep him? Pixies were said to ride horses until they were exhausted. Rose was glad they had escaped from the mischievous creatures, although they were cute in those little blue hats.

The woods seemed to grow even more mysterious as they traveled along, the trees larger and darker in the twilight. The path narrowed, forcing the pony to slow so he wouldn't trip on rocks or roots.

Rose felt around in her pocket, but she didn't find any more chocolate eggs. Her belly rumbled gently and she told it to shut up. They needed to find Princess Audrey and then they could all eat together. Maybe the princess would invite them to her castle for a feast. She pictured a table laden with roast beef, Yorkshire pudding, and all the vegs. Three kinds of pudding for dessert—

The pony stopped to drink at a stream and the girls joined him, cupping fresh cold water in their hands. "I'm hungry," Rose said, the words popping out of her mouth.

"I know," Poppy said. "So am I." She glanced around. "Oh, look. Raspberries."

The jewel-like fruit glowed in the near dark, beckoning them. They stripped the bushes, devouring the sweet morsels while Bramble found a patch of grass to nibble.

After every last ripe berry was gone, a few landing on the ground and another staining her shorts, Rose was still hungry. She was tired too. It was almost bedtime.

She spotted lights winking through the trees. "What's that, Poppy? Is it our home?" Her voice wavered.

"It's in the wrong direction," Poppy said. "Why don't we go see who lives there?"

They found a tiny cottage nestled among tall trees, and as they approached the back door opened and an elderly woman emerged. She began to cast grain around for the hens flocking to greet her.

"Look at all the chickens," Rose marveled. "And I see some kitties too." The cats were slinking around the garden, watching the hens.

"I'll feed you in a minute, you minxes," the woman said to the cats.

Poppy brought Bramble to a halt and slid off his back. "Hello," she said. "I'm Poppy and this is Rose." She glanced back at Rose, who was hesitating, worrying about the hens pecking her feet.

The woman's face creased in a welcoming smile.

"The Strawberry Girls. You're far from home, aren't you?"

"Yes, we are," Poppy said with a big sigh. "And we're hungry."

"All we could find were some raspberries," Rose said. "And we ate all the chocolate."

"That is a shame," the woman said. "Why don't you sit at the table here in the garden? I'll scramble some eggs."

"Thank you, missus," Poppy said. "That's awfully kind of you."

"Oh, no problem at all." The woman's eyes twinkled. "I enjoy seeing visitors." Her gaze went to Bramble. "Would your pony like a leaf of hay? You'll find it in the shed."

After she returned to the cottage, the sisters went over to the shed, where they found several bales of hay. Poppy broke off a chunk and fed it to Bramble, and then the sisters made their way to the table, Rose relieved that the hens ignored her toes.

While they waited, the cats came around, purring. One even leaped up onto a chair next to Rose, to her delight. "He likes me," she said, reaching out to pat his soft fur. He stretched out his chin for her to rub.

The woman soon returned with a tray, two bowls filled with fluffy scrambled eggs, a plate stacked with thick buttered toast, and a jar of jam. Two glasses of milk completed the meal.

"This should set you right," the woman said, placing the dishes on the table. "You need to keep your strength up so you can find Princess Audrey. She's counting on you."

Rose slid a look at Poppy. How did the woman know about the princess? She'd also known who they were. She must be a witch. But a good one, Rose decided. Only good witches made such delicious scrambled eggs.

CHAPTER 13

"Why don't you drive tonight, Molly?" Daisy said. "You have a license."

"Good idea," Mum said. "You really should give it a try." The three of us were walking down Magpie Lane to Aunt Violet's garage. At the last minute, Mum had decided to go shopping with Daisy and me, saying that she needed a new dress.

An unwelcome truth was hitting me broadside. Not only hadn't I been behind the wheel since we'd moved to England; I'd been actively dodging any opportunity to drive also. The idea of driving on the left petrified me and I had visions of causing an accident or looking the wrong way and killing a pedestrian.

"What is it, Molly?" Daisy asked. "You have a strange look on your face."

"I'm afraid," I blurted. "What if I wreck the car? It's Aunt Violet's baby." She'd owned the now vintage ride for decades. It was older than me.

Mum studied me for a moment. "How about this? I'll get

us out of Cambridge. You can try driving on the country roads."

I liked this suggestion. "Good idea. City traffic isn't the place to experiment. And no parallel parking in Hazelhurst, please." I didn't think I'd even attempted it since my driver's test, pathetic as that sounded.

"There's a big lot we can use," Daisy said. "We'll walk from there."

After unlocking the garage, Mum moved around to the driver's side. "Why don't you sit in front, Daisy?" I suggested, wanting to be polite. To forestall her disagreement, I opened the rear door—and discovered the manila envelope holding the original copy of Nate's journal. I'd forgotten to give it to Iona. "Can we swing by Strawberry Cottage after?" I asked Mum and Daisy, showing them the envelope. "I need to leave this there." It was also an opportunity to ask Iona about the characters in the book, if they had been based on Nate's friends like I thought.

"Fine with me," Mum said. "I'd like to check on her anyway."

"I don't care either way," Daisy said. "I don't have any plans."

We set off through the city, the route now familiar to me, but this time I watched the vehicles more closely. I could do it, I told myself, without killing my mother or my best friend.

Once we exited the highway, Mum pulled over. "Here you go, Molly." She climbed out and came to the rear.

I slid out and slowly took the driver's seat. Set for Mum, it was a little close to the wheel, so I adjusted it. The mirrors too, making sure I could see well. I glanced over the dash and found the lights, turn signal, and wipers.

"Any time now, Molly," Mum said from the back.

"Sorry," I said. "Just getting familiar with everything." At a snail's pace. I moved the signal to indicate we were pulling out, glanced in every direction, and hit the gas.

Fortunately, there was very little traffic this evening. I zipped along the country lane at a brisk 30 kilometers per hour, according to the dial.

"Um, Molly?" Daisy said. "Cows move faster." There were a few trotting along in an adjacent field and you know what? She was right.

Oops. Another detail to think about. Kilometers and miles weren't interchangeable. Trying to ignore my cognitive dissonance regarding space and time, I sped up to 50 kilometers per hour.

The high street was packed with traffic, but I white-knuckled it through to the turnoff to the parking lot. There I positioned the Cortina away from the other cars, pulling through so I wouldn't have to back out.

Naturally, the next car to enter the lot parked right beside us, although there were tons of other spots. Why do people do that?

As I opened my door, careful not to bang the other car, an older man got out. He looked familiar and, after a second, I recognized him. The head archeologist at the Thornton Hall dig, Dr. Holloway.

He glanced over and gave us a wave. "Hello. Molly, is it?" He locked his car with a beep and then pushed the keys into his trouser pocket.

"Yes, I'm Molly. How are you, Dr. Holloway?" I was working up to introduce my mother and Daisy, neither of whom had met him, I believed, when he sighed and shook his head.

"I'm rather staggered at the moment, to be honest. Did you hear the news?"

"No, I don't think so." My heart immediately began to pound. Although I had no evidence that something bad had happened, I braced myself.

He shifted his stance. "They found Poppy York's car. At the train station in Cambridge. No sign of her, though."

"That's good, isn't it?" I said, relief loosening my chest. She must have taken the train somewhere. Why or where was still unknown, but she must be alive. Then I wondered—why hadn't they seen it before now? Surely they would have checked there days ago.

"What would be better is Poppy returning to her job," he said, annoyance in his tone. "I won't be able to hold her slot much longer." With that, he gave a jerky nod of farewell and stomped away.

"And that is the man in charge of the Thornton Hall dig," I said.

"He's a right old grump, isn't he?" Daisy said, watching the professor cross the parking lot. "Sounded to me like good news."

"It is," I said. "But why didn't they notice her car before? She drives a vintage Ford Anglia and those are hard to miss."

"I see what you're saying," Mum mused. "It's possible someone else parked it there recently so it would be found only now." She reached for the door handle. "We need to go see Iona, make sure she's handling this all right."

"What about—" I sighed, seeing our shopping expedition go up in smoke. "You're right; we should. We can go shopping tomorrow. Or Saturday morning." Which would be cutting it very close, since the party was Saturday evening.

"Works for me," Daisy said, opening her own door. "Upset mothers come first."

I got behind the wheel again, doubly glad I'd pulled through. Dr. Holloway's car was parked so close it would have been tricky backing out. At least for me.

⚜

The front door of Strawberry Cottage stood open, golden light and classical music spilling out into the front yard. As we walked from the car, I recognized Prokofiev's *Peter and the Wolf.* The fantastical, atmospheric composition suited the setting perfectly.

"I feel like I've stepped into a fairy tale," Daisy said with a laugh.

"This place does that to you." I knocked on the door casing, but the music was so loud, Iona didn't hear.

After a moment of hesitation, Mum pushed past me and leaned through the opening. "Iona?" she called. "It's me, Nina." When she didn't get a response, she went inside while Daisy and I hovered on the steps. I'd remembered the journal this time, and the envelope was firmly clutched in my hand.

"They're old school friends," I said by way of explanation. "That's why she feels free to walk right in."

We waited, ominous music swelling in the background like a soundtrack.

Daisy grabbed my arm, her blue eyes wide. "Molly. What if Iona . . ."

She didn't need to finish the sentence. I'd let my mother walk into the house alone, possibly putting herself in danger—

"I'm going in," I said, stepping through the doorway.

"I'm right behind you," Daisy said.

The music was coming from speakers set up in the living room, which was empty. On a sideboard stood an open fifth of gin, along with an ice bucket and a bottle of tonic. Aha. Someone had been hitting the booze tonight. I put the manila envelope on the sideboard at the other end, where it wouldn't get wet if liquid splashed.

Moving in time to the lilting music, we tiptoed through to the kitchen. That, too, was empty, but the back door stood open. Aha, again. Iona was outside, which was why she hadn't heard us knocking.

Relieved not to have found a dead body—or two—we trailed out the back door, looking around for Iona and Mum. Soft voices drifted from the summerhouse, where they were seated on a swing, Iona pushing with one foot to make it rock.

"Molly," she said when I walked up the steps. "You're here too?" By the slight slurring in her tone, I knew she was feeling no pain, as they say.

"I am," I said. "This is my friend Daisy."

"Hi, Daisy," Iona said. "Pretty name and pretty girl. I like flower names. My daughters are called Poppy and Rose." As she spoke, she gestured with the glass in her hand, ice cubes tinkling.

"I love those names," Daisy said as she sat in a wicker rocker. I perched on the railing. "Your book is one of my favorites."

"So lovely to hear," Iona said. She stared at her glass as if realizing she was holding it. "Oh, I'm being rude. Would you like a drink?"

"Nothing for me, thank you," Mum said. We shook our heads. "We ran into Dr. Holloway in the village tonight and he told us they found Poppy's car."

Iona took a big swallow of her gin and tonic. "I heard that.

Now I'm more worried than ever. Someone else must have left it there, I'm thinking."

A weight slipped off my shoulders as I came to another conclusion. "Having it show up now also means that Robin wasn't involved in her disappearance."

Under the influence or not, Iona was still sharp. "Which would mean we might never find her. That's one small comfort, knowing whoever is responsible is still walking around."

Iona, like us, believed that Poppy hadn't vanished of her own volition, though there was a real risk the police would decide that she had and stop looking. I added this item to my list for Inspector Ryan.

"We'll find her," Mum said softly.

"Oh, I hope so." In Iona's tortured tone, I heard the frustration and fear I also felt, although to a much lesser degree, of course. How can you reassure someone who had already experienced a great and unjust loss? The worst can and did happen much too often.

"I'm going to keep looking for her," I said firmly. "One question is this: Where was her car all this time?" Poppy, and her car, had last been seen three days ago.

"It had to be hidden in a garage somewhere," Daisy said. "Or a barn."

"Does Thornton Hall have either?" I asked.

"Thornton Hall—you don't think—" Iona tilted her head and regarded me quizzically.

"I thought at first that Poppy might have gone back to Cambridge, to her flat," I said. "Rose and Ben thought so too. But what if she never left Hazelhurst?" One terrible possibility was that that Poppy had confronted Robin's killer and he or she did something to her.

Aunt Janice. I took a deep breath to ease the knot in my chest. Much as I didn't like my aunt, she wasn't exactly a criminal mastermind.

"Maybe she's still there," Iona said, her spine straightening. "In the barn or whatever. They moved her car to misdirect everyone."

"That's what I think," Daisy said.

"I'm planning to call Inspector Ryan," I said. "I'll run it by him." Although Mum and I had gone for a ramble on the property, I didn't feel comfortable searching Geoffrey Thornton's buildings. The police should do it.

"Please do tell him our thoughts," Iona said. "I would but . . ." Her lips trembled. "Oh, I'm such a mess."

"No, you're not," Mum said firmly. "You have a lot on your plate."

Iona found a tissue and dabbed at her eyes. "I knew about the crown."

That little bombshell stunned us for a moment. "You mean, when Nate had it?" Mum asked cautiously.

Ducking her head, she nodded. "He brought it home a few days before he died. He wouldn't tell me where he got it, only said that he was trying to 'save' it. I thought at first it was a costume piece and was like, 'What are you on about? It's a fake crown.' Geoffrey had trunks full of dress-up clothing at the manor that guests could wear, you see. Then I realized it was real."

"Save it how?" Daisy asked delicately.

"I don't know," Iona said. "I told him to take it back and he carried it off. I never saw it again and a few days later he was dead."

A loss so sudden and devastating, I guessed, that she didn't have the interest or the energy to find out where the crown was or where Nate had gotten it. Perhaps a bit of head-in-the-sand too, a fear of opening a can of worms.

Sir Jon had mentioned that Robin was helping Interpol regarding the black market in antiquities. Had Nate stolen it from a thief—or Robin—and one of them killed him? Now Robin had died, possibly while looking for the missing crown. Only a theory, but it worked.

"You need to tell the coroner about this," Mum said.

I saw her point. The coroner would rule on rightful ownership, and if Nate had stolen it then Iona wouldn't be able to benefit. I understood the temptation Iona faced, though. If she kept quiet, it might be assumed that Nate had found the crown on their property. Unless someone else filed a claim, like Geoffrey Thornton. That would beg the question why, if it had come from his property, Geoffrey had never reported the theft or notified anyone about the discovery. The coroner wouldn't like that either.

"I was kind of hoping the whole thing would go away," Iona said with a rueful laugh. "That's not going to happen, is it? And I lied to the authorities . . ." She took another gulp of her drink, then shook the glass, cubes rattling. It was empty.

"Here's something in your favor," Mum said. "You never did anything with the crown. It's been sitting up on the roof all this time. I think if you tell them everything you've told us, they'll understand."

"Do you really?" Iona gnawed at her bottom lip. "I'm afraid to risk it."

The tall lilac bushes behind the summerhouse rustled, a branch breaking with a crack. My heart jolted and I slid off the railing, feet planted wide. "What was that?"

"I don't know." Daisy's eyes were wide. "It sounded too big for a squirrel."

Anger rushed up the back of my head, burning off my initial alarm. Someone was spying on us. How dare they? Not stopping to think, I darted down the steps and around the side of the small building. The bushes rustled again and a dark figure burst out, running at top speed toward the woods.

CHAPTER 14

"Hey," I shouted. "Stop." I took off after the person, sneakers thudding on the grass. Naturally they didn't listen, instead putting on a burst of speed and disappearing among the trees. I picked up my pace.

"Molly," Mum called. "Come back."

Instead of listening to my mother, I entered the woods, glancing around to make sure I was on the path. It was almost totally pitch-black in here and I immediately stumbled on a protruding root and almost fell. Whoever it was obviously knew the terrain better than me, because they were already out of sight.

Unless they were lurking, waiting for me to come by . . . yikes. I turned around and bolted back toward the cottage. I had no chance of catching up with whoever it was and would only put myself in unnecessary danger—I was trying to work on my self-preservation instincts.

"Molly has a bit of a dangerous habit," Mum was saying as I returned to the summerhouse. "She likes to chase bad guys." She was referring to an incident during our first murder case.

"Mum," I said, panting. "You make me sound like a dog. 'Fetch, Molly, fetch.'" I began to laugh, bending over, hands resting on my knees, so I could breathe.

Daisy let out a peal of laughter. "I can just picture you dragging a bad guy home," she said. "Between your teeth." Mum and Iona laughed too.

"I know, I know, I'm too impulsive sometimes," I said, climbing the stairs and returning to my perch. "They made me angry, lurking like that. Loser."

Iona turned to Mum. "Your daughter is amazing. So brave."

"I think so too," Mum said. "Even if she does take needless risks."

I waved off her comment. "All right, I get it. I won't chase any more prowlers." Until the next time, which I fervently hoped was never.

"I'm glad to have you on my team, Molly," Iona said. "All of you. You're helping me stay sane right now."

My heart went out to her, but I had to admit, if it weren't for her missing daughter, I'd think Iona was involved up to her neck. The murder happened here, at her house, and she'd lied about the crown. Was she holding back other important information?

Mum slung an arm around her shoulders and squeezed. "It will all come right. You'll see."

"I hope so, Nina." With a sigh, Iona pushed herself to her feet. "I should let you go. I'll be sure to lock up tight after that little scare, but it looks like you got rid of whoever it was. My bed is calling me."

"Mine too," I said; though I was reluctant to leave Iona alone, I wasn't sure what else we could do for her. "Strawberry Fair tomorrow. I'll be up early." Earlier than I preferred, actually. Now that the event was upon me, I wished I hadn't agreed to go.

There was so much going on here in Hazelhurst, and I still had a dress to buy. Oh well. I'd have to make the best of it.

•٠•

At home, we gave Aunt Violet the latest updates before I headed upstairs, Puck right behind me. My bedroom was stuffy and warm, so I opened the diamond-pane casement windows to let in the soft night air. Despite being in the middle of the city, Magpie Lane was quiet, especially at this time of night when the only sounds were jovial voices as people left the pub. After changing into a sleep shirt, I settled on the bed next to Puck with my cell phone and copy of *The Strawberry Girls.*

Business before pleasure. With a longing glance at the book, I dialed the police station. It was probably too late to reach Inspector Ryan, so I readied myself to leave a message. To my surprise, he picked up his line.

"Ryan here." His voice was gruff, husky with exhaustion.

"Inspector Ryan? It's Molly Kimball. From the bookshop."

He gave a little laugh. "I know who you are."

Because of Mum or because I ended up meddling in his cases? Both, no doubt.

Now that I had him, I wasn't sure how to begin. "Um, I didn't expect to get you at this hour."

Papers shuffled. "What can I say? Burning the candle at both ends lately."

"I'll bet. Robin's murder and Poppy's disappearance are both big cases, aren't they?" Rather than try his patience further, I plunged ahead. "I heard that you found Poppy's car. I don't think she left it there; do you?"

"Molly, I really can't—"

"I know. It was a rhetorical question. Anyway, I was thinking that maybe it was parked somewhere else and moved to the station. Thornton Hall might be a good place to check out."

"Why? Do you know something?" he almost barked.

"Er, no. Not specifically. It makes sense, though, if she was last seen in that vicinity. There might be old barns, stables, sheds. Perfect for hiding a vehicle." I picked up my glass of water to wet my throat. "Before you hang up on me, there's one more thing. My aunt, Janice Marlowe." Despite not liking her very much, I still hated tattling on her. I quickly thought of a compromise. "You might want to talk to her. She used to date Robin, you know, and I think she might have some useful information, based on what she told me the other night." There. If she continued to hold out, that would be on her.

"Thank you, Molly." A warmer note had crept into his voice, as if he sympathized with my efforts to help. "As you know, I can't share any updates concerning what you've said tonight. There is one piece of information that I will tell you, though." He paused, probably just to torture me. "Your uncle has been cleared regarding Robin's death. A receipt came through for petrol, plus the owner of the station verified his alibi."

A whoosh of relief went through me, making me lightheaded. "That's awesome," I finally managed. "Thank you so much for letting me know."

"It's not often I get to deliver good news," he said, satisfaction in his voice. "Is there anything else?"

"Well, there was somebody creeping around Strawberry Cottage tonight. They ran off and we didn't get a good look at whoever it was."

Inspector Ryan grunted. "I'll send someone out to scout around."

"Thanks again, Inspector."

The second we disconnected, I was off the bed, leaving Puck glaring in my wake. "Mum, Aunt Violet," I called as I ran out of my room. "I have some great news."

The Strawberry Girls, cont.

Bramble came to an abrupt halt, jostling the girls. A fox sat smack in the middle of the path, licking his paws while remembering the delicious egg he had stolen.

Poppy jingled the reins, trying to get him to move. "Go on," she said. "Shoo."

The fox lifted his nose, his tail swishing around his feet. "I've been waiting for you," he said.

"He speaks?" Rose exclaimed. Then she wondered why she was even surprised. They'd seen butterflies turn into fairies and pixies roaming the Bluebell Wood. A talking fox was quite ordinary in comparison.

"I speak," the fox said. "My name is Aethelwulf."

"Aethelwulf?" Poppy asked. "But you're a fox."

"What can I say?" the fox answered. "My mother had great hopes for me." He stood with a stretch. "What are you two doing out so late? This is the time when nocturnal creatures roam. Shouldn't you be in bed?"

"We absolutely should," Poppy said. "But we're

looking for Princess Audrey. We can't go home until we find her."

"Princess Audrey, hmm?" His golden eyes flickered over Bramble. "I thought that was her pony."

Poppy patted the pony's neck. "He is. His name is Bramble."

"Have you seen Princess Audrey?" Rose asked.

The fox sniffed at the air. "Not today. Where have you looked?" They told him where they'd been, the paths they had followed. "Have you tried the fens? The hermit might have seen her."

"Mummy said we shouldn't go there," Poppy said. "It's not safe."

Aethelwulf snorted. "It's safe enough if you know where to put your paws. Come on, I'll show you."

He began trotting up the path, and after a moment Poppy nudged Bramble to follow. The crescent moon was higher now, flirting with them between the dark trees. White moths fluttered about and fireflies blinked in the trees. Rose wondered if they were fairies too. An owl hooted and then swooped down, wings wide.

"I've never been out so late," Rose whispered to Poppy. "I like it so far." She felt snug and safe on the back of the warm pony, nestled close to her big sister.

"Me too," Poppy said. "It's not scary at all."

The fox stopped and waited. "This way, gang. Mind you follow me exactly." Once they were close, he turned tail and slipped through a stand of willows.

It took some urging, but Bramble finally ventured into the thick bushes. The fox was waiting on the other side. "Thought I'd lost you," he said. "Watch out. It gets squishy."

Poppy and Rose soon understood what he meant. The pony's hooves sank into mud every time he stepped off the narrow track. In the pale moonlight, a seemingly endless sea of reeds spread before them, broken only occasionally by stunted and twisted trees. The fens.

Insects hummed. Things splashed in the reeds. Frogs croaked. Bramble's hooves alternately plodded and squelched.

Home seemed very, very far away.

"Do you know where you're going?" Poppy called, her voice wavering.

"I do," came the answer. "Try to keep up, won't you?"

On they went, the dark, empty marsh making it feel like forever. Plod, squish. Croak. Splash.

So Poppy did what she always did when she was lonely and afraid.

She began to whistle her father's favorite song. Her skillful notes flew up and down the scale, ringing out bright and sharp.

The fox turned and trotted toward them. "What are you doing?"

Before Poppy had time to wonder why he would care about her whistling, balls of light began to glow in the marsh. They bobbed, rising and falling as though carried across unsteady ground. Closer and closer, the mysterious lights came, beautiful but somehow menacing.

"What are those?" Rose asked.

Poppy's whistling died away as the fox practically spat, "The Lantern Men. Your whistling has called them and now they will lead you to a watery grave."

"A watery grave?" Rose cried. "Turn Bramble around and let's get out of here."

"You can't run," Aethelwulf said. He threw himself flat onto the ground. "They'll chase you. You must lie down and hold your breath."

The bobbing lights were drawing closer, accompanied by a wind whispering through the reeds. Danger is approaching, it seemed to say.

Poppy stared at the muddy track. "I don't want to get down in the mud. Are you sure that's the only thing we can do?"

"Yes," the fox said, his voice muffled. "If we're lucky they'll go right over us."

"What about Bramble?" Poppy asked.

"Him too. Now be quiet and get down here."

"We need to hurry," Rose said. "Make Bramble gallop away."

"No. He might hurt himself." Poppy stared out into the fens, at the lights coming their way. "What did Daddy tell us to do when trouble comes, Rose?"

"To . . . to stand our ground. But these are the Lantern Men, Poppy."

"I know." Poppy plucked the crown from the pommel and placed it on her head. She slid off Bramble, landing on her feet with a squishy, squelchy sound that would have made Rose giggle if she hadn't been so afraid.

Poppy stood with her feet widely planted and her arms crossed. Rose had seen that formidable look before, and while she didn't like it aimed at her, she appreciated it now. "Go on," Poppy growled at the lights. "Get out of here."

Rose laughed as the lights halted, wavered about,

and then floated in the opposite direction, bumping into each other as they fled. "You did it, Poppy. You scared them away."

The fox lifted his head. "It's safe? Really?"

"Yes, you scaredy-fox," Poppy said. "Get up and take us to the hermit. We need to find the princess."

Thankfully, they didn't see the lights again the rest of the way through the fens. All of them heaved a sigh of relief, especially Bramble, when they stepped onto solid ground again.

"Did we have to go through the fens to get here, Aethelwulf?" Rose asked.

The fox hunched his shoulders. "It's a shortcut. Not that I'll use it again."

"I wish you'd made that decision before," Poppy said in her big-girl bossy voice.

"Me too." Aethelwulf started trotting a little faster, and Rose had the feeling he couldn't wait for the journey to be over. She felt the same way.

They entered a grove of ancient oaks, thick, leafy tops hiding the sky. The air was mossy and sweet and a little stream trickled nearby. Through the trees, a fire snapped and glowed, and Bramble started moving faster, eager to reach some sort of civilization, Rose thought.

Fox, pony, and sisters burst into a clearing, stopping short to take in a very strange sight. A very tall man sat hunkered on a log, polishing a long silver sword with a rag. Beside him was a heap of other treasures— urns and cups, shields and helmets. Behind him was the opening to a cave carved out of the hillside.

"Who goes there?" he bellowed, resting the sword

across his knees. "Come closer, near the fire so I can see you."

"I think we're good right here," Poppy said, her voice shaking. "Since you have a sword and all."

The man laughed and held the sword up, then swished it through the air. He tested the edge with his fingers. "Yes, it's sharp all right. But I'm a peaceable man. Aren't I, fox?"

Aethelwulf had crept closer to the fire and was warming his paws. "You are indeed, hermit."

The hermit laughed and began to polish the sword again. "What is it you want, fox? It's late for visitors."

"We're looking for Princess Audrey," Rose said. "Have you seen her?"

"I have not," the hermit said. He turned to watch as a mole crept out of the cave, nudging a gold coin along the ground with his paws.

"I found the chest," the mole said in a squeaky voice, his nose twitching.

The hermit picked up the coin, examining it in the firelight before biting it. "Ah. Pure gold." He tossed the coin up and caught it, eyeing its glitter with a satisfied air. "Treasures hidden in darkness."

"I'm good at digging," Aethelwulf said. "If you need some help."

The mole squinted at the fox, eyeing his paws. "Sure, I could use you. Come on." Turning, he started trundling back toward the cave, the fox trotting behind him.

"Wait," Poppy cried. "We need to find the princess."

"I've done my best," the fox said. "You're on your own now."

CHAPTER 15

Midsummer Common was already a hive of activity when I arrived on my bicycle the next morning. Vendors were organizing their booths, a band was setting up at one of the stages, and vehicles were pulling in to unload. Over one hundred acts would be performing, I'd read.

Tim had texted me the booth location, so I found him fairly quickly, arranging bike shop merchandise under a canopy. "Good morning, Molly. Nice ride over?"

"Not bad," I said, dismounting. "It's a beautiful day." I parked my bicycle near my end of the table and pulled off my helmet. The provisions I'd brought—to-go cup of coffee, bottles of water, and a bag of warm scones—went on the grass next to what I guessed was my chair.

"Your boxes are under the table," Tim said, hanging helmets on a tree stand.

I peeked under the tablecloth and found them neatly lined up. The posters and stands were there too, on top. "Thanks again for bringing all this over."

"No problem," he said. "Are those scones I smell?" He glanced pointedly at the paper sack.

"Good nose. Fresh from Tea and Crumpets this morning." I picked up the bag and opened it, then held it out to him.

Tim selected a strawberry scone and bit into it, eyes half closed with pleasure. "Daisy is such a great baker, isn't she?"

"The best." I grinned at him. "Lucky you, that she's your girlfriend."

"I'll say. For many more reasons than this." He devoured the scone in several bites. "Thanks. Now I'd better get back to work."

I desperately wanted to drink my coffee, but instead I began to unpack the boxes of books, deferring gratification until after this chore. The new edition of *The Strawberry Girls* was gorgeous, the cover printed on luscious, glossy paper and the inside pages heavy, able to stand up to eager young fingers.

After arranging a few books standing up, I fanned out several more copies. One copy went in front with a note: Look at me. I wanted to avoid the other copies getting soiled or creased. Next I put two posters on stands, bracketing my display that way. Bookmarks advertising the bookshop were placed in a pile, and the final piece of the exhibit was a Thomas Marlowe banner, which I hung from the back edge of the canopy. The bike shop's banner was along the front of the table, plus Tim had hung a bicycle from the roof supports as well.

There. I was done. I plopped down in my chair and reached for my to-go cup and the bag of scones. I hoped I would sell some books and gain new customers for the bookshop.

"If you want to take a look around, feel free," Tim said. "We're not opening for another half hour."

I gobbled the last of my scone. "Maybe I will. I'd like to

check out the other vendors." Bringing my phone so I could take pictures, I began wandering the line of booths, stopping to admire the pottery, paintings, and handmade jewelry on display.

A tent decorated with real flowers and vines caught my eye. Titania's Bower, the banner read. Miranda's business. Ever since making the connection between the characters in *The Strawberry Girls* and Nate's real-life friends, I'd wanted the chance to talk to her again. This was the perfect opportunity because I had a reason to be here.

As I approached the tent, a man slipped out of the opening and strode away. Medium height, extremely buff, shaved head, and earring. Tough looking.

Miranda came to the opening and stood, gazing around at the hubbub. She noticed me and waved. "Molly. How are you?" Her clear voice cut through the noise.

"I'm fine. How are you?" As I drew closer, I saw she was dressed to coordinate with her booth—flowing white dress, flowers tucked in her long hair, rings and bracelets covering her hands and arms, dangling earrings. She wore sandals with long laces tied up her calf. Ever the Fairy Queen.

"Looks like it's going to be a busy day," she said. "If the weather holds."

We both glanced up at the sky, where wispy clouds were starting to filter in.

"I hope so," I said. "I've got books and I'd hate for them to get soaked." In response to her inquiring look I said, "I'm selling the new edition of *The Strawberry Girls*."

"Oh. I didn't know Thomas Marlowe sold *new* books." She stepped back into the tent and I followed, curious to see her displays.

"We do sometimes," I said. "Books with a local focus or updated editions of classics. This one hits both categories."

The merchandise she had on display reminded me of new age shops I'd seen in Vermont. Namely, heavy on the incense and trinkets, books, inspirational posters, herbal products, and jewelry. Her theme was a combination of flowers and magic.

"Love potion, Molly?" Giving me a sly smirk, Miranda held up a cute little bottle adorned with ribbon and dried flowers around its neck.

"I don't need one, thanks," I said, trying not to let her innuendo get under my skin. "It's pretty, though." Belief in its effectiveness or not, people would buy it because it was so appealing.

She raised her brows. "Are you sure?" Picking up a little cloth bag, she wiggled it. "I also have these sachets. Tuck one under a pillow for sweet dreams."

Now I was starting to wish I hadn't come in. Was she going to nag me until I bought something? I gritted my teeth, annoyed. "Maybe later. I'm just browsing around the booths right now." I noticed a dish of worry stones. Had the one we found in Ben and Poppy's apartment come from Miranda's shop?

She set the sachet down and rearranged the bags. "How about a reading? I'm not going to charge you," she added quickly. "It will be a warm-up for my day."

"Reading?" I asked, looking down at my hand. "My palm?" My immediate reaction was to say no. I didn't normally go for fortune-telling or psychics. Besides, I'd already met my tall, dark stranger and we were happily dating, thank you.

"No, tea. Plus it will give us a chance to chat." She put a hand on my upper arm and steered toward the back, where there was a small table covered with a cloth and two chairs. "Have a seat."

Wondering what I had gotten myself into, I obeyed, then quickly sent Tim a text so he'd know where I was.

On the job? he wrote back, followed by a thumbs-up.

I squinted at his comment, not getting it. Oh. *On the job* meant police work. I sent back a smiley face. Yes, that's why I was here, to see what I could learn from Miranda. Otherwise I'd certainly keep my distance from her attractive but toxic self.

Miranda switched on an electric kettle before bringing over a basket of teas, single servings in cellophane envelopes. "Take your pick," she said. "I grew and dried all the flowers."

Lavender, calendula, rosehips, honeysuckle. "Honeysuckle sounds good," I said, thinking of the flowers we used to pluck and chew on as children.

"It's one of my best," Miranda said. The water must have been hot, because it was already boiling. She deftly made two cups of tea and carried them over to the table. After a ritual stir—three times in each direction—she handed me my cup and saucer.

The china had a strawberry pattern. "Wedgwood Wild Strawberry," she said when she saw me studying the design. "I thought it was appropriate for today."

"It is." I picked up the cup and noticed tea leaves in the bottom. *Ugh.* I hated getting tea leaves in my mouth.

"Can't do a reading without them," she said, sitting down across from me. "Sip carefully."

No problem. I took a tentative taste, allowing the sweet liquid to sit on my tongue. Not bad. "I've been reading *The Strawberry Girls* again. I'm getting so much more out of it seeing the places that inspired the story." Not to mention Nathanial's notes, including the *M.* beside the Queen of the Fairies character.

"I'll bet." She propped her chin on her hand, her large eyes never leaving my face. Was this part of the reading process, her attempt to meld minds? That's what it felt like.

Uncomfortable, I shifted on my seat, which was one of those thinly padded metal chairs. "Have you read it?"

"I already know the story. I was there when Nate was working on it." She sat up, waving her hand dismissively. "I couldn't believe it when Iona went ahead and published. It wasn't *her* idea."

"Are you sure?" I asked. "If he talked about it with you, they probably brainstormed together."

Her face twisted in a sour expression. "I suppose. All I know is that I inspired him." That sly smile again.

What was she implying? I didn't believe for a moment that Nate had cheated on Iona with this self-centered woman. She was probably a femme fatale in her own mind, the type who believed every man was in love with her.

"What was Nate like?" I asked, curious to hear from someone who knew him, even if I couldn't entirely trust her opinions.

She thought for a moment. "Brilliant. Gorgeous." She pursed her lips. "Definitely eccentric. Iona told me before he died that she was worried about him working too hard. He'd stay up all night, holed up in his office. Or rambling around the countryside to the site of local legends. When he was in the middle of something, he'd often become obsessed."

My father had been a history professor too, and I'd witnessed his focus and absorption while on the research trail. I suppose this behavior could seem strange to people who had never engrossed by a project. I, on the other hand, understood it perfectly.

"You think that's why he was up on the tower?" I asked. "On the trail of some idea?"

Miranda pursed her lips, considering. "Maybe. He'd had a few drinks at the party. Not that I was counting, you understand." She shivered. "It was a foolish and dangerous thing to do, to go up that tower at night. Alone. I've often told Geoffrey he needs to block off the battlements. With a metal fence or something. They're a little too low."

"No one can get up there now," I pointed out. "It's boarded up." When her eyes narrowed, I said, "Mum and I went out to see it the other day."

"So it's still boarded up? I haven't been near it for years."

I nodded. "The rosebushes are so thick around it you can barely get through. It reminded me of Sleeping Beauty."

"I remember that," Miranda said. "Geoffrey's great-grandfather had a very whimsical side. The whole property is like something out of a fairy tale."

"No wonder Nate was inspired," I said. "I've also noticed that the characters seem to be based on his friends. Like the Good Witch, for example."

Miranda lurched back, color flaring in her cheeks. "That isn't me."

Which part? I wanted to ask. *The good or the witch?* She was probably offended since the Good Witch was elderly and kept cats. Not exactly a femme fatale.

Preferring to let her stew rather than ease her ego, I focused on drinking my tea. "This is really good," I said. "I want to buy some."

Her face brightened. "I have it in larger bags. You'll want one of those."

Now that she was in a better mood again, I dared to ask, "Do you know if any of the other characters are based on real people? Beside Poppy and Rose."

I could practically see her mind working as she decided what to tell me. "Um, let me think." Her lips parted. "Oh, the fox. That was Robin. He was always trying to lead us astray. We started calling him the ringleader." She sounded wistful.

"You must miss him." From what I'd seen on social media, Robin did look like a fun person, even if he might have been involved in antiquities theft.

Miranda shrugged and sighed as if trying to throw off her sad thoughts. "How are you doing with that tea?"

I peeked into my cup, where a thin layer of liquid covered the dreaded leaves. "Almost done."

"Let me see." She got up and looked into my cup. "We're ready. Pick up your cup." When I did, she slid a napkin onto my saucer. "Put the cup down, and using your left hand, turn it three times counterclockwise and think about your question."

Which one? I had so many. Who killed Robin? Where was Poppy? Was Iona innocent of theft? Would Kieran and I last? Actually, I wasn't even ready to contemplate the latter, even for fun.

Besides, I didn't believe in this at all, and if I did, Miranda wouldn't be my choice of reader. She had hidden agendas for days, I sensed.

"If you don't have a question, that's fine," she said, picking up on my hesitation. "We'll do a general reading. Sometimes those are the most interesting, anyway."

"All set," I said after spinning the cup. "Now what?" She instructed me to place the napkin and saucer on top of the cup and flip the whole thing over to catch the last of the liquid.

Then she took the cup, the tea leaves in a random design, and stared into it. Her lips pursed. "Interesting," she muttered. She cut a glance at me. "Did you choose a question?"

I shook my head. "I couldn't settle on one."

"All right." Her brow furrowed. "I see books. Several. All closed, which means secrets."

That fit, both literally and figuratively. You could say that books held secrets until they were read.

She squinted. "A butterfly. A fickle friend?"

I have to admit that my heart lurched at hearing that, since the obvious interpretation was that Kieran might be fickle. On the other hand, there were butterflies in *The Strawberry Girls* and Nate's death was related to a circle of friends.

Miranda's frown deepened. "This is strange. Something I don't see very often. A bag." She turned the cup to the light for a better look. "It's closed, which means a trap."

She set the cup on the table and stared into my eyes with a concern that seemed genuine. "Be careful, Molly."

"Just in time," Tim said when I arrived back at our booth. "The fair is officially open."

"Sorry," I said, stowing my bag of honeysuckle tea under the table. "I got caught up at Miranda's." As soon as Miranda finished the reading, I'd paid for the tea and bolted out of there, seriously unsettled.

Was that the result she wanted? Maybe so. That's why I'd been hesitant in the first place. Miranda was smack in the middle of Nate's death, Robin's murder, and who knew what else. She was probably trying to discourage me from poking around.

Fairgoers in singles and pairs and groups were strolling along the grassy aisle now, pausing at the various booths. A young woman pushing a stroller, accompanied by a girl aged three or four, stopped in front of us.

"See that book, Charlotte?" the woman said to the girl. "It

used to be one of my favorites when I was little." Throwing me a smile, she moved closer to pick up the sample copy. "It's called *The Strawberry Girls* and it's about two sisters."

"Like me and CiCi?" Charlotte asked, wonder dawning on her face. She reached out a starfish hand. "Ooh. They're riding a pony."

How I loved seeing children discover books. *The Strawberry Girls* was enthralling a new generation.

"Exactly like you and CiCi," her mother said. "They're brave and funny and kind."

She put the sample book back and picked up a fresh copy. "I'd like to buy this."

I'd made my first sale at the Strawberry Fair.

CHAPTER 16

Early the next morning at Thomas Marlowe, a former secret agent sat at the kitchen table, sleeves rolled up, digging into scrambled eggs and bacon. That was life in Cambridge.

"Sir Jon. I didn't know you were here." I detoured over to the pour-over coffee maker waiting for me on the counter. The kettle was steaming, so I bumped up the heat before scooping ground coffee into the filter.

"He stopped by to give us an update," Aunt Violet said. She sat in her usual seat, sipping tea and regarding Sir Jon with fondness.

"The fact that it was mealtime was purely a coincidence." Sir Jon winked at me before dabbing his mouth with a napkin. "I have something for you, Molly." He pointed at a cellophane-wrapped magazine on the table.

At Home was the title, and on the cover was a very familiar manor house, Thornton Hall, decked out for Christmas. The magazine date was December, almost twenty years ago.

I snatched up the magazine with a cry of excitement and slid it out of the sleeve. "How cool. Is there an article—"

The kettle whistled, so I set the magazine down and whirled around to grab it off the flame. After filling the cone with hot water, I picked up my gift and began leafing through, eagerly searching for the right page.

Ah, here it was. "Small and cozy, these classic homes offer holiday cheer." Several houses were featured, each with an exterior shot and one or two interior shots. Thornton Hall's interior photo showed the entrance hall, decorated with a huge tree and garland winding around the staircase banister.

Three formally dressed couples posed on the stairs. "Hosted by Geoffrey Thornton, a band of revelers make merry deep in the Cambridgeshire countryside," the caption read. I peered closer at the other people, who weren't identified. Iona and Nate, Robin and a woman I didn't recognize, Geoffrey of course, and Miranda, who was wearing a flowing velvet dress and a gold circlet in her hair. A circlet set with gems.

"That's the crown," I said, thrusting the magazine under Sir Jon's nose. "Or a darn good imitation."

He glanced up at me, one brow raised. "You can guess the probable response from Miranda Blake when we ask her, I'm sure."

"Oh yeah. She'll say it's fake." Still holding the magazine, I wandered back to the coffee and removed the cone, then poured a cup. Added a splash of milk. "I think they found it somewhere on the property and wanted to keep it. Or sell it."

"That's what we think too," Sir Jon said. "Although we can't prove it." He'd finished eating and now sat with his mug cradled in his hands. "The key question for the authorities is proving ownership. No one is likely to come forward with information about its origin. They can't without implicating themselves in hiding it all this time. Iona might win her case by saying that Nate must have dug it up on their property. Though on the other hand, since this type of artifact is usually found in burial mounds and there are none near Strawberry Cottage, she might have a hard time getting them to accept that."

Iona's confession sat like a lump in my throat. She'd known about the crown all along. I sensed Aunt Violet's eyes on me. Since we shared everything, she already knew what Iona had confessed under the influence of gin.

I sidestepped, coming at the subject from another angle. "Doesn't this picture prove Iona—and the others—knew about it?"

Sir Jon shook his head. "Not if they say it was costume jewelry. Robin might have helped us, but his climbing onto the cottage roof, apparently in search of the crown, has thrown his credibility into question."

I realized I didn't know much about Robin's background or why he was helping Interpol. "Was Robin involved in smuggling or had he just noticed some shady dealings?"

"Involved," Sir Jon said. "He's been under suspicion for years, operating under the radar just far enough that he wasn't caught. He was a slippery old fox."

Fox. Now I was certain Nate's fox was Robin. Leading people astray and into trouble, was that the message?

Sir John went on, "A few months ago, he was finally nabbed during a fairly small deal and that's when he offered cooperation, saying he knew of a major ring operating between the UK and the rest of Europe. A few of his tips panned out, so they decided to try to work with him."

"A major ring?" I asked. "Where? What were they selling?"

He ran a finger in front of his mouth, as if zipping his lips. "Sorry, Molly, but I can't say. Even without Robin, the investigation is still underway." His smile was wry. "They're now double-checking all the intel he gave them. We think he was going to skip the country with the crown. A person could live for decades on proceeds from that, in some places."

So Robin had been a fox to the end. A thought dawned. "That's probably why he broke up with Aunt Janice. Besides her terrible personality," I added. "He was going to take off."

"Molly," Aunt Violet said, trying to repress a smile.

"What's this about your aunt?" Sir Jon asked.

I told him Aunt Janice's version of events the morning Robin died. "We told her she should go to the police, since she was probably one of the last people to see Robin alive," I said. "I called Inspector Ryan last night to make sure he knew about it." I made a face. "However I feel about her, it didn't feel good to rat her out, believe me. She might know something, though, and not even realize it."

Mum appeared in the kitchen doorway, dressed in a robe and with a bad case of bed head. Her jaw dropped when she saw Sir Jon. "I didn't know we had company." Backing away, she tried to smooth her hair with both hands.

Sir Jon rose to his feet. "Please don't go. I was about to leave." He pushed his chair in. "Thanks again for breakfast. I'll keep you all posted and please, do the same." To our surprise and delight, he took a detour and kissed Aunt Violet on the cheek. "See you later, love."

Once he'd slipped out the French doors, Mum and I hooted in delight. "Love?" I said. "What's been going on down here this morning?"

Aunt Violet blushed deeply, trying to hide her confusion behind her mug of tea. "Nothing." She bit her lip. "Well, maybe a little something."

I jumped up and gave her a hug. "I'm so happy for you."

Sir Jon and Aunt Violet had been friends since college, over fifty years. I'd had the suspicion that he had held a torch for her all this time, judging by the way he looked at her in old photographs. Life had kept them apart and now they were having their moment.

Mum shuffled to the AGA with a yawn. "Fresh pot, Aunt Violet?" She turned on the gas under the kettle. "Molly, we need to go shopping today."

"That's right; we do." A thrill of panic went through me. The garden party was tomorrow night. "What if I can't find something to wear?"

"Don't worry," Mum said, emptying the teapot. "We'll scour the shops until we find the perfect dress."

"I really wanted to go to Bella Mia in Hazelhurst with Daisy," I said, thinking of Daisy. "It's only open regular hours today." When we'd driven by the other night, the dress I liked was still in the window.

"Give her a call and see when's good," Mum suggested. She dispensed fresh tea leaves into the pot, which reminded me of Miranda.

"Did I tell you about my tea-leaf reading at the Strawberry Fair?" They both looked at me. "With Miranda Blake." I gave them the gist of what she'd said, her mention of a fickle friend and a warning about a trap. Voicing it out loud gave me an icky feeling again. "It was creepy."

"Miranda is creepy," Aunt Violet said. "She's been involved with Geoffrey Thornton off and on for years, hoping he'll give in and marry her. Geoffrey, however, keeps her—and all women—at arm's length to protect his fortune. Remember how jealous she was when you mentioned the garden party? She was trying to sow doubt in your mind about Kieran. She couldn't stand to think you were happy."

"You think?" It had worked—for a minute. Even now I had

to deliberately push the nagging sense of uneasiness away. "She also called Nate eccentric. To me it sounds as if he was obsessed with his work, kind of like Dad used to get. Remember, Mum?"

"Sure do." She poured boiling water into the pot. "He'd go into his cave and come out only at mealtimes. If then."

"I'm the same way," I said. "Miranda also told me that the fox in *The Strawberry Girls* is based on Robin. Miranda called him the ringleader in their little circle."

"Interesting that Sir Jon also called him a fox," Aunt Violet noted. "Looks to me that Robin was playing both sides of the fence."

"What's this?" Mum asked.

I relayed our conversation with Sir Jon, including that the authorities now believed that Robin had been trying to find the crown and possibly skip the country.

Mum slipped the tea cozy over the pot and carried it over to the table to steep. "Sly behavior, indeed," she said wryly. "I wonder if the other characters are based on anyone real."

"Mrs. Dobbins is the Good Witch," I said. "In his notebook, he wrote *M.* beside the Queen of the Fairies. That's an easy-peasy one."

Aunt Violet fiddled with her teaspoon. "Beguiling and dangerous, yes, that's Miranda."

"And I think the hermit might be Geoffrey," I said. "The hermit digs artifacts out of the earth, which is quite a damning indictment when you think about it."

While whipping up a batch of scrambled eggs for Mum and me, I shared my thoughts about the crown and the events of twenty years ago. "I have zero solid proof, but judging by what Sir Jon told us about Robin, he and his friends might have been selling antiquities from Thornton Hall land. Nate either was involved and had a crisis of conscience or stum-

bled upon their criminal activity. So someone killed him."
I pointed at the magazine Sir Jon had given me. "Miranda
wearing the crown at a party tells me Iona also knew about
the crown before Nate brought it home. She might have
known about the smuggling too."

Mum groaned. "I hate to think Iona was involved. We've
been friends forever."

"Big money turns a lot of heads," Aunt Violet said. "If that
farmer hadn't plowed up an artifact, Geoffrey would probably still be selling antiquities from the property."

I stopped stirring the eggs. "Who says he stopped?"
Vague thoughts came into focus. "Okay, let's say Robin was
trying to find the crown. That doesn't mean he was the only
one who knew about it." Although, if a partner in crime
had pushed him off the roof, why hadn't they then grabbed
the crown? Realizing I'd almost let the eggs burn, I put my
speculations aside and began stirring again. Inspired by the
description in *The Strawberry Girls*, I wanted my eggs soft
and fluffy.

I was sitting down with my breakfast—after serving
Mum—when I remembered the shopping expedition. "Oops.
I'd better text Daisy." In between bites, I sent her a note.
"Good news. She has an employee working today so we can
shop this afternoon. If that's okay with you, Aunt Violet." I
tried to be mindful of leaving her alone in the store.

"I'll be fine," she said. "You cover plenty of hours for me."

Not so many of late, though: strange deaths and disappear-
ances had a way of getting the best of my schedule, but I
resolved to step up to the plate more than ever once this was
all over. Before we'd arrived—and after her brother, Tom,
had died—Aunt Violet had been alone and in financial trouble to boot. But with fresh energy from Mum and me, the
shop was experiencing a resurgence in popularity and sales.

Now over four hundred years old, Thomas Marlowe was killing it.

◀▶

"Oh, yay. The dress I like is still there." Before going inside Bella Mia, I'd stopped to check out the window. "Hopefully they have it in my size."

Daisy held the door for Mum and me. "If not, they have lots of other choices."

"I'm hoping for one and done," I said, since I really didn't like shopping. My phone bleeped, so I paused to read the text. "Rose is going to meet us at the café in an hour." Since she was working nearby at the Thornton dig, I thought this was a good opportunity for us to catch up while eating lunch.

"The food there is great," Daisy said. "Farm to table menu."

Since it was too late to start dieting for the garden party, I looked forward to trying a new place. There was always spandex underwear if my dress was a little snug, right?

The interior of the boutique was hushed, soft music playing on a hidden system. Mum and Daisy went to the dresses area and started sliding hangers along the racks, pulling out a few for a closer look.

"I'm interested in the periwinkle-and-red print dress in the window," I told the clerk behind the counter.

She glanced over my form with a practiced eye. "We should have something to fit you." She put down her phone and led me to a rack, where I leafed through and found a couple of sizes to try. "Changing rooms are in the back."

One dress was a little large, so I tried the other, which thankfully fit beautifully. Studying myself in the mirror, I tried to imagine how Kieran would see me. With the right shoes and my hair and makeup done, of course.

"Show us," Daisy called through the curtains.

I stepped out into the main room, where a three-way mirror was set up, and posed for Daisy and Mum. "What do you think?"

"It's perfect," Mum said. "You'll knock him dead. And the rest of the guests too."

A sudden stab of insecurity hit me. "What about his parents? Do you think I'll pass muster with Lord and Lady Scott?" I put on a fake accent for this last, trying to make a joke of it.

"They'll love you, Molly," Mum said softly. "How could they not?"

I wished I were as confident. "Thanks, Mum. I guess we'll find out." Twirling back and forth, I said, "So, thumbs-up, Daisy?"

"Thumbs-up," she said. "Now it's my turn."

In between Daisy modeling dresses for us, I helped Mum find the perfect outfit for her date with Inspector Ryan, er, Sean. Seriously, it would be too ridiculous to address my mother's date as "Inspector."

We settled on black wide-leg cropped pants paired with a silky gray shell, light cashmere wrap, and mules. "Oh, Nina," Daisy said when she modeled the outfit. "You look incredible. Sophisticated and *gorgeous*."

Mum shared a smile with the clerk. "I'm taking her shopping with me all the time."

"Whenever you like," Daisy said. "I had such fun today." She handed the clerk the dress she'd chosen, a flowing pale blue chintz with a wide ruffle at the bottom and buttons all the way up the front. "We'll be back."

✤

The Farmer's Table was a quaint little restaurant located in a pale blue brick building near Robin's shop. When we walked up, Rose was already seated at a table outside. She stood to greet us, pulling out chairs for us to sit. "I told the server there would be four. I had them bring water with lemon already. Hope that's all right."

"Perfect," I said, sitting down and picking up my glass for a long drink. "What's good here?" I turned the standing menu to face me, noticing it listed the day's specials.

"Everything," Rose said. "It changes every day, depending on what they can get from the farms. I love their bean cake." The black bean cake was served on greens and topped with goat cheese and balsamic.

"I think I'll try that," I said, relinquishing the menu so Daisy and Mum could see it. Daisy chose a grilled eggplant sandwich and Mum ordered a chickpea and veggie bowl.

By unspoken agreement, we didn't talk about anything heavy while we waited for our food. Rose gave us updates about the dig, showing us photographs of the latest artifacts. "I'm still hoping we get to excavate the barrows," she said. "Maybe there's a ship under there." She was referring to the magnificent vessel uncovered at Sutton Hoo.

"Barrows are tombs," I said, thinking of what Sir Jon had said about the crown, that it had probably come from a burial chamber.

"Yes, that's right." Rose leaned back so the server, a young woman, could place a dish in front of her. "They're similar to the pyramids in Egypt. In function, I mean. It's Poppy's dream to uncover one that hasn't been robbed. The contents are like a snapshot of life in ancient times."

"So fascinating," Daisy said, smiling thanks at the server,

who seemed unperturbed by our discussion of tombs. "I've heard that scientists can figure out people's diets and health from bones."

Rose's face lit up. "They absolutely can. For example, Princess Eanswythe, who lived in the seventh century. It's believed that her bones have been in a lead reliquary since around the year 800, in a church in Kent."

Thinking of the crown, I wondered if our princess had also lived in that era.

"Enjoy," the server said. "Do you need anything else?" We didn't, so she hurried off.

Mouth watering, I picked up my fork and cut into the bean cake. Oh my. It was savory and delicious, with hints of cumin and coriander.

"The church allowed a team to come in and analyze the bones." Rose paused to take another bite before continuing. "They discovered a female in her teens to early twenties, with very good teeth, meaning a refined diet, and her bones were strong, despite a couple of possible injuries. They think she died of bubonic plague and is possibly related to the Queen. She also founded one of the first convents in England."

I pictured a strong, healthy young woman with great faith and ambition. In the absence of written history, science was filling in some of the gaps.

"Fascinating," Mum said. "We should go see the mummies at the British Museum, Molly."

"Um, okay," I said, not sure if that was a field trip I wanted to take. Although the British Museum had lots of other cool stuff, including an extensive rare manuscripts collection.

A young man striding down the sidewalk caught my eye. When he noticed me and veered in our direction, I recognized Ben, Poppy's fiancé.

"Hey, Ben," Rose said. "Pull up a chair, if you want." She glanced at her plate. "We're already half-done, though."

"I'm not here for lunch." Ben's tone was terse. "It's your mum, Rose. She's been arrested. They're saying she killed Robin Jones."

CHAPTER 17

Guilt rooted me to my seat. Misplaced, perhaps, but strong enough to turn my stomach anyway. I pushed my plate away, appetite gone.

I had encouraged Aunt Janice to go to the police and she must have told them, as she had us, that Iona was home when she'd spoken to Robin. As a result, they probably believed that Iona had confronted Robin after Aunt Janice left. Maybe they had other evidence as well, or what they thought was evidence. Either way, a woman I liked, Rose and Poppy's mother, an author beloved by many, had now been arrested. I winced at the thought of the headlines.

Mum's complexion had paled. "They arrested Iona?" she asked, her voice choked. "I can't bloody believe it."

"Me either," Ben said. "I suppose they'll accuse her of doing away with her daughter next."

Of all of us, Daisy had the coolest head. "Why don't we get out of here? I'll take care of the bill. It's not the most, er, private place to chat." Everyone around us had stopped eating to stare, not bothering to hide their interest.

"Would you?" Mum said. "I'll reimburse you."

Waving that off, Daisy made her way through the tables to find our server.

Rose stood, her expression blank, her movements stiff and jerky. Mum put her arm around her. "Come with me, sweetie. We'll take you home."

"To Thornton Hall?" Ben asked. "Or to the cottage?"

Tears began to spill from Rose's eyes. "I suppose Thornton Hall. I can't bear to go to Strawberry Cottage if Mum isn't there."

"We'll take you," Mum said. "How did you get here?"

Rose had ridden her bicycle, so we arranged with the restaurant to keep it safely stashed until she could come get it. Ben was on his scooter, so he buzzed back to Thornton Hall while we packed up leftovers and made our way back to the car.

Nothing much was said on the ride due to the pall of shock and dismay that lay over all of us. If only Iona hadn't lied to the police about the crown. Us as well, I realized, my stomach filling with acid. When Uncle Chris had opened the box, she'd pretended to be surprised. Although I understood the temptation to claim ignorance, her lies cast a shadow of doubt over everything she said.

Another thing. Miranda wearing the crown in the magazine was more proof that Iona had known it existed. Sir Jon must have shared the article with the police.

I vowed not to say a word about any of this in case Sir Jon or Aunt Janice hadn't yet spilled the beans. The last thing I wanted was to give the police more circumstantial evidence against Iona. I still didn't believe that she had killed Robin. If she had, she would have removed the box before Uncle Chris could find it.

If the police were looking in her direction, that meant we needed to keep digging and find the actual killer.

"Go around back," Rose said, directing us. "Our digs are in the old stable block."

The tires crunched on gravel as we passed by the house and through an open gate into the former stable yard. The stalls themselves had been converted to garages, and above them was a line of windows. Ben's scooter was already parked near a side door, so Mum pulled up beside it.

Rose led the way upstairs, to a comfortable sitting room overlooking the house and gardens. Ben, who'd been sitting in a chair, rose when we entered. He went right to Rose and wrapped her in a hug.

"I can't believe it," Rose muttered, leaning against him as if he were holding her up. "Poppy and now Mum . . ."

"She didn't do it," I found myself blurting. "We need to find out who did."

Rose lifted her head, a tiny ray of hope shining in her eyes. "You think we can?"

I paced back and forth in front of the huge stone fireplace. "We have to try." Still knocked off-kilter by the news, I needed a moment to gather my wits.

Mum took out her phone. "I'm going to call the station. Your mum must have a barrister and we need to contact him or her." She perched on a wide windowsill to make the call.

Daisy had plopped onto an ottoman, chin propped on her hand. "I know one thing for sure. Iona wouldn't have harmed her own daughter. So there's that mystery still, isn't there?"

"Exactly what I was thinking," I said. "Why is Poppy missing? It has to be related to Robin's death. She either saw something and ran or—" I broke off, not wanting to voice my fears in front of her sister and fiancé.

"The killer put her somewhere," Ben said, his face stricken. "I'm beginning to think so too. I'm just praying that she's all right."

"Me too." I began to pace again. "The car showing up was a diversion. I suggested to Inspector Ryan that they search the grounds here." I pointed at the floor. "What if Poppy's car was hidden in the garage all this time?"

Ben frowned. "I never thought of that. You notice there aren't any windows on the bay doors. We always park outside, me, Poppy, and Dr. Holloway, when he stays here."

I gripped the stone mantel, my legs going all wobbly. My remark had been a wild guess and it could possibly be correct. Surely that would mean that Geoffrey was in on it. Had Geoffrey killed Robin? Maybe Robin was going to keep the crown for himself and Geoffrey found out. I'd thought the killer would have taken the crown, but maybe Robin said it wasn't there after all, either lying to protect it or having been unable to find it.

"What are you thinking, Molly?" Daisy asked. "I know that expression."

Mum disconnected her call, so I put up a finger to indicate we should wait to hear what she had to say. "Your mum does have a barrister and they're in with the police right now. I got her contact information if you want to give her a call later. Alexa Owusu is her name."

Rose pulled out her phone. "I'm ready." She entered the barrister's name and number as Mum recited them.

"Alexa Owusu," Daisy said. "I've heard of her, from articles in the paper. She's a rising star. Brilliant and aggressive."

"Exactly what Iona needs," I said. I had thought she might

call Sir Jon, who was also a barrister, but his involvement with the smuggling investigation probably created a conflict of interest.

"I'll call her later." Rose made a face as she turned to Ben. "I can't go back to the dig right now."

"Don't blame you a bit," Ben said. "I'll tell Holloway that you need to take the afternoon off." With a sigh, he moved toward the door. "But I've got to go. I'm supervising a couple of interns that really don't know what they're doing yet." A moment later we heard his footsteps thumping down the stairs.

Mum glanced at me and I knew what she was thinking. "We should probably get going too," she said. "Aunt Violet is expecting us back."

Daisy got to her feet. "And I need to cash out the register."

Rose touched my arm. "Do you have to leave, Molly?" Her lips quivered. "I really don't want to be alone."

My heart went out to her. Sister missing, mother arrested, left to stew with her own thoughts—it wasn't a healthy situation. I glanced at Mum, my brows raised.

"Stay, Molly," Mum said. "One of us will come get you later."

How could I say no? After reassuring Rose I would be right back to hang out with her for a while, I walked Mum and Daisy down to the car, wanting to touch base before they left.

"Keep us posted, okay?" Mum said. "I want to hear any news."

"I will." I studied her grim expression, girding myself to ask a difficult question. "How do you feel about this situation, about Sean Ryan's involvement, I mean?"

She shook her head once with an abrupt movement. "I haven't decided. I know he was just doing his job, as they say, but still. I can't ignore the fact that he arrested one of my friends." Frowning, she climbed into the car and inserted the key while Daisy went around to the passenger side.

"See you later, Molly," Daisy said. "Beer at the pub?"

"Sounds good," I said. "Give Kieran and Tim the update, will you? Tell Kieran I'll text him later."

"I will," Daisy said. "We'll take care of your new dress too."

I had totally forgotten about my delicious new outfit. Waving goodbye as they drove away, I wondered if Mum would cancel her date with Sean. If so, what would happen to their budding relationship? Dead on arrival, looked like.

Upstairs, Rose was wandering around the room, picking things up and setting them down. "I can't settle," she said. "Until I hear from Mum . . . or her barrister."

"Totally understandable," I said. "We went through something similar when Aunt Violet was a murder suspect." Thankfully, that case had never progressed to an arrest.

Hearing the crunch of tires on gravel, I went to the window. A gleaming white Range Rover slowed as the vehicle approached the garage, a rumbling starting as a door began to lift. *The garage.* "Hold on, Rose," I said, bolting toward the hallway. "I'll be right back."

Even as I ran down the stairs, I realized how far-fetched my theory was about the Ford Anglia being stored in this building. How would anyone drive it away without the upstairs occupants noticing? The rumble of the door going up was clearly audible. They would have had to move the car when no one was here, and at night, when people were less likely to notice such a distinctive car on the road.

By the time I got outside, Geoffrey Thornton was easing the Range Rover into a bay. The bay next to that one was empty, I quickly noticed before the door rolled down behind him. So there *was* room for the Anglia.

Deciding I should go back upstairs before he noticed me, I hurried across the gravel.

"Molly." Geoffrey emerged from a side door, sliding sunglasses down over his eyes. "I thought it was you."

Busted. "Yeah, it's me," I said. "I'm visiting Rose. Did you hear the news?" I threw that out there to, I hoped, distract him from asking why I was hovering around outside the garage.

"News?" He tipped his head in question.

"Iona has been arrested for Robin's murder." My chest knotted up and I could barely force the words out.

Behind the sunglasses, Geoffrey's expression was inscrutable. "*Iona* was arrested? Do you know the charges?" When I shook my head, he pivoted on his heel and stalked away, not even saying goodbye.

All righty then. That was weird. Feeling eyes on me, I glanced up. Rose was watching through the window. I gave her a wave and pointed, indicating I was coming back upstairs.

Rose met me at the door. "What was that all about?"

"I was trying to get a look into the garage," I explained as I eased past her into the flat. "There's an empty bay."

"You mean Poppy's car could have been in there *all this time*?" Rose's voice elevated, her cheeks flushing in anger. Her hands shook and she curled them into fists. "What did they do to her? Where is she?"

"We'll find her," I said, cringing inside at my rash promise, praying I could deliver. "Hang in there, Rose. Your mum didn't kill Robin." I wracked my brain for another topic, something to distract her. "By the way, with the help of your dad's notebook, I've been figuring out who the characters are in *The Strawberry Girls*. Their real identities, I mean."

Her fists unclenched, the fear and anger draining from her face. "You did?" She flitted over to a desk and pulled a book out of the pile, carried it to a sofa. "Tell me."

I sat beside her and we leafed through the old edition, which had worn corners, wrinkled pages, even a few fingerprints marring the pages. Well loved.

"Mrs. Dobbins," Rose said with a laugh. "How could I not see that? Of course she's the Good Witch. All those cats." She laughed when I told about Miranda's reaction. "Miranda has the biggest ego ever."

She agreed the fox was Robin, and we talked about how in the story, the fox led the sisters into trouble. "Was Dad saying he led people astray?"

"I think so, yes. It fits with . . . other things I've heard. That I can't talk about."

To my relief she didn't question me, instead turning to the scene with the hermit and the mole. "I always thought this was so cute, that little mole pushing the gold coins out with his nose. Me and Poppy used to say how much we wished we had a pet mole to dig up gold for us." She tapped a forefinger on the illustration. "Now, after seeing that crown, I wonder if Dad knew there were other Anglo-Saxon artifacts around here."

Bingo. Cautiously, mindful that I could be opening Pandora's box if I revealed too much, I said, "I wondered the same. Who do you think the hermit is?"

She squinted at the page. "He's tall, like Geoffrey, but that's about the only resemblance." Iona had drawn the hermit as shaggy haired, dressed in ragged clothing, and with bad teeth. Nothing like the handsome, sophisticated Geoffrey Thornton.

I saw the truth hit her like a thunderbolt. Her eyes flared wide and then she screwed up her features. "Hey, are you saying that they've been *mining* this place?" Her voice rang out in the room, bouncing off the high, beamed ceiling. "Geoffrey and Robin?"

Light footsteps tapped on the stairs. "Rose?" *Miranda.* "Rose? Are you home? I just heard the news, love."

A chill went down my spine. Had I left the door open by accident? I must have or else we would have heard her open it.

Rose rolled her eyes. "The last person I want to see," she whispered. She closed the book and put it aside, preparing to hoist herself off the deep sofa.

"Hold on," I whispered back. "You know who Miranda is, in the book?" She paused, waiting. "The Fairy Queen."

"That makes total sense." Rose pushed herself upright, pasting a smile on her face. "Miranda?" she called. "Yes, I'm here. Please come in."

Miranda swanned into the room, her steps faltering when she saw me. "Oh. Molly. I didn't know you were here." She set a straw tote on a side table.

I didn't bother to say anything and Rose and I both watched as she began rooting around in the bag.

"Here it is." Miranda pulled a small brown sack out of the tote. "A calming blend of chamomile, lemon balm, and mugwort. I'll brew you a cup."

"Um, thanks?" Rose's brow creased. "I'm okay, really."

Miranda bustled to the kitchenette at one end of the room, where she began banging cupboard doors and slamming drawers. "How can you be fine?" she shouted above the noise. "Your mother has been *arrested.*"

Rose winced as if hit in the gut, then rallied and said, "That doesn't mean she's guilty, Miranda. Mum is innocent."

"I know, I know." Miranda fluttered about, putting on the kettle and placing tea bags in mugs. At least she wasn't going to try to read these tea leaves. "We must keep our chin up."

For a nickel, I would have grabbed Rose's hand and escaped, leaving Miranda with her tea and dire predictions.

"My goodness." Miranda paused to put a hand to her chest. "What a shock. My heart is still pounding. I couldn't believe my ears when Geoffrey told me."

"She didn't do it," I said. "Iona wasn't home. Aunt Violet and I can attest to that."

Miranda blinked at me. "Yes. Right. I thought she'd left too. But the police must think she did it before, then drove around to cover it up."

"Get her out of here," Rose said under her breath, her fists clenched by her sides. "Please. Before there is a second murder."

"Of course." I popped up from the sofa. "Miranda," I said firmly when I reached her side. "A word?"

She glanced back and forth between Rose and the kettle before finally deciding to follow me. Once we were in the hallway leading to the bedrooms—I supposed, not having seen them—I said, "She's having a really hard time, which is totally understandable. I think it would be best if—"

The shrill ring of a cell phone interrupted me. Rose leaned forward and snatched it up. "Hello? . . . Oh, hello, Miss Owusu. What's going on with Mum?"

In one accord, we abandoned our discussion and edged back into the main room. The kettle began to shriek and Miranda ran to switch it off. To my annoyance, she filled all three mugs. So much for her leaving like I'd hoped.

After a couple of minutes, Rose hung up. She stared into space, unmoving for another long moment, as the tension in the room grew. Finally she said, "They're going to try to get bail. She's being charged with murder."

Miranda gave a loud gasp and Rose shifted to stare at her. "You're still here?"

"I'm sorry." Miranda's hands flew up. "I only wanted an update. Iona is one of my dearest friends."

Rose crossed her arms, her face settling into a ferocious glare. "Dearest friend, huh? Is that why you used to hit on my dad?"

CHAPTER 18

The room rang with a stunned silence. Miranda's eyes grew wider and wider, until they resembled the eyes of a gasping fish. Furthering the image, her mouth open and shut several times. Then she gathered herself. "You don't know what you're talking about."

Rose laughed. "Denying it won't work with me. I saw you trying to kiss him in the summerhouse. He laughed right in your face. And before you say I was too young to remember, I heard Mum talking about it not too long ago." She blinked as tears began to overflow. "My dad wasn't perfect, but he loved my mum."

Miranda's complexion had turned an ugly shade of red. Huffing, she pushed back her hair with both hands and tossed her head. "I know when I'm not wanted. I'll get out of your way." Hips twitching, she sauntered over to her tote and slung it over her shoulder before striding out of the room.

"Wow. Rose." I forced my own mouth shut. "You were amazing."

Rose shrugged, but a tiny smile crept around her lips. "I've been wanting to tell her off for ages. She's the worst. In love with herself and thinks everyone else is too."

"Yeah, I thought the same thing." I wandered over to the steaming mugs of tea. "Want one? I mean, I think it's safe. She was going to drink it too."

Rose laughed. "Sure. She makes good tea blends, I'll give her that." She sat on the sofa, curling her legs up on the cushion. "Did you ever have her read your tea leaves?"

I carried two mugs over to the sofa and handed her one. "I did. It was really creepy." Again, we'd found a topic to take the edge off Rose's situation, which must be absolute hell to go through.

Rose took a tiny sip, testing the tea to see how hot it was. "What did she say?"

"She warned me about a fickle friend—probably implying that Kieran would dump me—and that I was in danger."

"Nice." Rose's eye danced with humor. "She doesn't like you either."

"I guess not," I said. "It started when she found out I was invited to Lord and Lady Scott's garden party. She was miffed about not being invited."

Rose waved a hand. "Oh, they probably were. Or at least Geoffrey. But he hates going anywhere where there are lots of people." Understanding flickered in her eyes. "Like a *hermit*. I can't believe I didn't see that a long time ago."

Although he liked hosting. I'd met people like him before, more comfortable in his own environment. In light of the book, the logical conclusion was that Geoffrey was involved in digging up artifacts. Had Geoffrey ever read *The Strawberry Girls*? Maybe with Nate gone, he wasn't worried about betrayal by anyone else. Not if they were all involved.

Who was the mole? I had an inkling. "Did you know

Dr. Holloway before the dig? Before you went to college, I mean." Who better to portray as a mole than an archeologist, who spent much of their time delicately tunneling into soil?

Rose sipped tea, thinking. "No, not really. He was around, but I don't remember him visiting us at the cottage."

I picked up my phone and swiped to a photograph I'd taken in Thornton Hall, a group shot of Geoffrey and his friends. "Do you recognize these people?"

She used her fingers to enlarge the shot. "Oh, there's Mummy. And Dad. Miranda, Geoffrey, Robin. Don't know. Don't know. Don't know." She held the phone closer, wrinkling up her nose. "That might be him. Dr. Holloway."

The man in question was dressed in doublet and hose like the others. Short and slender, he had longish, wispy hair and a goatee and was standing with arms outstretched in a hammy pose. Take away the goatee and most of the hair, and yes, it was the professor.

"It is him." My pulse went up a bump. If my theory of a black-market artifact ring was correct, then Geoffrey provided access to the land, Holloway used his expertise to find likely spots to dig plus historical context to the finds, and Robin fenced their discoveries.

"What does this mean?" Rose asked. "Do you think he killed Robin for some reason?"

She hadn't put all the dots together, and I didn't want to voice my theories whether or not they were correct. Wrong, and I was smearing an innocent man. Right, and it could send criminals even deeper into hiding. I'd pass my thoughts along to Sir Jon, who was working on the artifact-smuggling case.

"Maybe so," I said. "They've all known each other a long time."

Rose's phone rang and she glanced at the screen. "It's the barrister. She said she was going to call me back." Her smile was sly. "Another reason to get rid of nosy Miranda." She picked up the phone, ready to answer. "Want me to put it on speaker?"

"Up to you," I said, hoping she would. Hearing an update directly was always better than secondhand.

She pushed buttons. "Another set of ears is always good, especially when talking about upsetting situations."

"Miss Owusu? It's Rose. I also have a friend here, Molly Kimball." I said hello. "She's going to listen in so I don't forget anything important."

"Hello, Molly." The barrister's voice was confident yet warm. "Thanks for supporting Rose right now."

"Of course," I said. "I want to do all I can to help." *Like find the real killer, for example.*

Computer keys clicked. "All right. First, some good news. We've got a bail hearing on Monday with the Crown Court. They don't often grant bail in these situations, but I may have twisted an arm or two." She chuckled.

"Oh, that's wonderful," Rose said. "Thank you."

"I'm hoping we can get bail set, and then your mum will be released until trial." She didn't offer any promises as to Iona's fate after the trial, I noticed.

"Miss Owusu," I said tentatively. "I have a couple of questions."

"Yes, Molly? And please, call me Alexa."

"Alexa." I cleared my throat, stalling while I framed my thoughts. "My great-aunt and I were with Iona when she found Robin. The reason I'm mentioning that is because she wasn't home when we arrived at the cottage. She drove in a minute or two after us, saying she'd been running an errand."

"We've confirmed that," Alexa Owusu said crisply. "The

thing is, they have another witness who spoke to Robin before he climbed onto the roof. This witness said Iona was at home during their discussion. The prosecutor's case is that Iona confronted Robin and went to the store afterwards, as her alibi. According to her own timing, she was gone a good half hour, much longer than was needed to drive to the market and back. Her story is that someone else came to the cottage and killed Robin while she was gone."

I understood immediately. "She has no alibi for the time gap?" As for the witness Alexa mentioned, that was my dear Aunt Janice, I was pretty sure. Regret tasted sour in my mouth. If I hadn't pushed her to go to the police, would Iona be free right now?

"Exactly," Alexa said. "Your mum says she took the long way to the store, Rose. Has she ever done that before?"

Rose gave a knowing laugh. "Every time she goes to town. She likes to drive out past some farms, especially at this time of year when the countryside is so pretty."

"Hmm." Alexa thought for a moment. "Unfortunately, she didn't pass any other cars or see any pedestrians that morning."

"What about Mrs. Dobbins?" I asked. "She notices a lot. She's the older lady who owns a cottage nearby, the opposite direction from Thornton Hall." It was possible the Good Witch had noticed Iona drive past that morning.

"Mrs. Dobbins. I'll have the investigator talk to her. Thanks, Molly. Just so you know, Rose, we have someone talking to all the witnesses and verifying details. We're not relying on the police case files."

I was grateful that Iona had such good representation. "Mrs. Dobbins told me that she saw a runner in pink the same morning," I said. "It was probably my aunt Janice, though."

"Janice Marlowe is your aunt?" Alexa's tone sharpened.

"Yes, she is," I admitted. "And Chris Marlowe, the thatcher, is my uncle. He was a suspect too. My family and I are in this up to our necks, I'm afraid."

"Why were you at Strawberry Cottage that morning?" Alexa asked. "Visiting your uncle?"

"No, we were there representing our bookshop. Iona was . . ." I swallowed hard, resolving to remain positive. "*Is* doing a reading of *The Strawberry Girls* for us. There's a new edition out."

"*The Strawberry Girls.* I love that book. One reason I was eager to represent your mum, Rose. She's practically a literary icon and I wanted to ensure she gets treated fairly." As opposed to being thrown to the media wolves as the latest celebrity to crash from grace? Alexa stopped short of declaring Iona innocent, which I suppose was due to barrister discretion.

"Thank you," Rose whispered. She had found a tissue and the poor thing was being destroyed by her fingers twisting it.

"Switching gears," Alexa said, the briskness back in her voice. "The crown. Were you aware it was tucked away on the roof? Any of you?"

Yes, according to Iona's own words. I'd cut my own tongue out before saying that in front of Rose.

"I don't know if Mum knew," Rose said. "Poppy and I saw Dad hiding the box on the roof. We didn't know what was inside, though." She thought for a moment. "Mum might have known about it. Miranda Blake used to wear one that looked just like it. I've seen old pictures."

So had I, in *At Home.* Maybe Iona also had a copy kicking around her house.

"All right. As you might guess, it's become pivotal to the police's case. They purport that she and Robin were fighting about it. She denies that, naturally. Another theory is that your mum was involved with Robin and they had a falling-out."

Rose scoffed. "No way. Robin was like a brother to her, an uncle to us. He used to drop by for tea—or a whiskey—and whine about his latest lady troubles."

Alexa laughed. "I see. Thanks for clearing that up." After a beat, she said, "There's something else I need to ask you. Did you ever hear Robin talk about his antiques business, especially European customers?"

She was indirectly asking Rose if her mother was involved in Robin's black-market activities. Were the agencies trying to tie Iona to the Interpol investigation?

A series of expressions flickered over Rose's features before understanding dawned. "I get it." Her tone was flat. "They think Robin was trading in antiquities. I have no idea and I'm pretty sure Mum doesn't either. She wouldn't have been so worried about bills, right?"

"Good point, Rose," Alexa said. "I know it's not easy to talk about."

"No kidding. I've known Robin all my life. His death was enough to deal with. And now—" She put a hand over her mouth, trying to hold back tears.

"It's early days," Alexa said. "One step at a time. Bail hearing is Monday. I'm also working on getting you in to see your mum later."

"You are?" Now the tears flowed. "Please do. I miss her so much." Turning to me, she collapsed into my arms, sobbing.

I patted her back, wishing I could give her what she really needed—her mother's freedom, and her sister's safe return.

"One more thing before I go," Alexa said. "Do not talk to

the press. Under any circumstances. They're going to be all over this case."

◆◆◆

When I pushed through the heavy doors of the pub that evening, I was emotionally exhausted, starving, and eager for a glass of my favorite ale. I'd stayed with Rose until Ben came back, and then shelved new bookshop inventory until well after closing, to make up for being out of the shop.

The pub was hopping tonight—three deep at the bar, all the tables full, noisy with chatter, laughter, and the clatter of dishes. By some strange alchemy, a man standing at the bar, one foot resting on the rail, turned the moment the door shut behind me. *Kieran.*

Our eyes met and a huge grin broke across his face. Leaving his beer, he pushed through the bodies and gathered me into his arms. "Molly. So glad you're here."

I looked up into his face with a laugh. "Me too." He bent to kiss me, a peck of greeting at first, then deepening into a real smooch. People were watching, probably even commenting, but at that moment I didn't care.

Then I remembered the tabloids and pulled back. Someone was probably snapping pictures of us to share on social media. "We're gonna see this on a gossip page," I whispered.

"Oh well," he whispered back, putting an arm around me. "Ready for a beer? Tim and Daisy are saving seats in the back room."

"Beyond ready," I said. "I had quite the day."

We made our way to the bar, where I picked out an ale, and then we moseyed through to join our friends. Daisy looked up with a wave. "You made it."

"Finally." I pulled out a chair with a sigh. "I ended up

working late because I'm so far behind." Kieran slid the specials card over. Scanning the list, I decided on Lancashire hot pot, a lamb stew topped with sliced potatoes.

After Kieran put in our food order at the bar, we sipped our drinks in contented silence, my friends kindly giving me time to unwind. At the nearby dartboard, our friend Ollie groaned as his opponent sank a bull's-eye. In another corner, billiard balls clattered when someone struck a new rack.

"How is Rose?" Daisy asked. And what's the latest with Iona?"

In between sips of beer, I took them through my time at Thornton Hall, including the encounter with Geoffrey, visit from Miranda, and conversation with Alexa Owusu. "Alexa is great. I'm pretty sure the judge will grant bail. She'll insist on it."

"I've heard of her," Kieran said. "She takes the high-profile cases." He gave a closed-lip smile. "And usually wins."

I held up crossed fingers. "Hope she wins this time. Iona didn't do it." I thought of something else. "Alexa has an investigator on her team. Maybe they'll figure out who killed Robin."

Tim shook his head. "Don't think so. They're focused on countering the prosecution's case so they can get Iona off."

He was right. The defense team's job was to establish reasonable doubt. Identifying the guilty party wasn't required. If Iona *was* found not guilty, would the police continue investigating? Or would they believe she'd gotten away with murder?

"Whoever it was took quite a risk," I said. "What if Iona hadn't left? Would Robin still be alive?"

Kieran spun his glass on the table. "Sounds like a crime

of opportunity to me. They might have seen her leave and decided to confront Robin. Maybe the argument got out of hand and they pushed him, not thinking he would fall."

"Or they climbed up there planning to push him off," Tim put in. "Hoping it would look like an accident."

I shuddered at the evil behind such intent. "Nate York died the same way. An unexplained fall from a high place. In his case they did rule it an accident."

"The killer might have been inspired by Nate's death," Daisy said. She screwed up her nose. "Sorry. That sounded awful."

An idea struck me like a blow. "Maybe it was revenge." Which would mean that someone—Iona after all?—had found out that Robin killed Nate and wanted him to die in the same manner. I put a hand to my forehead with a groan. "I'm so confused."

"It is confusing," Kieran said. "All we really know is that someone pushed Robin and he fell. Since the police look at means and opportunity, Iona is an obvious suspect."

I often thought more clearly when I jotted things down, so I fished for a pen in my handbag. Grabbing a spare napkin, I wrote *Motives* at the top, then listed *revenge, the crown, Interpol, love gone bad, other* below.

"Quite the list," Kieran said, reading over my shoulder. "Why is Interpol on there?"

I glanced around to make sure no one was listening. "Sir Jon told me that Robin was assisting with an Interpol case. Antiquities smuggling." I left it at that, since I didn't know details about Robin's possible criminal activity.

"Expert witness?" Kieran asked, his brows rising. "That could get someone killed." I was thinking more like deeply involved, but I let his assumption stand.

Tim stabbed a finger toward his friend. "Right on, mate. But a shot to the back of the head would be more like it."

The server arrived at our table, plates arrayed along her arms. She gave Tim a funny look as she began to distribute them but said only, "Hot pot, fish and chips, hot pot, burger and chips. Anything else I can get you?"

Kieran circled his finger around the table. "Another round, please." He listed our beer choices, pretending not to notice when I stole one of his chips. Why do they taste better off someone else's plate? A mystery for the ages.

After the server left, Daisy said, "You're right, Tim. A hit man wouldn't push someone off a roof."

"It might not have been a hit man," I said. "Maybe it was an accomplice." My suspicions about Geoffrey Thornton and Dr. Holloway crowded into my throat, but I held them back with an effort. This wasn't the time or place to mention them.

"Accomplice?" Tim gave me a quizzical look. 'You think Robin was a smuggler?"

"It's a possibility," I said. "What other reason could he have for being on the roof besides that crown? It's not as if he was fascinated by thatching techniques."

"Right on," Kieran said with a snort. "The crown is key. How did Robin find out it was there?"

I put down my fork. "Poppy might have told him. She and Rose saw their father carry the metal box up onto the roof. I don't know if she knew what was inside, but Robin might have guessed. Missing crown, hidden box. With half the thatch already stripped, it made his search easier." Though not successful. He'd been killed first.

"If Poppy did tell him about the crown, where is she?" Tim asked. "There has to be someone else involved. Whoever moved her car. It doesn't seem likely that she hid for days before taking a train."

"Only if she *was* involved in something criminal." I had to force the words out, they were so distasteful to me. "If that turns out to be true, I'll be very shocked."

"Me too," Daisy said. "An even worse possibility is that *she* killed Robin. If so, will she let her own mother take the fall?"

"I bloody hope not," Kieran said. "What kind of daughter would do that?"

My head was beginning to ache. "This case is way too complicated. I feel like Alice down the rabbit hole."

"Wrong book," Tim quipped. "That's next week."

We all laughed, which helped clear the air. Fresh glasses of beer arrived and I took a long, welcome draught. Time to put it all aside and take a break.

CHAPTER 19

"What's this?" I asked when Aunt Violet handed me a tabloid newspaper the next morning. After we opened the store, she'd run across to the tea shop to buy treats and, apparently, a paper. "Am I in here?" Seated behind the counter, I began to leaf through the slightly greasy pages.

"Not you," she said, opening a bakery box to reveal raspberry and lemon curd tarts. She set the box within reach. "Page three."

I found the article immediately. "Children's Author Makes Switch to True Crime?" the headline screamed. *Ugh.* They'd dug up an old publicity photograph of Iona signing books. An inset picture showed Strawberry Cottage, captioned "The Scene of the Crime."

Choosing a lemon curd tart, I nibbled as I read the article, horrified. They were very, very careful not to say that Iona was guilty, sprinkling *alleged* like confetti throughout.

"Oh, man," I said. "This is so bad." My gaze fell on the window, where I'd stacked the new editions of *The Strawberry*

Girls. Possible life in prison aside, how was this going to affect Iona's career? Would her publisher drop her like a hot potato? It had happened to other authors for far less.

Would one of the best children's books ever be tainted by these false accusations? I continued to staunchly believe that Iona was innocent. Innocent until proven guilty, right? I prayed we could find the real culprit. Slapping the paper shut, I vowed not to give up until every avenue had been exhausted.

"Yummy tarts," I said, refusing to even discuss that disturbing article. "Who knew something named lemon curd tasted so good?"

"My favorite," Aunt Violet said. Her gaze went to the front, to a trio of young women staring through the window. People often stopped to admire Clarence, who practically lived on the window ledge, but today they were taken by something else. The *Strawberry Girls* display.

Miffed, Clarence stretched dramatically with a huge yawn and, when that didn't attract attention, put his nose on the glass, tail twitching. One woman reached her fingers out in acknowledgement, but the other two ignored him. After a brief discussion, the trio entered the shop and grabbed copies off the stack.

"And so it begins," I muttered as they marched toward the counter. Clarence, surprisingly agile considering his bulk, leaped *onto* the books and curled up. *Way to go, Clarence.*

"I'll go move him," Aunt Violet said.

"Is it true the author *murdered* someone?" One young woman tossed her silky hair, her expression gleeful as she glanced at her friends.

"Early days," I said, taking another's card and swiping it. "Innocent until proven guilty."

The third woman leaned on the counter. "You have to say that, right? What do you think happened?"

"I have no opinion," I lied. As the card processed, I slid her purchase into a bag. "*The Strawberry Girls* is one of my favorites."

"Mine too," the customer paying said. "I was so excited to hear about the new edition."

The woman who'd first spoken put a hand on her friend's arm. "Oh. Get this. Iona York's husband fell to his death. Maybe she killed him too."

"Ugh, Stacey," the friend said, wrinkling up her nose. "That's gruesome."

"Isn't it?" Stacey giggled.

I had never considered that idea, mainly because Iona was home with her girls the night he died. I couldn't picture her leaving them alone to go out and murder her husband. How long would it take for the tabloids to leap to the same conclusion? A nanosecond, maybe?

"Enjoy." I ripped the slip off the machine and slid it into the bag. "Who's next?"

The young women were only the first of many. All morning long I fended off questions, comments, and theories about Iona York's probable guilt. The stack of books dwindled at a record pace.

"We're going to need to order more," Mum said. "I'll do it right now." She brought up the distributor website on her phone and logged in.

Aunt Violet peered over her shoulder. "I can't get over how you can do that on a cell phone. I still remember the days we sent orders by post."

"Slow books," I cracked, referring to the moniker given to handcraft movements like slow food and slow stitching.

"Very slow," Aunt Violet said. "Weeks, even months at times."

Mum groaned. "They're out of stock already."

"Let me see." She handed me the phone. "Huh. There isn't a back-in-stock date yet. They must have been caught off guard by influx of orders. Hopefully they'll do another printing right away."

Aunt Violet rolled her eyes. "Nothing like an arrest to make you a best seller."

"Not a route I recommend," Mum said briskly, taking back the phone. "I was thinking about throwing together some sandwiches. What would you like?"

She went off to the kitchen while Aunt Violet and I enjoyed a brief lull. "I'm going to get some air," I said, slipping out from behind the counter.

The cats following, I went out to the lane, where we'd placed two chairs. Leaning back in my seat, I turned my face to the sun, smiling as the cats did the same. What a gorgeous day. The clear weather was supposed to hold until tomorrow, which was perfect for the garden party tonight.

The garden party. Involuntarily, I glanced at the bike shop, my stomach beginning to churn with nerves and excitement. No sign of Kieran, but Tim was outside helping a customer try out a bicycle. I waved and he waved back.

A lean figure slouched down the lane, one arm steadying the heavy camera bags slung over her shoulder. Kelsey Cook, star photographer for the tabloids. I shrank back, hoping she wouldn't notice me. Kieran was friends with Kelsey, or should I say on good enough terms that he could ask her to back off and she would. In return, he sometimes gave her exclusives.

Of course she saw me and sauntered over, a grin breaking across her face. "Hey, Molly. Getting a little sun?"

Annoyed that my idyll had been ruined, my fingers tensed on the chair arms. "I was." I started to get up. "I'd better—"

"Sit, sit." She took the other chair, sliding her bag off and setting it gently on the cobblestones.

"Why are you here?" I asked. "The garden party?"

Uh-oh. Wrong question. Kelsey's face lit up. "Are you going to the garden party with Kieran, Molly?" Her tone was teasing. "Big step, huh?"

My cheeks heated, but I didn't respond. Much safer, as I'd learned to my chagrin.

She turned to look at the poster in the window, practically the only thing left of our Strawberry Girls display. "I'm not here about the party; well, I *wasn't*. I'm curious to hear your thoughts about Iona York. I understand you were there when Robin Jones's body was found."

Her words fired at me like demands, and thoughts whirling, I tried to compose myself, thinking of Alexa's warning not to talk to the press. *No comment*, that's what you say, I finally remembered. "No comment."

"Ah, don't go all coy on me, Molly," she said. "It must have been an awful shock. And to think you were right there with the *alleged* killer."

I crossed my arms, signaling that her needling was annoying me. If I told Kelsey what I thought of her and her newspaper right now, I'd pay for it. And so would Kieran.

"I thought you were a photographer, Kelsey," I said instead of answering. "Are you writing stories now?"

She ran a hand through her spiky hair with a laugh. "Yeah, I'm giving it a go. Figured if I can get a scoop, they'll let me do some articles."

"Here's a hint," I said wryly. "Ease into the questions. Otherwise your sources will clam up."

Kelsey pulled out a pack of cigarettes, holding it out as though asking permission. At my nod, she lit one, careful to blow the smoke away from me. "Yeah, I am kind of aggressive. It's my nature. Have to be, though, to get the pics. Obnoxious, really."

"Yes, obnoxious," I agreed, smiling to let her know I was joking. Sort of.

After she smoked a minute, she said, "So, about Robin . . ."

I really didn't want to be quoted or even have my name included in any articles about the murder. If it went to trial, I might be called as a witness and then my name would definitely make the papers. I hoped it wouldn't get that far.

"Kelsey," I said, deciding to try a Kieran tactic. "I don't want to talk about it, k? How's this, though. I'll send you an exclusive picture of me and Kieran at the garden party." I was guessing that Lord and Lady Scott wouldn't allow random photographers inside, plus I would make sure the photo flattered us. "I might even give you an interview about the murder later, depending on how things end up." After Iona was cleared. Nothing less was unacceptable to me.

Her head jerked up, eagerness in her eyes. "Deal." She took another puff, then stood, looking around for a place to deposit the butt. When she eyed our flowerpots, I said, "Sand bucket over there, near the lamppost." Deliberately placed a safe distance from our ancient building.

After putting out the cigarette, even checking to make sure it was fully buried, she threw me a jaunty, "Later," as she headed up the lane, equipment jingling.

I sat back in my chair again, this time in relief at dodging a bullet: I was pretty sure I'd come through that interaction unscathed. The last thing I wanted to do was say the wrong thing and have a quote end up in the paper. I didn't begrudge Kelsey trying to get a breakthrough story, but it wasn't coming from me.

◆◆◆

"Oh, Molly." Mum's eyes shone with pride. "You look lovely."

Standing in the middle of the bookshop, I twirled so they could get the full effect. To accessorize my new dress, I wore off-white sandals, a few bangle bracelets, and dangly faux gem earrings. A tiny purse with a long strap was slung across my shoulder, big enough for phone, lipstick, and keys. My hair was down, curled in ringlets.

Adjusting her eyeglasses, Aunt Violet looked me up and down. "Very nice, my dear. You'll certainly pass muster."

A surge of panic ripped through my body. I was meeting Lord and Lady Scott. Today. One half hour from now or so. I almost wiped my damp palms on my dress, barely stopping myself in time.

"Loo," I called over my shoulder to explain my dash out of the room. I wanted to wash my hands with warm water and dry them thoroughly, my trick for preventing clammy handshakes.

Imagine greeting Kieran's mum with sticky hands, I thought, turning on the taps. I might as well wear an *L* on my forehead. *Erk*. My train of thought was *not* helping. Trying to distract myself, I hummed "God Save the Queen" while I washed up.

A rap on the door. "Kieran's here," Mum said.

Show time. "Just a minute." I grabbed paper towels and dried my hands.

When I came back into the shop, he was standing by the counter, chatting with Mum and Aunt Violet—and looking absolutely scrumptious in his white shirt, navy blazer, and white trousers. He wore a bow tie with some sort of heraldic emblem pattern. The family crest?

His eyes flared when he spotted me. "Wow. Molly. You look gorgeous."

I fluffed my dress and preened, even batting my lashes. So not like me, but I couldn't help it. "You think? You're not bad yourself."

He held out an arm. "Your chariot awaits." Parked outside the window was a shiny silver Land Rover with, of course, bike racks on the back and roof.

"Oh, good," I said. "We're not traveling by bicycle." Since vehicle access was severely limited inside the old city, I'd never seen Kieran's car before.

"I considered it," he said. "But they were all out of tandems."

The image of us pedaling along the road in our finery made me laugh. The shop door was still propped open, but he leaped ahead to open the Rover's passenger door. I slid onto a buttery leather seat, enveloped by a waft of air conditioning.

After gently shutting the door, he went around and got behind the wheel. "Ready?" he said, checking to see if I was buckled. Then he leaned over and kissed me lightly. "Don't want to smudge the lipstick."

"You have been trained well," I joked. We set off along the lane, the tires bumping gently on the cobblestones. I inhaled deeply and released slowly, willing myself to stay calm and cool.

Kieran set the sound system to light rock, and we didn't say much as he made his way out of the city. Stealing glances at his profile, I wondered if he was nervous too. He threw me a smile. "How was your day?"

"We sold every last copy of *The Strawberry Girls*," I said. "They're out of stock at the distributor."

"Immediate best seller?" he asked dryly.

"Something like that. Oh, and I had an encounter with Kelsey Cook today." I filled him in about that, mentioning my promise to send a photo of us. I squirmed a little, realizing I should have asked him first. "I hope that's all right with you."

"It's fine," he said. "I wonder where we should take it." He thought for a moment. "I'll let you pick; how's that? We'll sneak out for a private tour."

"I'd love one," I said, thinking it would be a good excuse to take a break if the party was too overwhelming.

When we reached Hazelhurst, we turned at the sign for his family seat. Although I'd been to the village numerous times of late, I'd never seen his home in person. Online yes, once or twice. But then, feeling uncomfortable, I'd forbidden myself to take the virtual tour or even study photographs.

Suffice it to say, I wasn't prepared. At the open gate set between enormous stone pillars, Kieran stopped to check in with two security guards. They waved us on, down a winding drive leading us past a groomed forest, orchards, and kitchen gardens with greenhouses. A lush and extensive property.

We drove around a corner and the rambling stone manor, with its wings and towers and gables, came into view, water lapping at its walls.

Yes, it had an actual moat.

"Is there a drawbridge?" I muttered.

Kieran shot me a look. "Not anymore," he said, as if my question hadn't been tongue in cheek. "Only an open archway. We also built a bridge to the formal gardens. You'll see." As we drew closer, I saw lines of cars parked along the drive. "Normally we drive right into the courtyard. Tonight it's in use."

When we pulled up near the former drawbridge, a valet came over to the car. "Tony," Kieran said. "How are you?" He handed Tony the keys. "Park so I can make a fast getaway, okay?"

Tony leaned down to take me in through the window, a mischievous smile on his face. "You got it."

"Do you always make fast getaways from your parents' house?" I asked as we strolled toward the bridge, which was lined with globe lampposts. Crickets sang and a frog belched somewhere among the lily pads.

Kieran's arm tightened, pulling my hand against his side. "Not normally. Tonight I'll be ready to go whenever you are." He stopped walking to give me a kiss. "I couldn't care less about these parties. Seriously."

"Let's play it by ear," I said. What a wonder he was. Many, if not most, men in his situation would use, even leverage, their social standing to further conquer the world. Although, if he was like that, I wouldn't be here, that was for sure.

As we crossed the bridge, classical music drifted our way. We passed through the arch into the courtyard, where round tables set with linen cloths, buffet tables, and two bars filled the middle of the space. The small orchestra was playing in one corner, and straight ahead up a set of shallow, wide steps open French doors revealed a luxurious drawing room.

With an arm around my waist, Kieran guided me through the clusters of guests drinking and chatting. "Want something from the bar?"

"After I, um, meet your parents." My stomach clenched. The moment of truth was here and frankly I wanted to get it over with.

He accepted that with a nod and we continued on toward the manor. People along the way tried to catch his eye, even called his name, but he kept going, throwing them apologetic smiles. Curious eyes burned into me, raking me over for every detail. I kept my gaze straight ahead, chin up, trying to breathe.

As we drew closer to the steps, where Lord and Lady Scott were standing, my pulse began to thud in my ears. Lady Asha was petite with glossy waist-length hair, and she wore a fitted floor-length red sheath with a spangled shoulder wrap. She was absolutely stunning, her gestures gracious as she spoke with her guests. Beside her, Sir Graham was stately, almost stiff, with carved, handsome features.

Kieran's arm still around me, we climbed the steps. The older couple talking to the Scotts melted away. Lady Asha glanced around, her gaze landing on us, and a huge smile lit her face. I thought she was going to greet her son, but the outstretched hands and warm, crinkled eyes were for me.

"Molly." She took my—surprisingly un-clammy—hand between hers. "I am so happy to meet you." She slid a teasing look at Kieran. "He can't stop talking about you."

Really? Hoping I hadn't said that out loud, I gathered my wits. "It's so nice to meet you as well," I said, restraining the urge to curtsey.

"Tonight is too hectic to get to know each other," Lady Asha said. "You must come back soon. Sunday lunch?" The raised brows were for Kieran.

"We can do that, Mum." Kieran kissed her on the cheek. He held out his hand to his father, who pulled him into a brief embrace. "Dad."

After releasing his son, Lord Graham shook my hand. "It's wonderful to meet you, Molly. Please, enjoy the evening."

"I will. Thank you," I said. "This is a lovely party."

Guests were crowding behind us up the steps, eager to reach the Scotts, so Kieran and I exchanged last smiles with his parents and stepped aside.

Whew. That was over. It had gone well, I thought. Actually, his mother was perfect. She'd greeted me first, which had made me feel really welcome, not just an appendage to her beloved son.

"Drink?" Kieran asked as we trotted down the stairs.

Laughing in relief and joy, I took his hand, not caring about the people staring at us. "Drink."

The bartender whipped up a pair of cocktails, the party's signature drink. Gin based, it included mint, cucumber slices, apple juice, and Prosecco.

"Refreshing," I said after taking a sip.

Kieran clinked his glass with mine. "To us." He extended his elbow and we strolled the circuit, drinks in hand. As the son of the hosts, he knew almost everyone, of course.

I was introduced to so many people they all became a blur. Lady this. Lord that. The Honorable so-and-so. "Tell me there isn't a quiz," I whispered as we ascended the steps to the house. We were taking the promised private tour.

"I didn't tell you?" Kieran's face held mock surprise. "There's a door prize if you get the names right."

"Darn," I said, snapping my fingers. "I'm out of the running."

"Molly," a voice called. We turned to see Daisy and Tim right behind us.

"Did you just get here?" I asked, greeting Daisy with a hug. Her face was prettily flushed, her hair a little mussed.

"We did," she said, unable to hold back a grin. "Tim got lost."

"Right," Kieran said with a cheeky grin of his own. "She fell for it, mate?"

Daisy and Tim exchanged glowing glances, lacing their fingers together. "Put it this way," Daisy said. "I've now seen areas of Hazelhurst I never knew existed."

"Kieran is giving me a tour," I said. "Want to come along?"

"Love to," Daisy said, glancing around. "This place is fantastic."

"It's been in our family for five hundred years," Kieran said, a trace of pride in his voice. "Frankly, it's amazing we've been able to hang on to it." He wasn't being modest. Many families had been forced to sell their homes after the world wars or when death duties were assessed.

"I feel the same about the bookshop," I said. Our heritage, though not nearly as refined, was almost as lengthy as that of the Scotts.

We had reached the French doors. "Follow me," Kieran said, gesturing. "This is the West Drawing Room," he said in a formal tone like a tour guide, though the twinkle in his eyes gave him away. He was hamming it up. "Note the heraldic ceiling." We obediently looked up.

Coffered ceilings are normally squares or rectangles outlined by beams. This one had star-shaped decorations with the family crest painted inside at intervals. The room was spacious, with seating groups scattered throughout and two fireplaces on the far wall.

"The tea shop could fit in here three times," Daisy said. "What a room."

"In the old days, dozens of people lived here," Kieran said. "Plus the Scotts were always entertaining."

He led us through the room while we gawked. The place was teeming with artwork—painting, vases, figurines—and the furniture was definitely antique. "You're going to love the next room, Molly," he said.

We passed through a staircase hall featuring lots of carved wood before stepping into my dream library. Faded red silk wallpaper, gilded mirrors, and hanging crystal chandeliers added to the room's richness, but the bookcases were what I focused on. Thousands of volumes stuffed the tall shelves.

"I don't even know what's all in here," Kieran said with a laugh. "The catalog hasn't been updated for eons."

Wandering closer to a shelf, I inhaled the aroma I loved. Old paper, glue, and leather. "If you decide to, let me know. I'm in." What treasures would we find?

"Definitely," Kieran said. "I'll mention it to Mum."

"Show them the priest hole," Tim said. "That's about the coolest thing here." He sent me a teasing smile. "Besides the books, that is."

"Priest hole? That's a secret compartment, right?" Priest holes had been built to hide priests during a time when England's rulers had outlawed the Catholic Church.

"Exactly," Kieran said. "Come with me."

We returned to the staircase and went up a flight. Then we traveled several long corridors to a corner turret, where he showed us a brick-walled compartment.

"Is this it?" I asked. It was easily reached and not exactly hidden.

He shook his head. "This is the garderobe." The privy, he meant. "We're actually over the moat right now."

"Ew," I said, picturing the effect on water quality when this toilet had been active.

"I suppose they considered it another deterrent to swimming over," Kieran said, making us giggle.

Fiddling around on the floor, he lifted a section to reveal an opening. "And here you have it." Underneath was a space about three feet wide. The only saving grace was that its ceiling was over six feet. "Any takers? I've been inside dozens of times. Me and my brother used to play priest and soldier."

"No, thanks," Daisy said, peering inside. "I'd go crazy in there."

"Better than being hung," Tim said. "Or thrown in prison."

I shuddered, picturing the poor men who had crouched down there waiting to be released. What if someone forgot them? "You never found any bones down there, did you?"

"No, we did not." Kieran bent to move the floor back into place.

Thinking about ancient bones brought my thoughts back around to the dig at Thornton Hall. And from there, to the tunnels on the property. An idea struck me like a lightning bolt.

"Does Thornton Hall have a priest hole?" I asked.

"Not that I know of," Kieran said, standing up and brushing off his hands. "Why?"

"It has tunnels, though," I said, my pulse racing. "Where do they go?"

Kieran frowned. "I'm not really sure. What are you thinking?"

"Maybe there's a place to hide someone at Thornton Hall," I practically shouted, my voice echoing in the brick room. I just *knew* I was right. "What if Poppy never left?"

CHAPTER 20

My three friends stared at me. "But her car—" Tim started.

I waved my arm impatiently. "The kidnapper moved it, to throw everyone off. Worked, didn't it? Now they're searching for Poppy all over England and Europe when she's still in Hazelhurst."

Kieran clutched an elbow, using the other hand to rub his chin. "Hmm. It's a possibility, I suppose. If it happened here, then yes, we'd know where to look. I don't know much about Thornton Hall. Only the few places we poked around."

"I'll bet Rose and Ben can help," I said in triumph. "They're staying there. Why don't we go ask them?" Now that I'd discovered a new line of inquiry, I was raring to go. Poor Poppy had been locked up for *days*. I hoped someone was giving her food and water. If Robin had hidden her—I forced my mind away from that horrible possibility, which only made our quest that much more urgent. How long could someone survive without water?

"Let's do it." Kieran moved decisively down the hall, the

rest of us hurrying to catch up. I didn't want to risk getting lost in this labyrinth of a place.

He took us down a back staircase, along a corridor, and out through another set of doors to the garden bridge. Night was falling now, a golden glow in the sky, and topiaries and trees loomed up, dark and mysterious. Our footsteps crunched on gravel and fountains splashed.

"Ah, here we are." Kieran's Land Rover sat in lone splendor under an oak tree.

"But your keys," I said, thinking of the valet.

He fished around in his pocket. "Second set."

We hopped in and he left the estate via a long back drive cutting through woods and hayfields. There was a gate at the end, and Kieran punched in a code to open it.

I wondered briefly if we'd be missed at the party—with a little guilt about ducking out before saying good-bye to his parents. "Kieran," I started. "Your parents. Shouldn't—"

"Don't worry," he said, intent on the road unspooling a little too fast in front of us. "I'll send a text and tell them we left due to an emergency. They'll be cool with it. They know it's more their thing than mine."

I decided to take his word for it and focus on our next steps. The more I thought about it, the more convinced I became that Poppy was still at Thornton Hall somewhere. No one had seen her since the day of Robin's death.

Kieran slowed to take a turn onto a familiar lane. We had approached Thornton Hall from the opposite direction. He slowed to a crawl, watching for the entrance.

Lights bobbed out in the fields to our left. "What's that?" Daisy asked. "Are they still working on the dig this late?"

"Looks like they're in the mounds," Tim said. "Are they excavating there?"

"No, they are not." Alarm made my voice shrill. "Rose told me they were off-limits." Someone was digging illicitly.

Kieran braked and I grabbed his arm. "Keep going. Pretend we didn't see them."

"Why?" Daisy asked. "Shouldn't we call the authorities? Or at least Geoffrey Thornton?"

"Not yet," I said. "We don't know who's doing it." I had my suspicions.

Kieran slowed again at Thornton Hall's drive, and I said again, "Keep going. I want to pretend we're gone and then sneak back and see what's going on." I pulled my phone out of my bag and scrolled to Sir Jon's number. I wouldn't call him yet, but I wanted to be ready.

"Are you sure about this?" Kieran said as he drove past the manor. "It's really not our business."

I laughed. "It is if they're stealing our national heritage."

Tim whistled. "Good point. We'll be heroes."

"Pull in here," I said, indicating Strawberry Cottage's driveway. With Iona in jail until Monday, we wouldn't be bothering anyone.

Kieran drove partway down the narrow track and parked. "Don't slam the doors," I warned everyone as we got out. "And whisper from now on."

"Yes, ma'am." Daisy rose up on tiptoes to sneak along in a comical manner.

I put my hand over my mouth to hold back a laugh. "Cut it out."

A velvety dusk had settled, making visibility almost nil on this deserted lane. The four of us bumbled along in the dark, not daring to use our phones to light the way. Crickets chirped and the tall hedges hemming us in rustled.

"What's that?" Daisy asked when something especially large moved around.

We all stopped to listen. "Has to be an animal," Kieran said.

I thought of Poppy and Rose, worried about bears. If we were in Vermont, then yes, encountering a bear would be a real possibility. Moose and deer, too, maybe even a coyote or fisher-cat. England was pretty tame by comparison—if not for the murders.

The hedges fell away when we reached Thornton Hall land. The lights were still bobbing around out in the field, near the barrow surrounded by brambles. I studied the landscape, trying to figure out how to approach the area without being seen.

Kieran touched my arm and pointed, the movement barely visible. "Why don't we go up the lane to that stand of trees and cut in there?"

"If we go around the trees," I said. "Otherwise we'll stumble over roots and possibly break branches. Too noisy."

I sensed rather than saw his nod. "You're right. If we stay in their shadow, we'll be less visible, though."

Much less visible than if we cut straight across an open field. Despite the moonless dark, any movement might be noticed.

As we continued up the lane, I prayed no vehicles would come along. Even if we ducked off to the side, the headlights might reveal us to the diggers.

After what felt like hours, we reached the trees. One challenge met. Now we had a ditch to jump and an expanse of field to cross. And I was wearing heeled sandals.

"You okay, Molly?" Kieran asked.

"My shoes." I lifted one foot. "Maybe I should go barefoot."

"Don't," he warned. "The stubble will cut your feet to ribbons."

I would have to do my best, then, to navigate the field. If my shoes got trashed, then oh well, I'd be forced to buy a new pair.

We leaped the ditch, and naturally one of my feet landed smack in the water. Now I was squelching as well as hobbling along.

The distance to the barrow seemed endless. What if they stopped working before we got there? What if they saw us? Technically we were trespassing. Would we disappear like Poppy?

We skirted the trees, careful to stay in their shelter. The next obstacle was the bramble patch, which was extensive. No one had mowed this area for years.

When brambles snagged my new dress, I gently pulled the fabric away, hoping it wouldn't be ruined.

Finally we reached a position where we could see something. In the glow of portable lights, Dr. Holloway and Geoffrey Thornton were moving around, going in and out of a stone-lined entrance almost hidden by grass-covered humps. Various objects sat near the lamps—ceramic pots, something glittering gold, a small carved box. A farm truck sat nearby, ready to transport the goods.

"This isn't the way I like to do things," Holloway said in a complaining tone. "We're probably destroying all kinds of important archeological information."

Geoffrey rested his hands on his hips. "There's no time to excavate properly. Robin's death is like a lightning rod. The authorities are going to be watching this property closely from now on."

Holloway frowned, his features distorted by shadows. "Did he rat us out? I was starting to wonder if he was playing both sides of the fence. Remember how he dragged his feet on that last lot?"

"I certainly do." Geoffrey's tone was clipped. "Even more reason to gather the best things now." He gave a short laugh. "They won't be looking in my great-great-grandmother's tomb, now will they?"

Kieran jolted in surprise and I remembered the rumored tunnels he'd mentioned, including one connected to a burial vault in the Thornton Hall graveyard.

"I'm just glad they all have stone caskets in there," Holloway said. "I've had enough of bones." He picked up a water jug and drank, then wiped his mouth with his forearm. "Let's get to it, then. I'd like to finish sometime tonight."

His last comment revealed that they would be working here a while longer. I touched my friends' arms and indicated we should return to the lane. It was time to contact Sir Jon.

After we stumbled back across the field, we walked along the road a good distance to ensure we were out of earshot. I pulled out my phone and whispered my plan. Rather than call—and have to speak—I sent a text, hoping he would answer me. If not, I would have to call.

G & H tomb robbing. TH. Get here quick.

The answer came almost immediately. *On it. Hold tight.*

Hurray. "He's coming. Now we need to go find Poppy." The knowledge that the thieves were using the vault and probably the tunnels only strengthened my belief that she had never left the property.

"I have an idea," Tim said. "Why don't Daisy and I wait for Sir Jon while you two go up to the manor? When the authorities get here, I'll tell them what you're doing."

"Are you sure?" I asked, liking this idea. As long as someone was here to direct Sir Jon and the police, it didn't matter who exactly.

"Go," Daisy said, giving my arm a gentle push. "If poor

Poppy is underground with stone caskets . . . It's too ghastly for words."

"Wait further up the lane," Kieran suggested. "You'll be able to flag Sir Jon down and keep the operation covert."

"Yes, do," I said, already walking across the road toward Thornton Hall. Next stop, the converted stables, to talk to Rose and Ben.

Lights were on upstairs when we reached the stables. I rapped on the downstairs door, then tested the knob. Open. "Hello, up there," I called. "It's Molly. And Kieran."

Ben appeared at the top of the stairs, taking in our attire with a laugh, though his face looked as drawn as ever. His feet bare, he was wearing ratty shorts and a T-shirt. "Come to call, have you?"

"Not exactly," Kieran said, allowing me to ascend first. "Molly figured out where Poppy is."

A shriek rang out followed by thudding footsteps. Rose joined Ben at the top of the stairs. "You did? Where is she?"

"It's only a theory." I tried to breathe, walk up the stairs, and talk all at the same time. "One that's getting stronger every minute." Identical expressions of hope lit their faces. "I don't think she ever left Thornton Hall. I think she might be in the tunnels."

They exchanged glances. "Tunnels? Are they still passable?" Ben asked.

"When I noticed them on a property map," Rose said, "Geoffrey said they were all caved in."

"Geoffrey is a liar." I was tempted to tell them what he was up to but refrained. They'd find out soon enough, after he was arrested. Yes, technically he owned the mounds, but raiding them under the cover of night with total disregard as to their fragility and without registering his finds? He was on really, really thin ice.

Ben shoved his feet into flip-flops, ready to spring to action. "Let's take a look at the map. If Poppy is down there somewhere, we need to find her and get her out."

"It's in the billiards room," Rose said.

Sidling past us, Ben thumped down the stairs and, sharing his urgency, we followed. "Is Geoffrey home, do you know?" he called over his shoulder. "I'm hoping we can avoid seeing him."

"He's not right now," I said. "We saw him, er, out."

Ben opened a side door and entered the house, leading down a corridor lined with coat hooks and rows of boots. "The billiards room is along here . . ."

He slipped through an open door and flicked a switch. The overhead lights illuminated a room decorated with game trophies, displays of antique firearms, and oil paintings related to hunting. The billiards table sat at the ready, the balls racked and cues lined up on the wall.

"It's over here." Rose crossed the room, pointing to a framed drawing.

At any other time, I would have loved to study the hand-drawn property map, created over a century ago. Tonight I was focused on the dotted lines revealing the existence of tunnels, as the legend noted.

"The tower is closer to the house than I thought." I pointed to the circle denoting the structure. "The trails take you out and around."

Kieran studied that area of the map closely, tracing his finger above the map. "The tunnel goes to the tower. See? It starts here at the house. A branch comes in from the graveyard and connects."

"The tower is older than this house," Rose said. "It's part of the original structure, which would have looked more like a fortification."

"Where's the tunnel entrance in this building?" I asked, thinking that might be an option.

Rose shook her head. "I'm not sure. I don't think we should poke around in here right now. Why don't we start with the crypt, since Holloway mentioned it."

I inhaled. "The graveyard it is, then. Let's go." I glanced down at my muddy, battered sandals and then at Rose's feet. "What size do you wear? I'd love to take these off."

*

Rose not only lent me a pair of sneakers; she also gave me jeans and a T-shirt. Thus, more appropriately outfitted, we set off, equipped with flashlights, a bag of tools, and bottles of water, plus a pile of ham sandwiches Ben whipped up, in case Poppy was hungry.

That's how confident we were, invigorated by a certainty that we would find her. Except for our lack of a pony, we could have been the Strawberry Girls on a mission to rescue the princess.

We went through the formal garden and along a path lined with copper beeches. Located in a copse of trees, the small cemetery was fenced with wrought iron and stone blocks. Slipping through an arch, we picked our way through gravestones scattered like broken teeth. Worried about attracting attention, we didn't use any lights, instead relying on the contrast between white stone and the overgrown grass.

The vault loomed up suddenly, a squat rectangular structure. Brass plaques identifying those interred were fastened to the walls.

Ben tugged at one of the tall iron doors. "It's open," he said. "We won't need the crowbar." He pulled it open farther, so we could go in.

My feet froze to the ground in dread at what lay beyond. Visiting graveyards, sure. I didn't have any problem with that. I even enjoyed the history and humanity of admiring carved stones and studying the inscriptions.

Going inside a crypt where actual bodies lay? Uh, not so much.

"Molly?" Kieran was beside me, holding my hand. "You okay?"

"I guess so. I really don't want to go in there."

He leaned his head close to mine. "It won't be bad. You can't see anything."

I took a reluctant step forward. "If we weren't looking for Poppy . . ."

"In that case, you wouldn't catch me anywhere near this place." He squeezed my fingers and let go. "Shall we?" Ben and Rose were already inside.

Several stone steps led down into the vault. Ben had turned on a flashlight and, in its glow, I saw metal grates on both sides of the passageway. Beyond were the actual burials, I gathered.

"The tunnel is this way." Ben signaled with the light, toward the back. Rose waited there, next to a doorway. Stairs led down again, into the dark. Dank, cool air wafted from the tunnel, smelling of iron and soil and water.

"Ready?" Ben asked. "Kieran, why don't you take the rear, using this torch." He handed him the flashlight. "I'll go first."

Kieran switched on the light and I got into line behind Rose. "I'm glad you're both archeologists," I said. "Neither of you are nervous about going underground, are you?"

"I live for it," Rose said with a laugh that quickly trailed off. "Well, except when I'm looking for my sister."

She sounded so sad I gave her a quick hug. "We're going

to find her, Rose. I just *feel* it." I honestly did, a knowing beyond conscious thought.

"We're going to move slowly," Ben said. "I want to examine the tunnel walls and ceiling as we go. Any sign of a cave-in or the potential for one, and we're out of here."

"Got it," Kieran said. He ran the light over the closely placed blocks. "It looks well-built so far."

Ben descended the stairs, his light constantly moving as he surveyed the structure. I was grateful for the light behind me illuminating each step. They were steep and shallow and it would be very easy to fall.

At the bottom, the tunnel stretched into darkness. Before proceeding, Ben flashed the light around. "What was that?" Something had glittered along one wall. He brought the light back to the spot, revealing an alcove filled with objects, many of them packed in crates. "This is where they're storing the artifacts," I said.

"What?" Ben cried. "Are you saying . . ."

"You didn't know about it, did you?" I said, seeing that he was genuinely shocked. "Holloway and Geoffrey Thornton have been smuggling antiquities out of here for decades."

"The crown," Rose said. "I bet one of the mounds is her burial chamber." The Anglo-Saxon princess, Princess Audrey, although that name was probably Nate's invention.

"We need to stop them," Ben said through clenched teeth. "How much has been lost forever?"

"Sir Jon is already taking care of it," Kieran said. "We witnessed Thornton and Holloway excavating the mound tonight, so we called him."

"I didn't want to say anything until we knew they had time to get here," I said. "Not because we didn't trust you."

"I get it," Ben said. "You didn't know if I was involved."

Actually, I'd never considered that, which was probably a mistake on my part. Investigations—well, the two I'd been involved with—seemed to require thinking everyone guilty until proven innocent.

Rose hunkered down to study the objects. "A little more light, Ben." She pulled out her camera and took several shots. "At least we're going to save these." Rising to her feet, she tried to send a message. "No service, naturally. Thought I'd try." She tucked the phone into her pocket. "Let's go."

Ben shone the light on the floor ahead. "Someone has definitely been this way recently. There's a clean trail in the middle."

He was right. Thick dust and grime coated the floor on both sides, the accumulation of many years. Another indication that Poppy might be down here or in the tower.

We continued slowly, with Ben stopping frequently to make sure it was still safe. "Whoever built this is to be commended," he said. "The bricks are still tight and I don't see much water leaking in."

His assessment was a comfort, since the last thing I ever envisioned myself doing was exploring underground. I didn't even like subways or highway tunnels. *We're doing it for Poppy*, I kept reminding myself.

Rose had thought to snap a photograph of the map and she kept an eye on our progress, guessing how far we had gone. "We should be coming up on a fork," she said.

She was right. After a short distance more, a tunnel came in from our left, probably from the house, which meant we had almost reached the tower.

"She has to be in the tower," I said. "If she's here, on this property. If only I'd realized! Mum and I were there just a few days ago, exploring. But the door and windows are all boarded up, so I didn't even think . . ."

"They stopped anyone from going inside to check," Kieran said. "And prevented Poppy from signaling to anyone either."

I felt a tiny bit better about my assumption the tower was empty.

"We're going up," Ben said, shining the light on a flight of stairs.

I prayed fervently that we would find Poppy. Otherwise it was back to the drawing board. Another consideration was that we might have to break in to find out.

One step at a time, I told myself sternly. We could always ask the police to check the tower for us. That would probably be more prudent.

Ben reached the top. "Here we are." His voice was shaking. "I hope she's in there."

"You and me both," Rose said fervently.

When the flashlight picked out the gleam of a padlock, Kieran slid past me to examine it. "That's new. Look how shiny it is, hasp and all."

"She's got to be in there." Ben began to hammer on the door with his fist. "Poppy. Poppy. Can you hear me?"

A knock came from the other side. We quieted to listen. "Ben? Oh, Ben." She started sobbing. "You made it."

CHAPTER 21

Ben rummaged in his kit for a crowbar. "Stand back," he said. We edged back down the stairs, far enough so he could work. Working with the frenzy of a man rescuing his love, he snapped the lock off within seconds.

"Wait before you grab the doorknob," Kieran said. "Use your shirt or a handkerchief and try not to rub off any fingerprints. Or leave any."

"Good point," I said. "I wish we had a fingerprint kit with us." Unexpectedly, a gust of rage shook me. What kind of evil person would kidnap a young woman and lock her up for days?

"Okay, here goes nothing," Ben said. He lifted the hem of his shirt and used it to open the door with the shank, not the knob. We all held our breath as the knob turned and he gently pushed the door open.

"Ben!" Poppy threw herself into his arms.

He gathered her close. "Oh, my love. We were so worried."

"I'm okay," she said. "Hungry. And I stink."

"I don't care," he said, hugging her again with a groan of joy.

"Neither do I," Rose said, horning in on the embrace. Tears were running down her cheeks.

Kieran and I stood back, not wanting to interrupt the reunion. I opened Rose's knapsack and pulled out a bottle of water and a sandwich, for when Poppy was ready to eat, while Kieran shone his flashlight around the room.

We were on the ground floor of the tower. The floor, walls, and ceiling were all stone, and a stone staircase wound up the outer wall. Besides the heap of blankets, there were food wrappers, a water jug, and a bucket used for a latrine. That was all.

"Who did this to you?" Ben asked, his voice commanding.

Poppy was still clinging to her sister. "Dr. Holloway. I found out—"

Down the stairs, a breath huffed. We all froze, our faces masks of shock.

The professor appeared in the doorway. "What a surprise. You have guests, Poppy." He blinked when Ben shone the light into his eyes, throwing up one arm. "Cut it out."

Ben rushed toward him, rage tightening every movement. "You're lucky I don't wring your neck. How dare you kidnap my fiancée."

Kieran moved around behind Holloway and grabbed his arms. "Don't move if you know what's good for you. Any service in here, Molly?"

I checked my phone. "No, none." To Holloway, I said, "Why aren't you under arrest right now?"

A sly smile crept across his mouth. "I made it away before the police arrived. I was already on my way back to the manor." His mouth turned down. "My plan was to gather up some things and make my escape." He glanced toward the open door as if thinking about the objects we'd found.

"What about my sister?" Rose was aflame with anger. "Were you going to leave her here to rot?"

Holloway shook his head. "No, no, of course not. I was going to let her go. Well, tell someone where she was once I made it over the Channel." Again, he looked at the doorway.

"Really?" I said. "What about Robin? Why did you kill him?"

The professor jerked his head up. "Me . . . kill Robin? I'm sorry, miss, but you have the wrong end of the stick. I was nowhere near Strawberry Cottage when he fell."

"Are you talking about Robin Jones?" Poppy asked, her tone sharp. "What happened to him?"

"He fell off Mum's roof," Rose said. "The same morning you disappeared."

"What on earth was he doing up there?" Poppy shook her head. "How strange."

"We'll fill you in later," Ben said. "Right now we need to get out of here." He waved his fist under Holloway's nose. "After you tell me why you locked up my fiancée."

Holloway cringed, his eyes huge in the dim light. "Poppy followed me into the crypt. She was going to go to the authorities. So I . . ." His voice dropped to a whisper.

"What?" Ben practically screamed in his face.

"He hit me on the head, knocked me out," Poppy said. "When I woke up, I was in here, trapped. Believe me, I've been plotting how to get out."

Ben pulled his fist back, ready to hit the professor. "Don't," Kieran warned. "He's not worth it. And don't worry, he's going away for a while."

"Did you hide Poppy's car?" I asked. "Then move it to the train station?"

"I did," Holloway admitted. "It was in an old barn at the edge of the manor property."

One mystery solved. "Were you sneaking around Strawberry Cottage spying on us?" I asked next. "The night I was talking to Iona in the summerhouse?"

"That wasn't me," he said.

A slight scrape on the stairs from the tunnel caught my ear. Holloway heard it too, and his eyes shone with what looked like hope.

Miranda Blake appeared in the doorway, a vintage revolver gripped firmly in her hand.

"Oh, Malcolm," she said, her tone light and malicious. "It looks like you'll have a little company." She waved her gun at us. "Phones. Now. On the floor right there." When we hesitated, she said, "Don't test me. I'm an excellent shot."

"She really is," Malcolm said miserably. "If you remove your hands, lad," he said to Kieran, "I can get my phone. Or you can remove it from my trousers."

Kieran released him and Malcolm fished around in his front pocket.

Miranda Blake is involved in the black-market ring. Of course. Why wouldn't the Queen of the Fairies be queen of the criminals, as Nate had implied? She was probably the mastermind behind it all, manipulating hapless Geoffrey and feeble Malcolm like puppets.

"You killed Robin," I said as I came forward to relinquish my phone. "And it was you Mrs. Dobbins saw in your running clothes." She was probably also the runner I'd seen watching the dig while Aunt Violet and I were on our way to Strawberry Cottage.

The gun jerked up and I threw myself back, hands up. "He asked for it. The rat—or should I say fox—was going to turn us all in. What a nerve. He was as guilty as the rest of us."

"What did you say?" Malcolm's mouth gaped open. "I can't believe it."

"You'd better," she snapped. "He's been working with Interpol. Which is why I need to get out of here." She scooped up the phones and stowed them in her shoulder bag.

"Don't forget the crown," Rose said, a cheeky tone in her voice. "I know you liked to wear it."

Miranda's head came up and a calculating expression slid across her face. She wasn't startled enough to lose her grip on the gun, unfortunately. "The crown? Where is it?"

Rose crossed her arms. "At Strawberry Cottage. It was hidden there all this time. Before Dad died."

"That's why Robin was on the roof," I added. "Nate hid it up there, under the thatch."

Miranda was visibly taken aback. "That liar. He said he couldn't find it and Nate must have moved it."

Robin had probably planned to keep searching once he got rid of Miranda. Instead, she pushed him off the roof.

"Wait," Poppy said. "You mean a *crown* was in that metal box Dad carried up to the roof? I thought it was another treasure hunt for us, though he wouldn't let us climb up there, of course. Anyway, he died soon after and I forgot all about it until Mum had the roof done again." Understanding dawned on her face. "Robin was at the dig when I was telling you about our treasure hunts, Ben. Remember?"

"I do," Ben said. "You said they were what got you interested in archeology."

Miranda's eyes narrowed speculatively. "So the crown is at Strawberry Cottage. Thanks for the tip." Still training the gun on us, she whipped out a key ring and backed out of the room, taking our phones with her. The old-fashioned lock turned with a clunk.

Ben rushed to the door and tried to pull it open, growling

in frustration when it wouldn't open. He pounded his fists on the wood. "The tools. Why did I leave them on the steps?"

Rose put a hand on his arm. "Because you didn't know a psycho was going to lock us in. It's okay, Ben. We'll figure it out."

He seemed to calm down, shaking one hand, then the other. They had to hurt. "Why did you mention the crown? Don't the authorities have it?"

"Yes, they do," Rose said. "I wanted to delay her, if possible, send her on a wild-goose chase."

"The crown?" Holloway asked. "It's been missing for almost two decades. Your father had it, I'm guessing?"

"He did," Rose said. "Probably trying to save it from the likes of you."

With a groan of defeat, Holloway sank onto the floor, sitting with knees up and head resting in his hands.

Poppy was standing with her fists clenched and tears rolling down her cheeks. "I can't believe this. I was almost out of here."

I patted her shoulder, trying to comfort her. "I know. It's maddening." I showed her the sandwich. "But we've got food."

Kieran circled the room, shining his light on the walls and windows, of which there were three, all boarded up. Ben rushed to join him, helping him see if there was a way out.

For a moment I wavered. Would we be trapped in here forever, starving and without water? What if no one— With a huge effort, I pulled myself together. Daisy and Tim knew we'd gone exploring. They'd make sure someone tracked us down.

"You know," Poppy said between bites of the sandwich. "I was going to make a rope of my blankets and see if I could rappel down the outside. But I didn't have anything to cut them with."

I glanced at the stone staircase. "You can get out on the roof of the tower?"

"I'm assuming so, yes," Poppy said. "There's a trapdoor."

Rose came to stand beside us again, looking down at the bedding, then at the staircase. "Let's go check it out."

Up the three of us went, circling around on the narrow stone stairs. I had to stare straight ahead so as not to look down. There wasn't a railing, and under normal circumstances I wouldn't have been caught dead on this staircase.

The trapdoor was unlatched and we climbed up through to an open area surrounded by battlements. Rose went to the closest spot and looked down. "It's really not too bad on this side. See how the ground slopes up?"

Still working on her sandwich, Poppy went to join her. "How many feet is that?" She calculated in her head. "Yep. The bedding rope should work fine. We'll even be able to double up the fabric."

"This is exciting," Rose said. "We're following in Flambard's footsteps."

Who? I was glad that Rose at least found the idea of flinging herself over the edge a lark. I was petrified.

"Oh yeah," Poppy said. "The Bishop of Durham. He used a rope to escape from the Tower of London in eleven hundred and one."

"He lived?" I quipped as I edged closer to the battlements, which weren't all that high. It would be really easy to topple over the edge. *Like Nate?* I didn't want to think about that right now, and I certainly didn't want to remind his daughters, either.

"Bishop Durham?" Poppy asked. "Another twenty years or so."

"That's good." I scanned the hall grounds for a sign of Miranda—or anyone else for that matter. Were the authorities still at Thornton Hall? I was sure Daisy and Tim would tell them that we searching for Poppy and they'd look for us, but would they find us before Miranda got away?

A light flashed in the dark, a short distance away. "Do you think that's Miranda?"

The sisters stared in that direction, squinting in the dark. "Could be," Poppy said. "The graveyard is right there."

"Where is she going, do you think?" I asked, since they knew the property better than I did.

"Strawberry Cottage," Rose said. "You can count on it. Searching for the crown will slow her down. Hopefully long enough for us to notify the authorities."

Poppy looked over the battlements again. "I'm ready. Let's start ripping."

We trudged down the stairs to the main floor. "Ready to do a Flambard?" Rose asked Ben.

He got the reference immediately. "I suppose so. There's no other way out unless we claw off the boards over the window and door. I could kick myself for leaving the crowbar in the tunnel."

"Don't do that," Poppy said. "Have a sandwich." She handed him a half, with a kiss on the cheek. Even under these less-than-ideal circumstances, Ben looked happier than he had since I'd first met him.

Using Ben's knife, we ripped the blankets and sheets into strips, braided them, and knotted them into a makeshift rope. "Oh, I do hope this fabric holds," Kieran said, testing one. "Or else we'll be taking quite a tumble."

"I'm not trying it," Holloway said. He was still huddled in a ball, obviously feeling sorry for himself.

"We weren't going to let you, mate," Ben said. "You can

wait right here in dark, dismal comfort for the police." He glanced at Kieran and whispered something.

The two men moved toward Holloway with purpose. "We're going to tie you up," Kieran said. "Much easier that way. For us."

For a second I thought Holloway would resist, but he submitted and let them tie his hands and ankles with extra strips of cloth.

"We should probably go first," Rose said to Poppy and me. "We're much lighter than Ben or Kieran."

My stomach quivered. Was I actually going to climb over the battlements and slide down the tower on a cloth rope? Apparently so.

Feeling as if I was embarking on a death march, I climbed the tower stairs with Rose and Poppy, Ben and Kieran carrying the rope. Up on top, the men figured out how to best fasten it, using two iron rings and the edge of the trapdoor to secure it.

Ben tugged on the line. "This should work. Who's first?"

Rose stepped forward. "Me. Remember my rock-climbing adventures in Scotland? This will be a piece of cake."

Her assurance made me feel a little better. Holding our breath, we watched as Ben helped her over the edge. Propping her feet against the wall, she leaned out and walked her way down, hand over hand. "Sliding straight down will burn your hands," she called up. "Plus you might smack your face into the wall."

Poppy was next, after giving Ben a huge smooch. Despite her captivity, she was still limber and joined her sister on the ground within half a minute.

"Your turn, Molly," Rose called up. "Come on, Vermont, you can do it."

I glanced at Kieran, who shrugged. "The tabloids?" he guessed.

"All right." I rubbed my hands down my legs, trying to dry them off, and, head woozy, forced myself to breathe.

"Don't think about it too much," Kieran said as he helped me over the wall. There was a lip on the other side to rest one foot, I found with relief. Resting my right foot there, I grabbed the rope with both hands and swung over and down. Heeding Rose's warning, I walked my feet down the wall, holding them almost straight out from my hips. Initially I had to force my hands to move, but once I got the hang of it I did fine.

Until I was about eight feet from the ground. A terrible ripping, rending sound came from the rope. "Bend your knees when you jump," Rose called. "Don't land flat."

Or on my head. My hands and feet were a blur as I moved down, a race against time as the cloth continued to fray. Not wanting it to totally rip and dump me, I finally let go and landed hard, knees bent but jolting each and every bone. I sagged onto the ground with a groan.

"Are you all right?" Rose and Poppy knelt beside me, staring down with anxiety.

I rolled over and sat up. "I'm fine." I reached for their hands to help me up. "Or I will be."

We stared up at Kieran and Ben, who stared back. "Now what?" I called. "Can you fix the rope?"

Kieran shrugged. "Maybe. Why don't you keep going? Stop Miranda and find Sir Jon or the police."

Poppy waved at Ben. "Love you."

"Love you too," he said. "Please be careful."

"I'll take good care of her," Rose said. "Ladies, let's roll." She began to trot through the clearing, toward the arch in the bramble hedge.

"Onward." Poppy followed her sister.

Shaking off aches from the jarring drop, I kicked into gear, eager to see if we could put a spoke in Miranda's escape plans. Who would have thunk it? The Strawberry Girls and I were heading off on a mission in the Deep Woods. Sometimes truth really was stranger than fiction.

CHAPTER 22

The lights were on in Strawberry Cottage. "We caught her," Rose whispered as we crept through the garden. Through the windows, we could see Miranda tossing the living room, throwing books aside and spilling the contents of drawers. No sign of her gun or our cell phones, from here anyway.

"What should we do?" Poppy whispered.

Rose thought for a moment. "Why don't we distract her while you go for the landline, Poppy? Call nine-nine-nine."

Poppy nodded. "The extension in Mum's bedroom. I'll sneak up the back stairs." She tiptoed to the rear door, where she fished for a key along the lintel above.

"We'll go around front," Rose said, touching my arm.

"Do you think she'll shoot us?" I was being practical here.

Rose leaned close and spoke into my ear. "We only need to get her attention, not talk to her."

That made sense. We made our way around the far end of the house, well away from the living room and Miranda's rampage.

The gun was resting on the front step, where she'd set it

down while breaking into the house. No sign of our phones, though. I hoped I'd get mine back, although I had loaded my pictures and contacts into the cloud.

Rose pointed at the gun with a grin. "Big mistake." She scooped it up and, after checking the safety, tucked it into her waistband. With a wave, she gestured for me to follow.

"Hey, Miranda," Rose said, standing with hands on hips. "Enjoying your little look round?"

Miranda whirled around, surprise making her stumble. Recovering herself, she scowled. "What are you doing here?" Her gaze dropped to the gun.

Rose patted it. "It's all mine now. Police are on their way, so I suggest you sit down and make yourself comfortable."

A vase whizzed past Rose's head and crashed on the wall, the china pieces clattering to the floor. Miranda ducked back and forth, gauging which way to run.

"You won't get far," I said, grabbing the nearest weapon, a furled umbrella with a wicked point. "So give it up."

Miranda backed up against the fireplace. "I'll have you arrested for threatening me."

Waving the umbrella, I laughed. "Who is in a trap now, tea-leaf lady?" Her reading had been somewhat accurate, at least about me walking into a trap. I wonder what the latest about her future had said. *Go straight to jail?*

Poppy ran down the front stairs. "Police are on their way." She grinned. "They were very surprised to hear from me. Apparently I've been the subject of a countrywide hunt."

"We have a lot to catch up on," Rose said. "After this one goes to jail."

Miranda sank down onto an ottoman and began to cry. "It's not my fault. It was Geoffrey and Malcolm and Robin. I was an innocent bystander."

Her attempt to manipulate us enraged me. "Until you

pushed Robin off the roof. You probably killed Nate too."
The method seemed to be her M.O.

A series of emotions flickered over her face, as if she was
deciding what to say or how to present herself. "There's no
evidence I had anything to do with it," she said in a small
voice.

It was the exact wrong thing to say. "You bloody cow,"
Rose shouted. "You killed my father. Why?"

Miranda stared at the carpet. "He was going to turn us—
them—in. At first he accepted Geoffrey's rationale that anything on the property belonged to him, as the landowner. But
when they started selling off things . . . Nate flipped out. He
took the crown and wouldn't tell anyone where it was." She
snorted. "He acted as if the princess was a real person."

"She was," I said. "A thousand years ago, but still."

Both girls looked like they wanted to rip Miranda limb
from limb. I didn't blame them a bit. "Leave her to Inspector
Ryan," I said. "She'll be going away for a long, long time.
And you know what? This means your mother is cleared."

"What does Mum have to do with it?" Poppy looked confused. "Where is she?"

Rose put her arms around her sister. "Like I said, there's
a lot you don't know. I'll put on the kettle and we'll chat."

Blue lights flashed against the sky. Help was here. Or
should I call them the cleanup crew? In the rush of excitement, I couldn't help but toot my own horn: once again, I,
with the assistance of my friends, had cracked another case.

TWO WEEKS LATER, ON FRIDAY EVENING
Thomas Marlowe was abuzz with laughter and chatter as
people flooded in for Iona's reading. The shop was filled
with flowers sent by fans, and *Peter and the Wolf* was playing over the sound system. The lines of chairs were filling

up fast and we'd have standing room only, I guessed. This was much more than a typical event with wine and cheese. It was an outpouring of love for Iona and her work.

"For a while, I thought this would never happen," I said to Mum while arranging bottles of wine in the ice tubs.

"So did I," Mum said with a little laugh. "I was over the moon when Iona was cleared." She moved a cheese platter to a better position. "We're having coffee next week when she's in town. Such fun to have a bestie."

I gave Mum a hug. "Yay, you. I was hoping you'd make some friends here. Well, besides me and Aunt Violet."

"You'll always be my faves," Mum said, squeezing me back. "No doubt about it."

Speaking of faves, Kieran stepped into the room, holding a very expensive bottle of champagne. "Have you switched teams?" I asked. Like me, he usually preferred beer.

He shook his head. "No way. This is from my mum. A gift for the author."

"Lovely." Mum took the bottle, studying the label. "We'll put it aside."

"She wanted to be here," Kieran said. "But they had to run up to London." He frowned and I wondered if the trip had something to do with Lord Scott's health. Kieran had mentioned that he'd been under the weather.

"Sorry to hear that," I said. Now that the ice had been broken with Kieran's parents, I was excited to get to know them. In other words, I'd survived the first encounter and had high hopes for the long haul.

"Family dinner next weekend," Kieran said. "If you can make it."

I slid my arm through his and gave him a kiss. "I can." I didn't think I had anything on my calendar, but if so, it could easily be rescheduled.

"What's all this, then?" a deep voice asked. I turned to see George Flowers, family friend and bookshop fixture, standing behind us. Tonight the stout old gent looked handsome in an open-collared shirt and crisp trousers, quite a change from his usual work clothes, worn to fix something here or in his apartment building.

"George," I cried, flinging my arms around him. "We've missed you." George had become like a favorite uncle to me.

His broad face reddened as he patted my back. "Now that's what you call a warm welcome, lass."

"Where did you go for your vacation?" Mum asked. "St. Andrews?" George was a golf fanatic and the sport was said to have originated there.

To my bemusement, George's blush deepened. He cleared his throat. "I was actually on a literary tour of Yorkshire. The Brontë Beat, they called it."

"No shame in that here," Mum said. "You're among friends."

Despite the corny name, the tour did sound interesting. "I'd love to hear more about it," I said. "Oh, and back to your original question, Iona York is doing a reading tonight. Glass of wine?"

A wave of excitement ran through the crowd as Iona, flanked by her daughters, entered the room. All three were gorgeous in red, a nod to the book. Iona's choice was a silk pantsuit and the girls were wearing ruffled frocks and laced sandals. Ben was right behind them, beaming with pride and joy. I'd heard that he'd been hired by the University to teach courses next year, after the completion of his PhD.

Holloway's jail term for kidnapping and smuggling had created a gap, it seemed, and Ben's work was highly commended by his law-abiding professors.

Geoffrey was also facing legal challenges for illicit antiquity sales, and Thornton Hall was up for sale. As for Miranda, well, she had confessed to two murders and was facing life in prison. Perhaps she could earn some pocket money by reading tea leaves inside. The crown was going to the British Museum, along with other Thornton Hall artifacts.

According to reports, Holloway and Geoffrey had both claimed ignorance regarding the murders. Geoffrey had professed shock that his long-time girlfriend was a killer, although he admitted to having suspicions about Robin. The morning he died, Robin had told Geoffrey and Miranda that Interpol was closing in. Miranda, putting two and two together about Robin's treachery, had stormed off after him.

The last loose end was the break-in at Robin's shop. That had been Aunt Janice, scouring the place for any evidence that she'd been seeing Robin. She had also deleted the picture of their date that I'd found on social media.

Aunt Violet appeared at the front of the room. "Good evening, everyone," she bellowed. The audience gradually quieted down, a few whispers of "Excuse me," and "I'm sorry," as people slipped into their seats.

"Tonight we have a very special guest indeed, an author who has been brightening the lives of children—and their parents and teachers—for almost twenty years. After the tragic death of her husband, Iona York picked up his passion project and brought it to completion. Inspired by her beautiful daughters and the very special place where they live, I bring to you, Iona York and *The Strawberry Girls.*"

Everyone burst into clapping and cheers as Iona joined Aunt Violet up front. Rose and Poppy sat in reserved chairs in the front row. Clarence stalked down the aisle and, gathering himself, leaped up into their laps. Yes, I said laps. He's a big boy.

Iona smiled widely as the applause rolled on. Finally

she lifted a hand. "Please stop," she said. "My ego is quite large already, according to my girls." She winked and her daughters hooted denials.

"As you've probably heard"—Iona held up the most scurrilous tabloid—"I've gone viral lately. I'm happy to report that it was all fake news and no, I'm not a killer." The audience roared. "But my dear little book is killing the bestseller list, thanks to you."

Finally everyone settled down again, sighs of pleasure heard as Iona picked up a new copy of the book and cracked the cover. "'On a warm summer night,'" she read, "'under the light of the Strawberry Moon, a little girl was born in a thatched cottage on the edge of the Deep Woods.'"

I was still a little embarrassed that, as many times as I had read *The Strawberry Girls*, I hadn't thought to look for Poppy in a tower straightaway—that section was approaching. Then again, context was everything and I'd never read the book with the characters they represented in mind before. And we'd still managed to rescue the princess and stop the villain.

So as Iona's words washed over me, I leaned against the wall next to Kieran and listened, carried away into the magical world of the Strawberry Girls. Every person in that room, no matter their age, was enthralled. That was the power of a story.

Seriously, I had the best job, plus a fantastic boyfriend, fabulous friends, loving family. . . . As if reading my mind, Puck rippled through my ankles, a silky shadow, and I bent to pick him up. Oh, and the greatest cat ever—next to Clarence.

What a lucky woman I was.

The Strawberry Girls, finale

As the Strawberry Girls turned to continue their search, the mole stopped moving, his feathery nose sniffing the air. "Have you tried the tower? Every time a princess goes missing, she's usually locked in a tower."

Poppy looked at Rose. "He's right." She turned back to the others. "Where is the tower?"

The hermit stopped polishing the sword with a sigh. "Go up that trail and keep going until you bump into the thorny rose hedge." He gave a hoarse chuckle. "Well, don't literally bump into it. The thorns are quite sharp. Go around until you find the gate. Go through and you'll find the tower." He saluted them with a grimy hand. "Good luck and Godspeed."

The pony plodded along the path, slowly but with determination.

"What will we do if Princess Audrey isn't at the tower?" Rose asked. "And if she is, how are we going to get her out?"

"Don't think about all that," Poppy said. "One step at a time."

She sounded so much like Mum that Rose was comforted. She rested her cheek against Poppy's shoulder and foraged in her pocket, hoping to find a stray chocolate or two.

A whole candy bar was nestled there—no, make that two. "Poppy, look what I found." Rose pressed the chocolate into her sister's hand. "It just appeared in my pocket."

"Awesome," Poppy said, ripping the paper. "Yum. It's my favorite kind."

As they drew closer to the tower, a fierce wind

began to blow, almost ripping the candy wrapper out of Rose's hand. She tucked it into her pocket quickly, not wanting to litter.

Bramble dropped his head and slowed, the wind so strong that he had to struggle against it. Next icy drops of rain pelted them, running down their faces and trickling inside their collars.

"Why is this happening?" Rose asked, pushing back sodden locks of hair.

"It must be magic," Poppy said. "Trying to keep us from the princess." She shook a fist at the sky. "You've overplayed your hand. Now we know she's there."

A huge thunderbolt rent the sky, accompanied by a deafening thunderclap that echoed around the valley. Poppy threw back her head and shouted, "Bring it on."

"You're awfully brave," Rose said.

"Never let them see you sweat." Now Poppy sounded exactly like her father, who had sayings of this type for every occasion.

Snowflakes began to mix with the rain, creating a slushy mess on the path. The intrepid Bramble slipped and slid but kept pushing along.

Then the rain turned to all snow, the flakes growing larger and larger until snowballs were falling from the sky.

Rose laughed when one smushed onto her head. "This has to be magic." She held out her hand and let a snowball land in her palm. She threw it at a tree with a squeal of delight. Poppy did the same and soon they were tossing snowballs left and right.

The snow stopped, melting away as if by—yes, magic. A huge bramble hedge loomed up in front of them, cutting across the path.

"Now what?" Rose asked, rubbing an old scar on her calf. Pushing through that wouldn't be fun, as she knew from experience.

Bramble lifted his head and sniffed the air before setting off with a jingle of his harnesses. His step was lighter, almost perky.

"He senses that his owner is nearby," Poppy said. Sitting back, she let the pony lead as he skirted the hedge, looking for a way through.

They found the open arch and Bramble pranced through eagerly. The tower loomed ahead, a single light in the top window.

"Princess Audrey," the girls called out. "Are you there?"

The window flew open and the princess leaned out. Seeing the sisters and her pony, she clapped her hands in delight. "You found me. Help me get out of here."

"How?" Poppy asked. Princess Audrey's answer was lost in the flapping of wings as a murder of crows descended upon the tower. They perched on the battlements, cawing.

Rose wished she had snowballs to hurl at them to scare them away, although she probably couldn't throw that far.

The girls slid off the pony, hoping that moving closer would help. Poppy held up the crown so the princess could see they had it. She smiled and reached down, indicating that she wanted it back.

Another clap of thunder sounded overhead and the crows flew away, cawing. A cloud descended from the sky, swirling around like a tornado.

"It's the Queen of the Fairies," Princess Audrey cried. "She's the one who locked me up."

Taunting laughter rolled around the clearing, raising the hair on the back of Poppy's and Rose's necks. A glowing figure appeared on top of the tower, forming into a beautiful woman with black sparkly wings. "The Strawberry Girls. So nice of you to visit. I see you have something of mine." She lifted her wand and pointed.

Nothing seemed to happen, but then dozens of tiny creatures appeared, swarming over the pony and running toward the girls. Rose gasped. Brownies.

The brownies circled Poppy, tugging at her clothes and reaching for the crown. When several tackled her knees, knocking her off-balance, Poppy cried, "Catch," and spun the crown like a flying disc.

Holding her breath, Rose leaped up and caught the crown. The brownies stopped, blinking. Bramble turned his head. The Fairy Queen flew up with a scowl and hovered mid-air.

"Now what?" Rose asked. Her heart was pounding.

"Put it on your head," Princess Audrey said. "And command the door to open."

Using both hands, Rose set the crown gently on her head, then pushed it lower so it wouldn't tip off. "Am I a princess now?" she asked.

"Always," Princess Audrey said. "Now get me out of here."

Rose threw up her hand. "Open, door," she commanded. The tower door flew open. Then, since she could, she turned to the mischievous elves. "Brownies, go home."

They scrambled and scattered, climbing over each other in their haste to be gone. Rose rested her hands on her hips, returning the Fairy Queen's scowl. "Don't you have somewhere to be?"

Grumbling, the Fairy Queen fluttered her wings and vanished, leaving behind a very nasty aroma.

Princess Audrey ran out through the open door, laughing. "Thank you, thank you," she cried. "All she gave me to eat were dry peanut butter sandwiches with the crust still on. And an apple with a worm inside."

"Well, it's the middle of the night," Poppy said. "But I'm sure we can find something at home. Why don't you come with us?"

Rose handed the princess her crown, with reluctance but knowing that she would never forget the thrill of using her authority for a good purpose.

To give Bramble a rest, the three girls set off for Strawberry Cottage on foot, with Rose allowed to hold his reins.

Along the way, they told the princess about their adventures. Behind them, the full moon rose over the tower and all was well in the Deep Woods.

The End